MR. KNIGHTSBRIDGE

LOUISE BAY

BOOKS BY LOUISE BAY

The Mister Series

Mr. Mayfair

Mr.Knightsbridge

Standalones

International Player

Hollywood Scandal

Love Unexpected

Hopeful

The Empire State Series

Gentleman Series

The Wrong Gentleman

The Ruthless Gentleman

The Royals Series

The Earl of London

The British Knight

Duke of Manhattan

Park Avenue Prince

King of Wall Street

The Nights Series

Indigo Nights

Promised Nights

Parisian Nights

Faithful

Sign up to the Louise Bay mailing list at
www.louisebay/mailinglist

Read more at www.louisebay.com

ONE

Dexter

She was the kind of beautiful that could send a man straight to the asylum. Just a glimpse of her had the hairs needling the back of my neck and my fingers stiff, desperate for a simple touch.

Exotic. Glorious. And bloody expensive.

"Very pretty. You should be extremely proud," Gabriel, one of my best friends, said while staring at the display case in the middle of the Dorchester's ballroom.

"She really is glorious," I replied. I hadn't seen her for a long time, but you didn't forget beauty like hers.

"You know that's a headband thingy and not a woman, right?" asked Tristan, another of the group of six of us who had been friends since we were teenagers.

"Tiara," I corrected him. To Tristan, it was just something women wore on their heads. To Gabriel, it was a collection of pretty stones. But to me, the tiara was beauty, life force—it was my fucking legacy.

"Right," Tristan said. "And your parents made it?"

"My mother designed it. My father made it."

"For the queen?" Tristan asked.

"The queen of Finland. She wore it on her wedding day." As a child, sprawled in a heap of Lego underneath the display cases in their shop on Hatton Garden, I'd felt like the only thing my parents did was work on this design. Hearing about the tiara was the soundtrack of my childhood. Though their lives were dominated by the tiara for just one summer, it consumed them entirely. Seeing the piece again now, for the first time since their death, I understood why they had been so consumed. It was gorgeous, an audaciously modern design still classic enough to be regal.

My parents' passion for their work had percolated through the air I breathed, and I grew up in the enviable position of knowing exactly what I was going to do with my life—follow in their footsteps and be a jeweler. But when my parents died and my brother sold their shop without me knowing, my desire to become a jeweler wasn't enough. For them, for their memory, I wanted to be the best in the world at what I did. I wanted their name—my name—to be known internationally for the most beautiful jewelry in existence. It was what they deserved.

"I still don't understand why we're in London and not Finland," Tristan said.

"The princess is marrying a British man, so they're holding the competition to design her jewelry here. It's raising a lot of money for charity. Pockets are deeper in London."

"Makes sense," Gabriel said.

Tristan pushed his hands into his pockets and nodded. "Well, it's nice stuff."

I grinned. Tristan might be clueless at times, but he didn't flinch when I asked him to come tonight. Far more comfortable in jeans, in front of a computer, he put on a dinner jacket without hesitation because he was as loyal as you could want in a friend. He needed a drink. I caught the eye of a waiter with a tray of champagne. He came over and we all grabbed a glass.

"To diamonds?" Tristan offered in toast.

"To your parents," Gabriel corrected. He had been the dad of our friendship group since we were seventeen, long before he was actually a dad—wise, measured and always armed with the right thing to say.

"Thanks, mate," I replied, clinking my glass to his. "To my parents. And to winning this bloody competition."

"I predict that if you do, you'll open your first store in London. It would be a great way to burst onto the scene," Tristan said.

I took commissions in London, and our workshop and design studio were based here. But I had yet to open a Daniels & Co storefront in the UK. My flagship store was in New York, with locations in Paris, Rome, Beijing and Dubai. We'd just opened in Beverly Hills and Singapore.

But not London.

In London, I existed in my own tightly controlled bubble. I lived and worked here, but didn't interact with the local industry. There were too many memories from the bleakest part of my life—my parents' Hatton Garden store that no longer existed. Sparkle's shop, which only survived because of my parents' designs. And David, my brother, the man who destroyed my parents' legacy and gave Sparkle theirs. There was too much here to forget.

I was asked about a London offering all the time, but continually dodged the questions and kept quiet. A Daniels & Co London shop wasn't going to happen. I believed in moving forward, not looking back. There was no need to dredge up the past when it could stay properly buried and undisturbed.

"And cheers to being mate dates," Tristan said. "I'm quite enjoying being on your arm. Just as long as you don't try to kiss me at the end of the night."

"You should be so lucky," I replied.

"I've been that lucky—that weekend in Prague, remember? I don't want your wandering hands near me again," Tristan said.

"Shut it," I replied, only half concentrating on Tristan as my gaze caught a woman in a white dress, strands of treacle-colored hair tumbling down her back. She was carrying a glass of champagne and an old-fashioned reporter's notebook, though she was focused on neither as she squeezed by us, nearly tipping alcohol over Gabriel's very expensive jacket. "It was fifteen years ago and I was asleep," I said as the woman passed. I tracked her as she headed toward one of the display cases, where her face lit up with a huge smile as she took in a pair of earrings my parents had produced to go with the tiara. Happy at the thought of someone else enjoying my parents' designs, I tuned back into the long-running debate with Tristan.

Tristan rolled his eyes and nodded. "So you say. But asleep or awake, you tried to spoon me."

Gabriel was a man of few words but Tristan had enough for both of them. How the three of us, plus Beck, Andrew and Joshua had managed to remain friends all these years was a miracle. We were brothers more than friends.

"The six of us should go back to Prague," Gabriel said.

"Definitely now we can all afford our own rooms, and I don't have to sleep with this guy," Tristan said, nodding his head toward me. "I'll look into it."

A break with my best mates sounded like a great idea,

but not until I'd won this competition. I had a lot of work to do over the next few months. Putting together the designs for the princess of Finland's wedding collection wasn't going to be enough. The quality and rarity of the stones, plus cutting and setting them, was going to set us apart. My contacts with stone suppliers were the best in the business, and I was going to need the best of the best. There would be no taking breaks in Prague or anywhere else for a while.

"We can make it a celebratory trip when Dexter's won this competition," Gabriel said, once again guessing my thoughts.

Tristan shrugged. "If you like. I still don't get why you have to enter some stupid competition. It's not like you need the work. Or the money. Do you?"

Tristan was right. I didn't need the money or the work.

But I *had* to win.

Partly for my reputation—it would be more evidence I was the best at what I did. But mostly for my parents. To win the competition a generation after they had was what they would have wanted—proof that their passion had been passed through their genes—and I was carrying on the torch for them.

"I'm not knocking on the door to the poor house, don't worry," I said.

"Pleased to hear it. But at the same time, if you want to offload that DB5 of yours at a knockdown price, I'd be happy to pay cash."

"Find your own Aston Martin and stop trying to buy mine," I replied. I turned to Gabriel. "If you ever find me dead under suspicious circumstances, point the police in this guy's direction," I said, nodding toward Tristan. "No doubt they'll find him with my car keys in his grasp."

Tristan shrugged as if it would be a fair assumption.

He'd borrowed my car too often for me to count. He didn't need to bump me off for it.

"You know we're huddled here like Macbeth's witches. You should mingle," Gabriel said.

It was probably true. I was here to prove to the industry that contrary to popular belief, I didn't think I was too good for them. I scanned the room for a safe place to land—ideally, a small group of people who wouldn't immediately bombard me with stories about my parents. And of course, I had no desire to run into anyone from Sparkle. A conspicuous trail of empty champagne glasses led to the woman in the white dress, who was standing in front of the earrings my parents had produced for the queen's wedding. "Okay. I won't be long," I said, heading in the direction of the earrings. The woman in white seemed to be the only person in the room focused more on jewelry than socializing, and by my standards, that meant she was someone worth getting to know.

As I passed the entrance, a list pinned to an easel caught my eye—the names of the attendees. Primrose, my head designer, would be keen to see who was here tonight. I pulled out my phone and took a picture before trailing my finger down the alphabetical list to find my name. I pulled away abruptly, as if the board had emitted an electric shock. I'd expected to see my name there, but there were two "Daniels" on this list.

David was here.

The brother who'd tried to destroy my parents' legacy. The brother I'd vowed to have nothing to do with. The brother I hated.

Heat flushed through me and I turned quickly to survey the room. He couldn't be here, could he? Would I even recognize him fifteen years later? At thirty-seven he might have lost his hair, like dad. Or—

"Dexter Daniels!" An avuncular stranger in his mid-fifties grabbed me by the elbow and thrust his palm against mine, shaking my hand vigorously and effectively pulling my thoughts from the black hole they'd been circling. "Gosh, you make me feel like an old man," he said. "If Joyce McLean hadn't said it was you, I never would have believed it." He grinned at me as if I should recognize him, but I was sure I'd never seen him before in my life. "The last time I saw you, you had a bottle of vinegar in one hand and tissues in the other, cleaning the glass in your parents' shop."

I exhaled and imagined an invisible shield surrounding me, stopping his words from penetrating, from reaching the places I'd spent so long protecting. This was why Tristan and Gabriel were here tonight. Sure, Tristan liked free booze and the chance to mingle with a ballroom full of women, but he and Gabriel both were here because I'd asked them to be my buffers. "They were good people," I replied. This was why I'd avoided situations like this for as long as I had. I knew how great my parents were. I didn't need strangers to remind me, to poke at the open wound created by their absence.

"Talented. And kind. It was a long time ago but the industry still feels their loss."

"You're right," I said. "It was a loss on a personal level but their talent and hard work meant it was a loss for jewelry more generally." My rehearsed response emerged automatically, not for the first time tonight.

Usually this short, polite exchange would end with a handshake here, but the man, whoever he was, wasn't going anywhere.

"Do you know what I miss most about them?" he asked. "Your father's rather rare laugh."

I smiled—a real smile, not the forced one I'd been wearing all night. My father had been a serious man at work. But not around his family. Our house was full of tickles and laughter.

"It was your mother who was always able to coax it out of him," the man said.

I nodded, remembering how she'd tell him jokes in the shop, trying to get him to lighten up. "They were a good team."

"She would say how his stern face made it look like he was being possessed by his father, your grandfather."

I'd forgotten that. She'd chase me around the shop making scary noises, and inevitably my father's stern expression would give way to something softer, more familiar.

"You know all the big houses were after your mother— Bulgari, Harry Winston—they queued up to offer her design roles. She could have written her own check. But she only ever wanted to work with your father."

I tried to keep my surprise from showing. I'd never heard her mention how she'd been offered other roles. I guess it hadn't been important to her. The only person who ever mattered was my father—and her boys, of course. "My mother was very talented."

I'd been dreading coming here tonight. I hadn't wanted to hear the sorrow and sadness in people's voices when they discussed my parents, or be constantly reminded about how much I'd lost. But hearing about them from someone else's perspective was gratifying, and reigniting beloved memories was deeply comforting. I'd pushed so much of my past away to stop it from hurting me that I'd lost some of the memories that were important.

"She was. And from what I've seen, the apple doesn't fall too far from the tree. I've followed your career."

I still didn't know who this man was but he seemed to know me well enough. "Can I take your card?" I asked. Perhaps I might have reason to do business with this man at some point in the future.

"Of course," he said, flipping open his wallet. "You've not shown your face much around London."

"No, sir," I replied. "I go where my clients are." It was a lie but a believable one.

"Yes, I was surprised your brother never went into the industry," he said, holding out his card.

The warmth that had gathered in my belly at his words about my parents turned to ice when he mentioned my brother. The realization that David was here tonight, enjoying the champagne, no doubt at the Sparkle table, pulled the air from the room. I needed space. I needed to breathe in the goodness my parents brought to this room, not the betrayal my brother did.

"Would you please excuse me," I said, shaking the man's hand once again. "I've just seen someone over there I must speak to." The girl with the treacle-colored hair was in the corner, looking at one of my favorite pieces.

TWO

Hollie

I glanced over my shoulder to check I was going unnoticed in the ballroom full of men in tuxedos and women wearing dresses that cost more than our trailer back home in Oregon. I'd only ever seen scenes like this in movies, yet here I was, one of the guests.

I didn't belong here.

My new colleagues had disappeared as soon as we'd entered this vast room, and given the number of people here tonight, I'd probably never see them again. That was okay. The bus to take us back to the office was leaving at eleven, which meant I had limited time to study the incredible royal jewelry on display.

A tall waiter thrust a tray of drinks under my nose, like being offered free champagne was just completely normal. I'd never tasted champagne before, and was determined to keep a clear head, but if my sister, Autumn, was here, she'd tell me I shouldn't miss out. I took a glass and headed toward one of the displays of jewelry from the Finnish royal family. I was here to work. Learn. Invest in my future. My three-month internship was my one shot—my opportunity to escape the life my parents had led, a trailer-park existence I was ready to quit.

"Wow," I said out loud as I came to the first of the display cases dotted throughout the room. I took in the two-tiered tiara, not quite believing what was right in front of me.

I'd seen it online. The queen of Finland had worn it on her wedding day. Seeing it up close and personal was an entirely different thing. It was almost overwhelming, there was so much to look at. The bottom layer was a headband of huge solitaire diamonds, each one as big as my knuckle. The top was like a string of bunting of alternating rubies and diamonds. From a distance, just the bigger stones were visible, but as I got closer, I could see a top string of small stones that had been strung together with even smaller stones. It was so unusual I wanted to pull out a sketch pad and start to make drawings. I had a notebook and pen stashed in my bag, but I couldn't see anyone else writing anything down and I didn't need to draw attention to myself tonight. I stood out as it was. If I didn't keep my head down, I'd probably get arrested by the plain Jane police likely patrolling here tonight. I was wearing a cheap, slightly too big A-line white dress my sister had loaned me. I'd sewn a line of black sequins around the collar in the hope of passing it off as cocktail attire. I'd even borrowed Autumn's slightly too small shoes and had newly formed blisters to prove it.

Blistered feet were a small price to pay for being in this room. I was the intern for a jewelry house that had a real chance at winning the competition. The sheer luck of it all was enough to dull any pain I might otherwise have felt.

The thought of being part of the team that would

bejewel the princess of Finland on her wedding day was the cherry on top of the cake. I'd have been happy with three months' experience with one of the most successful jewelers in London. This was the push I needed to get a job in New York at one of the big jewelry houses. A dozen job applications had sent the message loud and clear—no experience, no job. But a letter of recommendation from Charles Ledwin, CEO of Sparkle, would open every door that had been slammed in my face. It was my ticket out of my dead-end life in Oregon.

I glanced around at the display cases dotted throughout the room before clocking the burly security guys at every exit point. There was a lot of money here tonight. A lot of talent. It was intimidating and completely exhilarating at the same time. It felt as if I was about to start a supermarket sweep of knowledge. I'd have three months to grab as much as possible and then the buzzer would sound and my fate would be sealed. Hopefully I'd have done enough, seen enough, learned enough to change my future.

Why wasn't there a line to see this tiara? It was so freaking beautiful that I wanted to shout at the top of my voice for people to come see. I guess this way I had it all to myself. I glanced around to ensure no one was paying any attention to me—of course they weren't—abandoned my champagne glass on a nearby table, pulled out my notebook and scribbled down some ideas.

The next display case contained a silver hair comb incrusted with pavé diamonds. Another tall waiter hovered next to me with a tray of champagne. Jiminy Cricket, I must have left my glass behind at the tiara display. I never even got to taste it. Could I just take another one? I glanced at the waiter but he wasn't taking any notice, so I swiped another glass and turned back to the display.

The comb must have been Victorian, from the date written on a card placed discreetly beside it, but the design was so simple it seemed much more modern. If I'd been to art school or any kind of college, perhaps I'd recognize the jeweler. I'd done my research these last few years, but I barely had time to make and sell the few pieces I could afford to make—let alone find time to study the history of jewelry design. The designs I'd come up with had started as doodles in my break time at the factory. At some point I'd found a soldering kit on eBay, and when I drew something I loved so much I couldn't just leave it on the page, I saved up for some silver and made my first piece. When I hung that first pendant I'd made—a silver oak leaf—around my neck, something took hold of me. For the first time in my life, I had a goal that was just about me—not making sure my parents made the rent on their trailer or my sister's tuition was paid. This was a desire for me and me alone. Jewelry was *my* thing.

I made a few notes and sketched out a couple ideas. I knew Sparkle wouldn't consider any of my designs for the competition, but I wanted to learn how to create my ideas on the company's specialty software.

This room was full of inspiration, and I wanted to soak it all in while the opportunity lasted. I'd missed out on a lot by not going to college, but I was determined to get as much of an education as I could out of my time in London, squeeze out every last drop of experience.

I ducked and weaved through the canapes, crystal glasses and cummerbunds to the next case, and then the next and the next. If heaven turned out to be just like this, I wouldn't be surprised.

As I circled a display containing three bracelets, I overheard a group of people standing to my left, whispering about Dexter Daniels. Daniels entering the competition had been a huge deal. He was a virtual recluse and as famous for not having a London store as he was for being incredibly successful despite his youth. He was one of the favorites to win and, I'd heard, devastatingly handsome.

He'd obviously inherited the family genes—his parents had designed the tiara I'd been ogling. Meanwhile, my family business was dodging landlords and skipping out on rent. To have come from a family who made their mark in history by designing jewels for royalty . . . Dexter must be so . . . Did he even know how lucky he was? To grow up with all this? No wonder he was so successful.

As I sketched in my notepad, someone on the other side of the display case nudged her friend and stage-whispered, "Over there by the bar. The tall one. That's him. Dexter Daniels."

I glanced up and followed the woman's pointed finger as a man on the far side of the room turned in our direction. His furrowed brow and pained expression came as a shock. What on earth could make someone so miserable on a night like this, in a place full of beautiful things? He pinched the bridge of his nose, the exasperation of being uber-successful obviously too much to bear.

He was the most handsome man in the room.

Perhaps the entire city of London.

His thick, wavy, almost black hair was the perfect length—long enough to thread fingers through, but not so long it could be tied in a ponytail or even worse, a man bun. He seemed to be the only man in the room who wasn't wearing a tie with his suit, the open shirt displaying a bronzed v at the notch in his throat. He stood out but not because he lived in a trailer park or was wearing borrowed shoes a size too small. It wasn't how tall he was, or how confidence seemed to radiate from him, or how his jaw was shadowed by a couple days' worth of stubble. He stood out because rather than looking like he was among colleagues, he looked like he was a client of the jewelers in this room. He seemed like the guy who could throw a couple mill' down on a necklace for his wife and pick up something for his girlfriend at the same time. Someone came up to greet him and the pain drained from his face, replaced by a wide grin. It was a smile that could close a deal, make someone feel like the most special person in the room and no doubt had panties falling to the ground.

Not my panties though. Mine were staying firmly on. I dropped my gaze back to the bracelets and resumed sketching.

I finished off my notes and scanned the room to see if there were any display cases I'd missed. In the far corner there looked to be a smaller case I could have sworn wasn't there earlier. I wasn't sure how I could have skipped it. I checked my watch—still a few minutes before I had to meet the bus.

As I got to the case I froze and nearly dropped my notepad. Inside was the most beautiful ring I'd ever seen. Far simpler than most of the pieces here tonight, it boasted a large emerald flanked by baguette diamonds. While most of the jewelry on display had demonstrated original designs or brilliant engineering, this ring did neither. It was a classic design with a straightforward setting, but it was quite simply stand-out gorgeous. It must have been an engagement ring. But it was huge. I put my hand next to it to get some perspective on its size. The contrast was almost alarming—my rough hands, subjected to a home manicure, and this elegant, dignified, perfectly polished ring. A week ago, I'd been home at the Sunshine Trailer Park, with an

Etsy shop that brought in a couple of necklace orders a month. Now I was across the world, surrounded by beautiful people and more-beautiful jewelry, at the start of a three-month internship for one of the best jewelers in the world. Even if hands like mine would never be graced by jewelry this fine, I could still use them to make something beautiful.

THREE

Hollie

I needed to leave the party to make sure I found the bus on time, but I just wanted to steal a few more moments with this ring. I shoved my notebook and pen back into my bag and circled the display case again. When was I going to get another opportunity to see jewels like this, with this kind of history, demonstrating this kind of talent and creativity?

It was only now I understood Lord of the freaking Rings. I could happily suspend my disbelief for wizards and hobbits, but I'd never bought into the idea that some mystical band of gold could inspire such risk to life and limb. Looking at this emerald, though, I totally and completely understood how it might be worth a trip to Mordor. There wasn't much I wouldn't do to put that ring on my finger. Again, I held my hand alongside it. The stone was big, but that was part of its charm. You wouldn't see anything else when this ring was in your eyeline. My smudged manicure and hand-me-down dress would go unnoticed with this gem on my hand. I might even fit in with the other guests in this ballroom tonight. All it would take was a multi-million-dollar ring.

"It suits you," a man said from behind me. His gravelly voice sent an involuntary shiver racing down my spine, as if someone had run a finger across the bare skin of my back.

I snapped my head around to find the impossibly gorgeous Dexter Daniels grinning at me, his eyes twinkling in amusement. If I'd thought he was handsome from across the room, being face-to-face with him didn't disappoint. He was broad, filling up the entire space in front of me, and so tall I had to tip my head back to look him in the eye. He was standing close, as if we were already sharing secrets, and a faint woodsy scent came from his custom suit. A curl of shiny black hair fell onto his forehead, and I couldn't help but wonder how it would feel to push it back into place.

I turned away, unsure if I would be able to form a coherent sentence if I was looking at him. "Sadly, it's out of my price range," I said, flattening my hand on the glass case.

"I'm not sure it's for sale," he replied. "But if it was, you should have it."

"Right," I said. "I also deserve a castle in Scotland, but that's not on this week's grocery list either."

I looked up at him, waiting for a response, but instead he just stared right back at me. When he finally spoke again after a too-long beat of silence, he said, "Your eyes are quite the most beautiful shade of green and have the most glorious flecks of blue, just like a Zambian emerald."

I wanted to giggle at his straight-up crazy mixed with a hunk of cheese, but before the corners of my mouth had turned up, he stepped back and his cheeks reddened as if he was embarrassed by what he'd said. As if it had been a slip of the tongue.

"God, sorry, I sound like I'm coming on to you." He

pinched the bridge of his nose and instinctively I reached to remove his hand.

"Don't be sorry. I treat cheese as its own food group. I'm a fan. My name's Hollie."

He chuckled. "Dexter Daniels, and I swear I'm not usually so cheesy. Some people have even accused me of being too smooth." He narrowed his gaze. "But your eyes are really quite extraordinary."

"Yeah, Zambian-emerald extraordinary. I get that all the time, whatever it means."

"Wait. You've not seen a Zambian emerald?" he said, pulling his cell from his pocket. "Are you not in the gemstone business?"

I shrugged. "Just an intern."

"We all have to start somewhere."

"Right," I said. "This is just the first step." I thought my Etsy shop would be the first step and in many ways it had been. I just didn't have the time or money to make enough pieces to turn a profit. My online shop was a hobby, but one that had ignited hope in me, a belief that there was a life for me outside the trailer park once Autumn graduated.

Dexter handed me his phone, which displayed a huge emerald on it.

"It's not as pretty as this," I said, handing back the phone and nodding at the ring in the display case.

"Or your eyes," he replied.

With a face that pretty and a body that hot, surely this man had women throwing themselves at him left and right. Why was he over here, talking to me about my eyes? Sure, he was gorgeous, but I didn't need gorgeous unless it could cut glass. I had to stay focused on my internship. I wasn't in London for a holiday romance.

"Sorry, more cheese," he said. "So apart from the ring

that goes with your eyes, did you see anything else you like?"

"What's not to like? I'm from Nowheresville, Oregon. It all looks good to me. What about you?" I asked.

"The tiara." He thrust his fingers through his hair as if he were uncomfortable all of a sudden.

"It's very beautiful," I replied. "The settings for that top layer are genius."

He nodded but didn't elaborate. It was as if his mood had flipped. Maybe he was thinking about the tiara and how hard it would be to design and produce anything as stunning.

"It sets the bar for this competition pretty high," I said.

"I was born for the challenge," he replied. His mood flipped again and he grinned widely. "My parents designed and made that tiara."

"I heard that. So, winning this competition is your . . . destiny?"

"More like my responsibility."

That hadn't been what I was expecting him to say. I was starting to see that beneath the near-offensive level of hotness and the oh-so-relaxed attitude, Dexter Daniels had hidden depths. And the longer I stood here, breathing the same air as him, the more I wanted to know.

"That's an interesting way of looking at it," I replied. "Holy Hercules," I said, catching a glimpse of Dexter's watch. "I was supposed to meet my ride fifteen minutes ago out front."

"Let me walk you out," he said, putting his hand to the base of my spine and making me shiver again as he guided me out.

I hoped the bus would wait. I didn't have money to splurge on cab fare and I hadn't figured out the subway yet.

"Who's lucky enough to be taking you home?" Dexter said. "Jesus, everything I say to you sounds positively fondue-like. What is it with you?"

I laughed. "You think it's me? I'm cheese-inducing? That's like the best compliment ever," I said as we reached the entrance of the hotel. I craned my neck but couldn't see the bus at the promised pick-up point. Would they just leave me? Weren't the British too polite to do something like that? "I was meant to be meeting my colleagues." I was stranded. I didn't pick up my UK phone until tomorrow, and my thousand-year-old flip phone with an American number and no international roaming plan was back in my room at my short-term rental. It wasn't like I'd swapped numbers with my new Sparkle coworkers anyway. What use did they have for the intern's phone number?

I needed to find a way home, but not before I cut Dexter loose. He'd already distracted me and made me miss my ride. God knew what would happen if I let this go on even one minute more.

I held out my hand. "It's been good to meet you, Dexter Daniels."

He grinned as he gripped my hand with his.

"But if you'd point me in the direction of the subway, I'll be on my way. These Zambian eyes need their beauty sleep."

"Please," he said as a car pulled out in front of us and he opened its back door. "I'll drop you. Where are you going?" He gestured for me to get inside.

"This is your car?" I asked. "My mom warned me about getting into cars with strangers." Of course, that was a lie. It was the kind of thing I warned my sister about, but that my mother would have positively encouraged if it meant we saved on bus fare.

"We're friends now, though, aren't we?" he asked. "Not strangers."

Silently I weighed my options. Get into the car with the most handsome man in Europe, who would either take me safely home or he'd chop me into tiny pieces and feed me to his dog? On the other hand, I could wander the streets for the evening and end up meeting a murderer anyway. Seemed like even odds on getting home or getting axe-murdered. "You promise me you're not a serial killer?"

"Scout's honor," he said, holding up three fingers.

The way his eyes twinkled as he said it suggested Dexter was about as far away from Boy Scout as it was possible to be. But I was lost in a big city, and whatever decision I made would be a risk.

I took his hand as he helped me into his car. When the door shut, the man at the wheel said, "Good evening, ma'am."

He probably thought Dexter was taking me home. Which he was, but not like that. No siree. I wasn't shopping for distractions.

"Where are we going?" Dexter asked as he got in beside me.

I leaned forward to give the driver my address and Dexter chuckled from behind me. "What?" I asked.

"Nothing," he said as if he'd just discovered a secret about me I didn't know I'd revealed.

"You want me to tell you my address so *you* can tell the driver? Do you have control issues you need to discuss with your shrink?" I teased, grinning. I just hoped he was a guy who could take a joke. "You may be surprised to learn that in America, women can give out their addresses without any male assistance."

"Across the pond, but an entirely different world," he said, unable to contain an answering smile.

After I gave the driver my address, I settled back into the plush leather seat.

"So how long have you lived in London?" he asked.

I counted on my fingers. "Six days. Well, six and a half, if you count the time difference. I arrived last Saturday morning."

"Oh wow. Not long. Is it your first time in England?"

"Yeah. I didn't even have a passport before this trip." I wasn't about to tell him I hadn't made it out of Oregon until a week ago. He was a super-successful, sophisticated guy who no doubt travelled all the time. I bet he'd never met someone before who'd never made it out of state, let alone lived in a single-wide trailer.

"And how do you like it?" he asked.

"Mostly it's amazing, though some of the guys are a little cheesy."

He nodded, pressing his lips into a thin line. "Positively fondue-like, I'm afraid."

"To be honest with you, I've never had fondue," I replied. "But I'm guessing it's something close to heaven. I think the next three months are going to feature a lot of firsts for me. Let's hope fondue is in there somewhere." There had already been more first-time experiences than I could have imagined. Tonight had more that I could count on both hands. It was the first time in the ballroom at some fancy hotel. First time drinking champagne. The first time seeing millions of dollars' worth of the most gorgeous jewelry up close and personal.

The first time being driven home by a handsome stranger who also happened to be one of the most successful fine jewelers in the world.

"Well I'd be delighted to make sure it is. It seems only fair, considering my cheesiness distracted you from meeting your colleagues this evening. I should make it up to you."

He had nothing to make up. But he knew that already.

"Like on a date?" I asked.

"A cheese date," he replied.

It had started raining, and I traced one of the raindrops trickling down the other side of the window so I didn't betray how I beamed inside at his invitation.

For most women, it was an invitation too good to pass up, but this guy had already distracted me enough. "I'm not sure that's a good idea."

"I like to talk cheese with you," he said, looking at me as if he was unpeeling the dress from my shoulders. "I want to take you to dinner."

I wasn't asked out on dates often. And when I was, I rarely wanted to say yes. Fondue with Dexter sounded great, but felt wrong. It seemed self-indulgent and stupid. I was already in London on my dream internship. That was enough fun, wasn't it?

Back in Oregon, I was used to making sure there was enough money coming in to pay the rent on mine and Autumn's trailer, and my parents' trailer, along with tuition payments for my sister's college and then gas and food. Grilled cheese was a staple, and anything creative we could figure out with that week's sale produce. I spent a lot of my life worrying, adding up the *out* column and making sure it wasn't bigger than the *in* column. London should be enough without dinner dates, period. I didn't even want to calculate the karmic cost of spending more time with Dexter Daniels.

We turned onto my street and my heartrate began to pick up. I didn't want to say no, but I didn't see how I could say yes.

"Can I think about it?" I asked him.

He chuckled. "If that's what it takes. Let me have your number."

"Actually, why don't you give me your card." I didn't know what my UK number would be, and there was no point in giving him my US cell, which I was afraid to turn on for fear of incurring massive charges.

He pulled his business card out from his inside pocket. Even if I never called him, I'd have a memento of him asking me.

We pulled to a stop outside my flat and before I had the chance to say goodnight, Dexter had slipped out, rounded the trunk and was opening the door.

"Thank you," I said as he helped me out of the car. "For the ride. And the offer of cheese."

He chuckled. "I hope you call." He lifted my hand to his lips and pressed a kiss to it.

Despite my brain telling me I never would, another part of me, the part that believed anything could happen, hoped I did too.

FOUR

Dexter

I'd never been one of those businessmen glued to his phone. Like my father, I believed business was personal and better done face-to-face. But this morning, I must have checked my mobile a thousand times.

"Are you waiting for a call?" Primrose asked as she sat opposite me and pulled out her tablet.

"No." I slid my phone into the top drawer of my desk. Perhaps not having it in my hand might be a start at ignoring it. "How are the designs coming along? Seeing the wedding tiara last night was a reminder of how good we have to be."

"I was sorry to miss the reception. How was it?"

"Sorry?" I asked. "Don't be. It was an awful industry event. You did the right thing to escape." In many ways it hadn't been as bad as I had expected it to be. Remembering things I'd forgotten and hearing things I didn't know about my parents—like how my mother had been courted by all the high-end jewelers but had stayed working with my father—was both wonderful and reassuring. If I hadn't gone last night, I would have missed out.

But seeing David's name, and worrying about running in to him? That was beyond uncomfortable. I had no idea what he was doing on the list of attendees. As far as I knew, he was still working the back office of a bank. Why would he attend last night?

Then there was Hollie.

Meeting her had been an experience. I eyed the top drawer of my desk. I needed to get a grip. Even if she called in the next few minutes, she could wait. I was in a meeting.

The fact was, I'd expected her to call by now. Frankly, I was pissed off with myself for not insisting on taking her number.

"It was my thirty-third wedding anniversary—I wasn't escaping. I heard you ran into Ben Lewin."

Ahhh, the chap who liked my father's laugh. "Yes, he was one of several people I talked to. How the hell do you know that?"

Primrose tapped the side of her nose. "You might have been avoiding London jewelry circles all these years, but this old bird knows most things that go on in this town."

Primrose had been born in the same month as my mother. She lived for this business in the same way that I did, the same way my parents had. It wasn't work. It was passion. And that's why Primrose felt like family. She was built the same way.

Unlike my brother.

He couldn't wait to be out of the family business after our parents died, so why was he going to industry events?

"I didn't see a single person from the organizing committee. There was no need for me to have gone at all," I said.

Primrose sighed. "Do we have to go through this again?"

"I don't see why we can't just design the shit out of some jewelry. Pick the best stones in existence, cut them like motherfuckers and win this award."

"Dexter," Primrose said, her voice deep and chastising.

"Sorry, cut them like the best in the fucking business." Primrose tolerated my bad language, but *motherfucker* was where she always drew the line.

"We are going to do all those things," she said.

"Then why all the cocktail parties and dinners and charity luncheons?"

She laughed. "For the first time in your life, you're going to have to play by someone else's rules. You've snubbed this industry your entire career. You're going to have to use some of that charm of yours and play the game if you really want to win."

"And I do," I replied, "really want to win."

She nodded. "Me too. So, during this competition, you'll shake hands, swap small talk, play nice with the other kids and not look like you thought you were too good for these people all these years."

Primrose knew as well as I did that the reason for staying away from London was nothing to do with being arrogant, however much that accusation was thrown around.

It had everything to do with not looking back. With looking to the future rather than the past.

"Okay, so let's talk designs. What have you got to show me?"

Primrose pulled up images of the earring designs she'd been working on. "I'm not sure I've quite got the effect of the snow yet," she said. They were the shape of a snowflake and covered in a kind of pavé, but with larger, more exaggerated stones.

"I like this version though. The smaller stones are better. And not so small that they don't look special."

"Absolutely. I think sourcing the stones and making key parts of the jewelry is important," Primrose said. It had taken a while to accept that design and production had to work together on what Daniels & Co put out. At first Primrose felt it was too much pressure. Over the last fifteen years, she had started to see my perspective.

"It's how we've been successful up until now." Beautiful jewelry designs weren't enough. I had to find the stones and have them carved into the right cuts before I could be sure a design would work. Oftentimes, we changed the design to bring out the best in the stone. Some things that looked beautiful on the page, or even in a 3D render, just didn't work if the stone wasn't right. Understanding how to bring out the natural beauty of each stone in our designs would give Daniels & Co the edge.

The first stage of the competition was focused on design. It wasn't until after the three finalists got picked that any actual jewelry was submitted. Because it was so expensive to make these pieces, the other jewelers would hold off production as long as possible, focusing on the design in case they didn't get through to the next rounds. But we were cutting the stones and making parts of the pieces even as the designs continued to take shape. It was the only way to know how strong a design was before it was submitted. We would pick designs not because of how they looked in theory, but how the stones brought them to life.

"I've also been thinking about sourcing the emeralds," I said. "I think if we can find good Zambian emeralds, that's how we should go."

"Really?" Primrose said. "Why wouldn't you go Columbian?"

Hollie's eyes last night really had been spectacular.

"Because of our theme. Columbian emeralds are thought to be the best because of the intensity of color."

"Yes, exactly."

"But what we're trying to recreate is the feel of Finland."

"Yes," Primrose replied, elongating the word, which either meant she thought I was stupid or she was growing impatient.

"The color saturation of the northern lights isn't intense. They're ethereal. Green but blue, full of patterns and movement, light and dark. They're mysterious and otherworldly and uniquely fascinating." I wasn't sure if I was describing the northern lights or my encounter with the mysterious and fascinating American I'd met last night. Both maybe, but when I went to sleep last night, all I could see were those eyes—layers on layers of color. I wanted to find that in a stone. "Mystery and romanticism, that's the northern lights. That's what we're trying to achieve." I'd thought of nothing else since I'd come face-to-face with Hollie yesterday. I'd noticed her earlier in the evening and hoped I'd get a chance to speak to her, but being up close, looking into those eyes—she drew me in.

Fuck, I should have got her number.

"Well you know your stones better than anyone," said Primrose. "So, if you say so."

"I've got to find a supplier. Zambian emeralds aren't as consistent in color, so we'll have to be picky."

Primrose let out a laugh. "Well, picky is your middle name. Sounds like a job for you."

I'd never apologize for being difficult to please. As far as

I was concerned, it was a huge part of what made me successful. Good enough wasn't good enough.

"If you didn't enjoy last night," Primrose said, sliding her tablet back into its sleeve. "Did Stacey at least?"

For a second, I had to think who she meant. "Oh, didn't I say? Stacey and I broke up a few months ago."

"Dexter! What happened?"

She was acting like it was a big deal. "Nothing. Just came to the end of the road, I guess." I tried to remember who had actually ended it. Her, I think.

"The end of the road? She was such a nice girl and so supportive."

"Yeah. She was great," I replied, glancing at the top drawer of my desk and wondering if Hollie had called. If I'd not been so distracted last evening, I would have remembered to get her last name.

"So, if you admit she was great, why aren't you together anymore?"

Primrose was looking at me as if I had some bomb I was about to drop, but really, it was the same story as it had been with the last few women I'd dated. They wanted things to "progress" or to "take our relationship to the next level" or began suggesting we move in together. I was always content to stay in the early, less-intensive phase of relationships, but the women I was with always wanted more. I knew I couldn't give them more, but I wasn't the guy to lead them on, either.

"Do you think you ever got over Bridget?" she asked.

I leaned back in my chair. "Bridget and I had something great, and I messed it up. It's that simple. I couldn't make it work with her, so why would I think I could with anyone else?" When I'd tried to make things right with Bridget, she'd already moved on to someone more worthy of her.

Last time I heard, she was happily married. At least that had been closure.

"It was a long time ago," Primrose said.

"Yes, but a mistake is a mistake. The important thing is, I'm not repeating it." My mum always used to say the same to my brother and me—messing up is to be expected. It's part of life. What's important is that we learn from the mess.

"So you cut these women loose as soon as they hint at wanting more from you, instead of trying to make it work."

I didn't want to talk about this with Primrose. She just wanted me married off to whoever was around. She'd liked every girlfriend of mine she had ever met. And I got it. She wanted to see me happy. But I wasn't the guy to get married and have a family. Bridget had been the only chance at that kind of life. And if I couldn't manage it with her, I wouldn't be able to give any woman what she needed from me. "I think you're almost there with the earrings. I can't wait to see one actually made. But let's progress the others in case these are too on-the-nose once they're made. When do you think you and Frank will have something for me?"

Primrose sighed and stood up, knowing better than to push the issue. There was nothing more to be discussed between us on the subject of my dating life. "By the end of next week."

"I really want to get tiara drawings with the Zambian emeralds in place of the Columbian tomorrow. Is that possible?"

"Of course. I can put that change through on the three designs we're still working on," she said as she opened the door to leave.

I waited exactly three seconds after Primrose left before I yanked my desk drawer open and pulled out my phone.

Nope. She still hadn't called. Bloody hell. I was acting like a teenager. And what was the point anyway? We'd just end up dating and eventually come to the end of the road, just like I had with everyone who'd come after Bridget. I probably shouldn't have even given Hollie my card. Better to imagine what might have been than to disappoint her like all the rest.

Who was I trying to kid? I wouldn't rest until I saw her again.

I flipped to my messages. Nothing.

Maybe attending all the competition events wouldn't just be about showing people I didn't think I was too good for the London jewelry trade. Maybe I'd get to run into Hollie again, and maybe this time I'd convince the new-to-London American to share fondue with me. The next event was a charity luncheon next week, and for the first time in a very long time, I was looking forward to some small talk and warm wine.

FIVE

Hollie

Everyone had left the office some time ago, leaving me in the dark with just the glow of my monitor lighting the way to understanding the specialty design software. At some point I'd have to master my new company smartphone as well.

I'd been over Sparkle's designs for the competition again and again. They were . . . nice. I was sure they had qualities I didn't fully appreciate, but at the same time, to my untrained eye, they seemed kind of . . . dull. I got that a design fit for royalty would have to be conservative. The tiara Dexter's parents had designed set the bar for an innovative but classic piece, timeless and elegant but forever in style. Sparkle's entries were definitely on the classic end of the spectrum, and I had yet to be convinced of any innovation. I had some ideas and wanted to see if I could use the computer to bring my design to life instead of relying on my trusty notebook.

The longer I sat at my desk, the more error messages I

saw. I was worried I was about to blow the entire computer to pieces.

I nearly jumped out of my skin when my new smartphone began to ring.

Propping the cell on a stack of stationery, I pressed the accept button.

"Hey, you did it," Autumn said, beaming at me from the screen.

"I just had to move my finger, Autumn. It wasn't that hard. I wish I could say the same thing about this computer program. This stuff is so complicated." I needed to be proficient at the program, which all the big houses used. Adding the skill to my resume would be important during my job hunt.

"You're smart. You'll figure it out." Easier said than done. Despite the fact that I worked in a semi-conductor factory, I wasn't great with technology. In preparation for doing an internship, I'd spent the last twelve months getting familiar with my sister's old laptop, so at least I knew the very basics. I probably should have bought a smartphone before coming to London, but those things were just so expensive. I couldn't justify it when there were so many bills to pay.

"Speaking of smart," I said, "how are your classes? You don't have long to go so you need to get—"

"I know, get my head down, get the work done and get out of this town. You've been telling me the same thing since I was eight years old. I'm just as motivated as you are." Hearing how Autumn was keeping things on track was almost as gratifying as my internship at Sparkle. Knowing my sister was destined for something more than the Sunshine Trailer Park was something that kept me going when I was working double shifts at the factory to pay her tuition at Oregon State. I'd been determined for as long as I could remember that she and I would not end up stuck where we weren't happy, just because that's where we'd been born. Autumn was smart—so smart she'd gotten a scholarship for half her tuition and most of her textbooks. Some months I had to juggle—take on extra shifts, pray for a necklace sale on my Etsy site, even do a spring clean for Mrs. Daugherty across the street. But Autumn would graduate this summer and it was as if I were graduating too. Since I was four years old and my mom had brought Autumn home from the hospital—a bundle of limbs and peepy eyes—I'd vowed to take care of her. Her graduation would be confirmation that I'd done what I set out to do. After that, I just had to get her to leave Sunshine and make good on all her amazing potential. She would do something spectacular with her life—if her boyfriend didn't make her want to stay right where she'd always been.

"How's Greg?" I asked.

Autumn laughed. "You know I can see your gritted teeth when you ask me that because you're on video."

I rolled my eyes. "I'm trying to be supportive."

"No, you're not. You were just hoping I'd tell you he'd been crushed by his dad's muscle car."

"I'm not a monster. I don't want Greg dead. I just don't want him . . ."

"Anywhere near me."

I couldn't lie. I would be very happy if Greg disappeared from Autumn's life. Not because Greg was a bad guy—he wasn't. But I could guarantee he was going to spend the rest of his life living within a hundred yards of his current home, which just happened to be the Sunshine Trailer Park, managed by none other than Greg's dad. I wanted something better for Autumn. I dreaded her getting pregnant or announcing she and Greg were getting married or something. She was almost twenty-two and I wanted more for her. Or I at least wanted her to have options. If she took a job in Portland or New York or something and decided she was happier at the trailer park, that was one thing. But not having a choice? I couldn't live with myself.

"Don't sweat it," Autumn said. "Greg does whatever I tell him and it's convenient. It's no big love affair."

"How are Mom and Dad?" I asked. Keen as I was to change the subject, I was just jumping from the frying pan right into the fire.

"Okay, actually."

"Have they asked you for money yet?"

"I gave Mom twenty yesterday but it's no big deal."

I sighed. I'd begged Mom not to ask Autumn for money.

"It's not a big deal. She seemed okay actually, talking about applying for a job at Trader Bob's."

"Really?" I said, wondering if I'd heard her correctly. I couldn't remember the last time my mom had been interested in working. Occasionally she'd get offered something through a friend, but it never lasted long. She'd shoot her mouth off or lose something important. She never lasted more than a week. But I covered their rent and gave them money here and there. I just didn't want Autumn to have that burden. It wasn't fair.

"Yeah. Her friend is working there or something. We'll see how long it lasts."

"How's Dad?" It had only been a week since I'd left but if Mom was job hunting, maybe Dad had taken up lion taming. Apparently anything was possible.

"No idea. Mom says he has a cold."

Maybe I was overreacting. My dad took to his bed with

a cold most months. It was an excuse to watch a lot of TV and not clean up after himself.

"But enough of boring old Oregon," Autumn said. "Tell me about last night. How was the dress? Did you get to try on any jewelry?"

"You know." I sighed dramatically. "Another evening, drinking champagne and rubbing shoulders with the beautiful people." I grinned. "I didn't get to try on the jewelry, which is just as well because I'm pretty sure I wouldn't have wanted to take it off again."

"You look so happy," she said. "I bet you looked beautiful."

"Well I didn't get thrown out because my dress wasn't expensive enough, which at one point, I thought was a real possibility. I even got to drink the champagne." That wasn't quite true. I'd tasted it, but I kept putting down my glass and forgetting about it. The jewelry had been all-consuming.

"You were born to drink champagne," Autumn said. "I'm glad it's not just work, work, work. I know what you're like. I know you're there to learn but try and have some fun too."

"Actually, I got asked out on a date," I said and then immediately wished I hadn't.

Autumn scooted closer to the phone. "Tell me everything. A British guy?"

Not just a British guy. *The* British guy. Anyone who was anyone knew Dexter Daniels. I still wasn't sure why he'd singled me out. "Of course a British guy."

"Tell me you said yes."

"I took his number."

Autumn groaned. "I suppose that's better than a straight no."

Except that I had no intention of using the number, so it wasn't much better.

"You should enjoy yourself," Autumn said. "You can work hard *and* go out for drinks with someone you know."

It was tempting. Dexter had been sweet. And although he couldn't have been as good looking as I remembered, he was undoubtedly handsome. But he had thrown off my concentration long enough for me to miss my ride. God only knew what the man was capable of during the course of an evening of fondue.

"You don't need to worry about me. I'm in London. I'm having more fun than you could possibly imagine." Compared to life in Oregon, the past week had been a kaleidoscope of fresh, exciting experiences.

SIX

Hollie

Jiminy freaking Cricket.

I'd convinced myself he couldn't possibly be as good looking as I'd imagined, but sitting across the other side of this gigantic room from Dexter Daniels, it was clear I'd just been delusional. And it wasn't just how he looked. It was the way he carried himself. It was as if he were the sun and we were all orbiting him, our only option to surrender to his gravitational pull. He was so confident and relaxed, as if nothing could faze him. What would happen if I went up behind him and tickled him under his arms?

He'd probably forgotten about me by now and moved on to Gigi or Bella. Or some other tall, leggy supermodel who didn't have one boob half a cup size bigger than the other. I glanced down at my chest. Autumn swore she couldn't tell but she also told me I was the best jewelry designer in the world, so she was clearly full of it.

There was no doubt he was gorgeous, the kind of man who was every girl's type. Was there such a thing as being universally handsome? His suit was blue—not navy—and the color emphasized the black of his hair. His voice was deep with a hint of roughness, like the sound a five-o-clock shadow would make. His hands were capable and strong. We didn't get many men like Dexter at the Sunshine Trailer Park. Or maybe in all of Oregon.

Out of nowhere everyone started clapping and the plates that had held our lunches were being whisked away from in front of us.

Our table was the eight-member competition team of Sparkle. Most other jewelry houses had their own tables, and some had even filled two. We all shifted to see the two people standing behind the lectern at the far end of the room.

I glanced over at Dexter to see if his attention had also been captured, only to find him looking right at me. The corners of his mouth twitched as we locked eyes, as if he'd just been told a dirty joke in his grandma's house. I quickly looked away.

I tried to resist covering my heating cheeks, knowing the movement would just draw attention to my embarrassment. I pretended to be engrossed in what was happening behind the lectern. While the two women in front of us were speaking, I tried to stay focused. In the end I pulled out my notebook and started making notes, just so I'd be forced to follow what they were saying, which wasn't very much. Something about having the honor of hosting the competition. How the best of the best were all in the same room. They were looking forward to unveiling the designs. Then someone else was welcomed on stage. A tall, slender guy with a shock of white-blond hair. I'd missed who he was, but he looked like he'd be in the airport, welcoming everyone to Finland. When he started talking about his mother and his soon-to-be-married sister, I figured out we were in the presence of royalty. *Actual* royalty, and I'd nearly missed it because of darned Dexter Daniels. We'd only had one conversation and already I was missing vital pieces of information because he was so distracting.

That was it. I was determined not to look in his direction again. I wouldn't even think about that chiseled jaw, those blue eyes and large hands that fit so deliciously in the small of my back. No siree.

I scribbled furiously for the rest of the presentation, completely focused on what was being said. The prince talked passionately about Finland and the environment and how the charitable causes being supported through this competition were important to his entire family.

As he stepped off the podium, everyone stood and applauded.

While I was clapping, there was a tap on my shoulder. I turned and found myself face-to-face with Dexter.

So much for pretending he didn't exist.

"Hollie," he said. "Good to see you again."

"Hi," I said as breezily as I could manage. "Great speech, right?"

"Inspiring," he said, grinning at me as if I'd said something hilarious.

I glanced around, checking that no one from Sparkle was scowling at me for fraternizing with the competition, but no one was paying any attention to me. I turned back to him, staring at his Adam's apple as if looking him in the eye would turn me to stone—mush more likely. "So, I didn't call," I said, feeling awkward at our closeness and slightly ridiculous not meeting his gaze.

"I figured you must have mislaid my card," he said.

I rolled my eyes, irritated at his arrogance, and finally

looked him in the eye. This guy didn't have the power to turn me to mush. He overestimated himself, just like most men, and I wasn't going to indulge him. "Nope. I know it's hard to believe, but there are women in this world who actually don't want to have dinner with you."

He paused, his grin never faltering. "I can think of a number of women who fit that description. But you're not one of them."

Was this guy for real? I'd refused to give him my number, for crying out loud. And I hadn't called him. Why would he assume I wanted to have dinner with him? "It must be the way I keep calling and texting you that has you thinking like that," I said, folding my arms.

He chuckled, and a voice in my head told me to turn and walk away. This guy was trouble. Not because he was cocky but because he was right. I did want to have dinner with him. And I didn't like that he knew that.

"Nope. Not that," he replied.

"Is it the way I sent you panties in the mail?"

"They were from you?" he asked, and I had to bite back a smile when I rolled my eyes this time. "I've not quite worked out why you didn't call, but I know it's not because you don't want to have dinner with me."

"Actually, I don't," I replied. A pit started to form in my gut at the prospect of him taking me at my word, and finding some other woman to badger about going to dinner.

I liked being that woman.

"I don't find you attractive. I'm not into British guys."

He nodded as if he were carefully considering my words. "Give me your phone."

I pulled out my brand-new company *mobile*. I swear, I had never touched anything that expensive. I bet Dexter was going to check if I'd saved his number—to use that as proof I really did want to go on a date with him. "Here," I said, having unlocked it.

He scrolled through my four contacts, and I waited for him to hand it back with his tail between his legs when he saw he wasn't listed. His phone started to ring and he ignored it, then passed me back my phone. "There," he said. "Now I have your number and mine is saved in your phone. This way I get to convince you to have dinner with me."

Well, he wasn't lacking in confidence.

"Have you heard of the Me Too movement?" I asked. "You know no means no."

He pulled away from me just a fraction and, holding my gaze, blinked once. Then twice. "Hollie, sexual harassment is something to be taken seriously. If you're uncomfortable, tell me now and I'll delete your number and walk away. If we're flirting, having fun, and for some reason you're a little scared to come to dinner with me and need some convincing, then that's another matter."

My head buzzed with heat. I needed to flee from this place as if it were on fire. Dexter had an answer for everything and seemed to have the measure of me. More reasons to run for the hills. I kept telling myself I didn't want to be distracted by some guy in London, but the truth was, I had a sinking feeling Dexter wasn't just *some guy*. "A lot of convincing," I corrected him. Darn. I hadn't meant to show him a chink in my armor. I'd meant to tell him I was absolutely not interested in him and that I didn't want him to call.

But the way he looked at me as if he wanted to uncover all my secrets and tell me all his . . . The way his hand felt as he'd helped me out of the car—as if he could protect me from anything. And the way he said my name like he'd never heard anything quite so exotic. It was all too overwhelming. Despite the logical side of my brain telling me to run far away, the thumping in my chest and the pulsing ache somewhere far below it overruled my head. Like it or not, I wanted him to convince me to go to dinner with him.

"Challenge accepted," he said, before turning to disappear into the crowd.

SEVEN

Dexter

Hollie Lumen. She'd finally confessed her last name. It had only taken two days and God knows how many messages. She was a challenge indeed.

"Have you fallen victim to Fortnite?" Beck asked me as I set his water in front of him.

"What are you talking about?" I replied and slid my phone onto the table and went back to the bar for my whiskey.

"You've looked at your phone about ninety times since I said hello three minutes ago," he said as I pulled out the stool and took a seat. Beck and I were almost always the first to arrive at our weekly mates' night. It gave us a chance to catch up before everyone else arrived.

"No, I haven't." I *had* been kind of caught up with my phone in the last few days, but Hollie was funny. I looked forward to her messages.

"Yeah, you really have. Is work okay?"

"Yeah, it's fine. How's Stella?" I knew mentioning the

love of his life would be the best way to throw him off the scent of the phone obsession I didn't have.

"Oh, you know. She blows my mind every day."

"You know if you say things like that, it's almost mandatory that I have to make an oral sex joke."

"Why? Because you're fifteen? Or you've turned into Tristan?"

"You just make it so bloody easy. It's ridiculous." He'd left the door open, true, but we both knew Stella was the best thing that had ever happened to Beck. I was pleased for him. I knew what it was to find the love of your life. I'd been there. And Beck had done better than me. He'd hung on to his and was living their happily ever after.

"You need a woman who blows your mind," he said. "That's your problem. It's all about the sex for you, but there's more to a relationship."

"Sorry, did you just become my mother?" Ever since Beck had finally sorted it out with Stella, he'd become the world's biggest proponent of serious relationships. I got it. But he needed to understand—I wasn't looking for Mrs. Daniels. That ship had sailed.

"You talked sex with your mother? I just want to see you happy."

That's why I couldn't even stay mildly irritated at Beck. All he wanted was for all of us to be as happy as he was. Judging by the grin on his face, that was pretty bloody happy.

"So, what's going on?" he asked. "You stressed about the competition?"

"No, that's not it," I replied. I had nothing to hide. And maybe if I threw him a bone, he'd get off my case. "I've actually been messaging a woman I want to take to dinner. She's funny. And . . . pretty." I couldn't help but grin like a ten-year-old who had been given a United season ticket as I thought about her.

"This is news. You never talk about women."

"I'm not talking about her. I'm just explaining—"

"I'm not complaining. Who is she? Do we get to meet her? I have to tell Stella."

He grabbed his phone from where it lay face down on the table. Before he could start to gossip with Stella, I pulled it from his grasp. "None of your business and no. We've not even been on a date yet. Put a hold on that hat."

"Wait, what do you mean you've not even been on a date? You lost your bollocks and haven't asked her?"

"When I lose my bollocks, you can take an ad out in the *Times*."

"So why haven't you been on a date?" he asked.

It was a good question. We had chemistry. And I didn't normally have trouble getting a woman to have dinner with me. But there was something about Hollie that made her scared to say yes. That only made me more intrigued about what lay beneath her beautiful surface—what had made her so scared. I wanted to take her to dinner more than ever. "I'm not sure."

"So, you've asked her?"

"Yeah. She said no and then confessed that she'd wanted to say yes. We're messaging back and forth." I'd thought about calling her but I didn't want to spook her. I couldn't tell Beck that, because Beck would ask me why I cared—and I wouldn't have an answer. I also wouldn't have an answer if he asked me why I was checking my phone incessantly in case she messaged me back. I wouldn't have an answer if he asked me why my stomach flipped whenever a message finally came through.

"The thrill of the chase," he said. "I was never like that but—"

"It's not that." I had never been into the chase. "That's Tristan, not me."

Beck nodded, and I could tell by the controlled movement he was dying to ask more questions.

"I don't know what it is," I said. "She's American. And . . ." I had dated American women before, so that wasn't the reason I liked Hollie. It was more that she managed to be both wide-eyed innocent and devilishly suspicious at the exact same time. She was direct enough to refuse to give me her number and to ask for my card, but not so open that she'd tell me why she was refusing to have dinner with me

"Maybe it's because you like to torture yourself a little," Beck said, fishing out the lemon from his water and placing it on the table. "Bloody lemon."

"I like an easy life. That's why I end things whenever they get heavy. I'm not into self-torture at all."

"That's total bollocks," Beck said. "I can't let you get away with that, mate."

"What?" I said, offended. "I like women. I like sex with women, friendship with women, but I'm not into torture. I'm not a masochist, physically or emotionally."

Silence echoed off him in waves. Beck rarely held back telling me what he thought. None of us did. Meeting when we did—facing the challenges we'd faced together—had created an intimacy between us that meant we were brutally honest with each other, and as open as it was possible for six guys to be.

"You don't agree?" I asked him.

"What about Bridget?" he asked.

"What about her?"

"You like to torture yourself about her."

"I blame myself. That's not the same as torture." I'd been young when it had all fallen apart, but that was no excuse.

"I'm not sure about that. I think you two breaking up has become almost mythical to you."

"What the fuck are you talking about? It is what it is. We were together. We were happy. We were in love. I screwed it up by ending things over some stupid argument. When I finally got my head out of my arse and tried to get her back, she'd moved on. I'm an idiot. That's not self-torture. That's facts."

"Well they're not the facts as I see them."

I liked Beck. Loved him. Not just like a brother, but as my best friend and confidante. Tonight, though, he was pissing me off. I checked the time on my phone. Where the fuck was everyone?

At that exact moment Gabriel swept in. "I swear to God, if I was ever gay, it would be Gabriel I'd have the hots for," I said, watching him as he strode over to the table.

"Is this your coming-out party?" Beck asked.

"You're gay?" Gabriel asked, looking at me as if he'd just asked me whether I was enjoying my water.

"Nope but if I was, I think you'd be my type."

Gabriel rolled his eyes and pulled his pint of Guinness from the small circle of drinks in the middle of the table. "Good to know."

"He's trying to distract us because I just told him some home truths."

"Interesting," Gabriel said, taking a seat beside Beck. "Go on."

"No, you didn't. You just floated some ridiculous theory about me enjoying self-torture."

Gabriel's gaze flitted between us like he was at Wimbledon.

"Because of the Bridget thing," Beck said as if that explained everything.

"Oh, right, yes," Gabriel said as if he completely understood.

"What do you mean, yes? Beck is being ridiculous, right?"

"Look, mate. I just got here—you two keep your playground fight between yourselves. I'm going to sit and enjoy my Guinness until some sane people arrive."

"You'll get splinters sitting on that fence," I replied. "Beck just said I like to torture myself about Bridget and I said stating facts wasn't the same as self-torture."

"I'm not sure it's self-torture," he said, giving Beck a look that said *don't be so dramatic*, "but it's weird how you just write yourself off as never being able to find happiness because things didn't work out with the girlfriend you had at nineteen."

It took all my effort not to stand up and walk out. Was he serious? These guys knew me inside out, or at least I thought they did. Maybe they didn't at all. Maybe I knew them. Understood how each of *them* ticked, what their strengths and weaknesses were, but perhaps that knowledge wasn't reciprocated. Because I *wasn't* torturing myself about Bridget. I was accepting responsibility. I wasn't bitter or broken by what happened. I just understood that I'd messed up and would never be in love again. "What we had was special and that doesn't come along twice in a lifetime. I'm completely at peace with that. No torture. No drama."

Gabriel started to chuckle. "Yeah. No drama at all." He raised the back of his palm to his forehead. "I'll never love again. It only happens once in a lifetime."

Beck began to copy him. "She's the only woman in the entire world—Jesus, mate, you were basically a kid. Get over yourself."

Harsh.

I leaned back in my chair as if pinned by a sudden g-force. Honestly, I thought I'd been the opposite of dramatic as far as Bridget and I were concerned. And it wasn't as if I'd sworn off women or anything. I'd rarely been single in the last decade.

I looked up to find Tristan glancing around our silent table.

"What did I miss?" he asked.

"We're giving Dexter shit," Beck said.

"I think we should stop," Gabriel replied, shooting me a sideways glance. "If you want to torture yourself, that's your business. We're here for you whatever."

"So, what's your solution to me being dramatic about Bridget? I barely talk about her . . ."

"We're talking about Bridget again?" Tristan asked before collapsing on his stool. Gabriel pushed him a pint of beer.

"You make it sound like I'm mooning around, constantly talking about her—"

"No, you don't talk about her," Gabriel conceded and I gave him a nod in appreciation. "It's just that the women you hang out with—your relationships are all a reaction to Bridget. Still."

"That's a good way of putting it," Beck said. "They're a reaction."

"You assume you'll never meet anyone to be with long-term—commit to, fall in love with—*because* of Bridget."

Well that was true. "I'm not complaining. I'm not heartbroken." I was an idiot, that I could accept. But it's not like I was pining over lost love.

"Doesn't mean you're over her," Beck said.

"No," Gabriel corrected. "Getting over *her* isn't the solution. You need to get over your *relationship*."

I was pretty sure that was a distinction without a difference. I'd had enough. I'd come out tonight to relax and kick back, not to suffer a character assassination.

My cell buzzed in my hand.

Okay dinner. But only if it's fondue. And you must not distract me at competition events. We're strangers if we ever bump into each other outside of cheese. Agreed?

Finally. And even though I didn't understand her terms, I didn't care. I needed to be distracted from thinking about whether I was still hung up on Bridget.

"Did I tell you that David was there at the launch of the competition?" I said in a final ditch effort to stop these guys going on about Bridget.

"David who?" Tristan asked. It had been a long time since I'd brought up my brother in conversation, so Tristan's confusion could be forgiven.

"Your brother?" Gabriel asked.

"Apparently," I said. Seeing his name on the list of attendees had reignited the anger inside me. "I guess he and Sparkle are still colluding. Fifteen years later, they're still making money by rereleasing and rehashing my mother's designs. I guess they have a lot to be grateful to him for." Maybe he'd taken some kind of shareholding in the company when he sold them my parents' business? Were we competitors now?

"Sparkle? You think he took additional money from them?" Beck asked.

"It wouldn't surprise me. He has the moral compass of

an alley cat. Why else would he be there? I looked him up. He still works at a bank. Not in the industry."

"Wow, that's low," Beck said.

"And fraud," Gabriel pointed out, ever the lawyer. "Potentially. If he was offered an incentive to sell to Sparkle and didn't tell you about it."

"He didn't tell me about any of it," I reminded Gabriel. I hadn't gotten a say in what happened to my parents' business. David had made all the decisions and had taken the opportunity to betray me in the process.

When I'd entered the competition, I'd every intention of winning. I'd wanted to carry on my parents' legacy—to link my business with theirs by bejeweling the next generation of Finnish royalty. But now winning wasn't enough.

I was going to have to destroy the competition.

EIGHT

Hollie

I'd never cared what I'd worn on a date before. Tonight was different, not just because I was going on a date with the best-looking man I'd ever seen, but because we were in *London*. People here were *sophisticated*. They went to the theater and spoke a thousand languages and read books I'd never even heard of. I was going to give myself away as some trailer park chick as soon as I rocked up wearing my favorite skinny jeans and a blue shirt that looked like silk even though it was one hundred percent rayon. Actually, it wasn't my outfit that would give me away—my shirt really did look like silk, and it seemed that in London there were fewer rules about what you could or couldn't wear than in Oregon. But I hadn't gone to college, my favorite book was *A Woman of Substance,* and the only language I spoke was English, with an American accent.

I rubbed my pendant between my thumb and forefinger, trying to get up the courage to go inside Urban Alpine, the restaurant Dexter had sent me the details of yesterday.

He'd offered to pick me up but I told him I'd meet him here. Now I was hovering on the step, wishing I'd said yes to a ride. At least that way, there would be no chickening out at the last minute.

It wasn't that I was nervous. It was more that I just felt out of my depth. Dating wasn't my forte, but it was much easier when you didn't want to strip the guy naked in public and take shots off what I just knew would be deliciously hard abs. It would be much, much easier if he didn't make me laugh so darn much, even by message. And the way he was so completely sure that I'd eventually say yes to dinner and that it didn't seem to faze him that I'd kept him waiting as long as I had. It was annoying because he was so freaking attractive, and spending time with an attractive man wasn't on my list of things to do while I was in London. And I had a long list.

"Here goes nothing," I said out loud. I gripped the door handle and pulled with such force that it smashed into the wall, and the few tables nearest the door all turned to look at the lunatic who apparently didn't know her own strength.

I grimaced. "Sorry," I said. I immediately caught Dexter's eye. He was grinning at me from a corner table on the far left of the room.

I couldn't help smiling back, despite the fact he was probably laughing at my ridiculous entrance.

Awkwardly, I grunted at the hostess and pointed at Dexter. She let me make my own way over to our table.

He stood as I approached and leaned in to kiss me on both cheeks. I was getting used to the two-kiss thing, and managed not to accidentally turn it into a kiss on the mouth.

"So," I said. "Fondue."

"*Finally,* fondue," he replied. "You look beautiful."

"So do you," I replied. Weird thing to say to a guy

maybe, but I wasn't about to get arrested by the truth police. He looked freaking phenomenal. Just the way he sat—arms stretched along the top of the booth, taking up as much space as possible, like he was the King of London—had my heart racing.

He chuckled. "Okay."

I sat at the v-shaped booth, him on one side, me on the other, our knees almost touching.

"So, what's good?" I asked, picking up the menu.

"I heard the cheese is amazing."

I laughed. "Well if it's not, I'm off. I'm all about the cheese."

"Don't I know it. I think if I'd suggested any other type of place, I'd have got a hard no. It was difficult enough to get you to say yes to cheese."

He was looking at me like he knew I thought he was as hot as Hades but was happy to play along with my I'm-not-that-into-you routine. And gosh-darn it, that just made him all the more attractive. No doubt he'd gotten more female attention than he would know what to do with his whole life, yet here he was. With me.

"Yeah, well, I'm not in London for the guys." Although it would be the place to come.

"Certainly not. You're clearly here for the cheese." He beckoned the waitress over, and after checking with me, ordered fondue and wine.

I wasn't sure if it was just that he was supremely confident or whether he was just the first grown-up man I'd ever gone on a date with, but tonight felt different from any date I'd had before. "I've never had a date order for me," I said, tearing a piece of bread from the board in front of us. I wondered if Autumn would approve or think he was an overbearing jerk.

"Do you mind? I know you don't like me giving your address to my driver." He raised his eyebrows.

"I don't think I do. I mean, you checked with me first. If you hadn't, I think it would have been weird."

"Given we've only met twice before."

"Right," I said. "But I kinda liked it, and I figured maybe you majored in hot cheese at college or something."

"What a relief." He smiled as if it wasn't a relief at all. As if he'd known all along that I'd like it. That it would make me feel looked after. Special. "I like that I get to hear your inside thoughts. On the outside."

I swallowed down my bread. Was that the British equivalent of "bless your heart?" Was it meant to sound like a compliment but was actually a ginormous put down? "What do you mean?"

"You're open. Direct. Say what's on your mind. And I get it in real time as you're thinking it."

Hmmm, he was kinda right. The filter I had was in need of repair in places.

"Mostly," he added. "I can't wait to uncover the rest." He raised his glass. "I've never worked so hard to get dinner with a woman. Let's have a great evening and not worry too much about anything but cheese."

It was as if the bits I was hiding, he had discovered anyway. He knew exactly what to say to put me at ease. And that was amazing and horrifying. Part of me had agreed to this dinner so I could get to know his flaws, find something irritating about him. This wasn't going to go well if he just got *more* attractive.

"That's a pretty necklace you're wearing," he said.

My fingers went to my throat. "Thanks. It was the first piece I ever designed." My oak leaf was plain silver. No stones or fancy settings, but it was priceless to me. "I have an Etsy shop," I said. There was no point in pretending to be anyone I wasn't. This guy was as big as anyone could be in the industry. Nothing I said was going to impress him. "No diamonds or Bolivian emeralds."

"Zambian."

"Those either. No emeralds of any kind."

He grinned at me, his eyes fixed on my face as if he couldn't quite believe his luck that I was his date. "You make your own stuff for the Etsy shop or do you get it made?"

"I make it myself." He didn't have to know I had a couple of orders a month.

"I like the leaf. Is it you? Away from home, looking for a place to land?"

I took a breath before I answered and popped a chunk of bread in my mouth, trying to give myself some extra time. But even those additional seconds didn't give me an answer. "I don't know," I said. Maybe I was. I wasn't connected to the trailer park in any sentimental way, and although home should have felt like anywhere Autumn was, at the moment, I didn't know where I belonged. I wanted more than I had in Oregon. Being here, in London, gave a sense of freedom I hadn't expected. Sometimes I felt the pull of home, but I hadn't been homesick. The feeling was usually accompanied by a rush of worry about what was going on when I wasn't around to clean up after my parents or look after my sister. "When I think of an oak tree, I think of strength," I said without thinking.

"Yes," he said, an intense look on his face. "I like that."

He didn't elaborate and seemed much more comfortable in the following silence than I was.

"Do you design things?" I asked, wanting to shift him away from whatever it was he was thinking about.

He shook his head. "I leave that to more talented people."

"So you're the business brains?"

"I like to think I've got an instinct for what will look good when it's translated from paper into reality," he said. "I see myself as an editor—a curator of the design, if you like. And of course, I love stones. When I see an uncut stone, I can see the gem it will be. I can picture it when it's cut and polished and in its setting."

He had creative vision. With business brains. Argh. Why couldn't he have been a bean counter? I guess that's what made him one of the most successful people in the industry.

"I haven't worked with stones. That's why I'm here."

"I'm not sure you'll find any in the fondue."

"Whoever told you that you were funny was lying."

He laughed, perfectly satisfied with his joke.

"That's why I'm here *in London*," I clarified. "More experience. I want to turn a hobby into a career."

One side of his mouth began to curl upward as if he was enjoying listening to me speak. Maybe it was my accent.

"So, if jewelry is just your hobby, what's your career now?"

"I have a job, not a career. It pays the bills. Let's not talk about it." While I was here, I wanted to imagine that this was my only life now. The less I had to think about the worries that awaited me back home, the better.

A hint of a frown crossed Dexter's forehead and I longed to reach across the table and smooth it down.

"What about you? What would you have done if you hadn't been a jeweler?"

"There was no other path for me," he answered without hesitation. "I was born to do this."

"Because you love it or because it's what your parents did?" It was amazing to me that anyone could be so sure about what they were meant to do with their lives.

"Most definitely both," he replied. "What do your parents do?"

I groaned. "Not a lot." I really didn't want to talk about life back in Oregon.

Our fondue arrived just in time to save me from the question. The waitress placed a small saucepan on the burner in the middle of the table, with an array of bread, meats and vegetables alongside. I hadn't thought this through. This blouse was rayon, but that didn't mean it would wipe clean. Who came to a fondue restaurant for a first date?

"Who knows you best in the entire world?" I asked, desperate to steer the conversation away from my life in Oregon.

He offered me the bread basket and I stabbed a cube with my long fork.

"I have five best friends—we've been close since we were teenagers."

"Nice," I said. "Like a pack?"

"They're human. Not wolves." He growled, low and deep, and I swear I was a second away from pulling a Meg Ryan. Only I wouldn't have been faking.

"You tell them your deepest, darkest secrets?" I asked.

"To the extent I have any. I'm pretty much an open book." A hint of the frown again and my fingers buzzed with the urge to press it away.

"I read a thing online about you," I confessed. "Because, you know—" Obviously I was going to google a guy before I shared cheese with him. "It said you had 'shunned the London jewelry industry' for years. That true?" I didn't need an internet search to tell me that—his reputation preceded him—but he didn't need to know that.

"Yes and no," he replied.

I waited for him to elaborate but he just dipped a mushroom into the cheese, popped it in his mouth and chewed.

"Well, that's not an answer."

"No. That was me saying I don't want to answer." His lips curled around his words and he scanned my face before adding, "In British."

I laughed. "I'm not fluent yet." I met guys who kept things secret, but I wasn't sure I'd ever met a man who was completely open about what he was hiding.

"You didn't tell me which one of my competitors you're interning for," he said, clearly trying to change the subject.

"Sparkle," I said, still proud I'd managed to secure an internship at such a well-renowned firm. Daniels & Co were arguably a better brand, but Sparkle wasn't far behind.

Dexter froze, his breathing shallow and his eyes fixed on me. It was as if he had an invisible gun to his head and he was trying to warn me to run. And then all of a sudden, he was back to normal—all smiles and easy charm.

"Rewind there for a minute." Okay, so it was a first date and he didn't have to tell me why he'd stayed away from London or what his mother's maiden name was, but we had to have some kind of exchange of information, something deeper than cheese talk. "What was that?" I asked. "When I mentioned Sparkle?"

"What?" he asked, stabbing a piece of pepper.

"Put down the vegetable and tell me why you looked like you'd seen a ghost when I mentioned who I was interning for."

"No ghosts," he said, setting down his fork and taking a sip of wine.

This date had only just begun and already it was full of negatives. I was avoiding telling him things, and he was clearly holding his cards close. "You know what I think?"

He paused and looked at me, waiting for me to go on.

"I think we're doing a dance," I continued. "I think you're not saying some things. I'm doing the same, even though you said you like it when *I'm* completely open and you said you were an open book. We're skating on the surface and it's nice and all. I mean—you're great to look at, and fondue is a riveting topic of conversation, but what are we doing here if we're both trying so hard not to share who we are?"

He blinked but didn't move. I wasn't sure if he hadn't liked what I said or he wanted me to elaborate.

I sat back and pushed my glass away. "I'm trying not to give away that I live under a gray sky in a single-wide trailer and work in a factory. And that I'm wearing a one hundred percent rayon shirt. You?"

There—I'd thrown down a challenge. He might walk out, but just like Dexter had known I wanted to say yes to dinner despite saying no at first, something told me he wouldn't balk at my invitation to tell the truth. These three months in London would come to an end all too soon, and I wanted to make the most out of every second, including tonight. I had to have the truth, because I didn't have time for lies.

"It's all connected," he said, as if that made perfect sense. His gaze scanned the room, like he was checking for exits or perhaps deciding whether or not he was going to open up. "My parents died in a car crash when I was nineteen."

This time, I couldn't hold back—I had to touch him. I leaned and slid my hand over his.

"And my brother sold their business to Sparkle, right out from under my nose. I had no rights under the will because I wasn't twenty-one. Dealing with the estate was all up to my brother. I lost my parents and their business to Sparkle. All in one."

"Oh, God. I'm so sorry." I squeezed his hand.

"Sparkle had tried to recruit my mother—over and over —as a designer. And had poached other members of staff. My parents' business was small but it produced beautiful jewelry. Sparkle had wanted to own them for years. When they died . . ."

"Sparkle pounced."

The warm, flirtatious smile had disappeared and the ridge between his eyes was deeper now. I wanted to fix it. I wanted to make it better. "They took advantage," he said. And I'd bet he'd spent his entire life making sure no one else was ever going to take advantage of him again.

"What did your brother say? Was he sorry?" I asked.

"I wouldn't know. We haven't spoken since." He flipped my hand over and linked his fingers through mine.

I couldn't imagine going a single day without my sister, let alone years. "Wow. And did he start his own jewelry business like you did?"

"Last I heard he worked in the back office at one of the banks in the City."

His brother should have been protecting him, not selling off the family business. "I bet that's a huge motivation for you. Creating Daniels & Co and being so successful."

"A little," he replied. It was just two words, but they unlocked a lot about the man in front of me. I couldn't imagine what such a betrayal by a member of my family would do to me.

Dexter's brother wasn't the only one who had betrayed him. Sparkle shared the blame. I was working for the enemy. "I bet you want to beat Sparkle in this competition, huh?" I asked.

"A little," he repeated. "I want to kiss you more."

I bit back a smile. He was lying. But I could live with that. "What are the odds, do you think?" I asked, thinking out loud.

"Of me kissing you? That's up to you. What do *you* think the odds are?"

"Hmm, well, given your form, I'd say . . . three to ten?"

"Three to ten?" he asked, his brow crinkling in confusion. "That's specific."

"I have no idea what I'm talking about," I confessed. "I'm not a girl who makes bets."

I liked this guy. Against my better judgment, I was here at dinner with him. "It would be complicated, wouldn't it? Me on the Sparkle team and everything?" I had my reservations about Dexter. He was devastatingly handsome and I wasn't in London to be devastated. And I wasn't exactly the ideal woman for him. I hadn't had anything to do with taking over his family business, but I was working for the people who had.

He sighed and sat back a little in his seat, cold air filling the distance between us. Despite myself, I wanted him to kiss me. And that was the problem. Because I couldn't remember ever being on a date and wanting so badly to be kissed. First dates were all about thinking about whether the date would end in a kiss. Until tonight, the answer had always been *absolutely not* or *maybe it wouldn't be so bad*. Once or twice it had even gotten to *you never know, it might be amazing*. But the idea of kissing Dexter didn't make me think. It made me feel a thousand feelings—the fluttering swirl in the base of my belly, the shiver at the bottom of my spine, and the pulsing heat under my skin. I couldn't *wait* for him to kiss me.

He glanced up at me as if trying to weigh the pros and cons.

"It's not like you were the one who bought my family business. We just won't discuss the competition," he said, nodding as if it were the easiest answer. I'd suggested the same thing, hadn't I? It was the only way I could justify sitting here tonight. Work was work. This was . . . not work. And even if I was in London to lay the foundations for the rest of my life, Autumn would be quick to tell me I couldn't work one hundred percent of the time. I needed time to recharge. That's what Dexter would be for me—a trip to the spa, but in male form.

"I'm not the enemy?" I asked.

"You don't look much like the enemy," he replied, leaning forward, closer than before, the air between us thickening.

The clatter of the restaurant faded into the background, and all I could focus on was the rise and fall of Dexter's chest, the way his lips parted and his gaze burned into me.

He slid his hand around the back of my neck and dropped a kiss on the side of my mouth.

I shut my eyes, as if blocking out at least a part of Dexter —the sight of him—would make this moment more manageable. Otherwise, I ran the risk of being completely overwhelmed.

"I'm not your enemy," I whispered as he pressed his lips on the other side of my mouth.

He growled and I opened my eyes to find him shifting away from me.

"The things I want to do to you," he said, his voice raw

and coarse. I reached out to him, stroking the five o'clock shadow covering his jaw. I ached to know how the rough stubble would feel between my legs.

"Tell me," I said. I wanted details, to know what he was thinking. I knew that whatever it was, in that exact moment, I would have said yes. To anything.

NINE

Dexter

"I can't wait to meet this woman," Beck said, craning his neck to survey the bustling room as if he had a clue what Hollie looked like. He was overly invested.

I'd been light on detail when he'd pumped me for information about my date with Hollie. Partly in an effort to throw him off the scent and also because it had taken me by surprise. Yes, she was fun and warm and so beautiful. But the way she'd called me out—us both out—for hiding things on our date, the way she'd confessed what she'd been trying to hide and had me do the same . . . It wasn't what I'd expected, which made her all the more intriguing. I'd thought she'd just be another date, just a bit more of a challenge. And I suppose I thought she'd be funny, given her messages after we'd first met. But I hadn't imagined her to be so . . . beguiling.

I never talked about what my brother had done, conspiring behind my back to sell off everything my parents loved to a predator. As much as I'd like to put it down to the cheese, I knew differently. She'd been right when she'd accused us both of dancing around secrets and half-truths, but we'd been on a date at a restaurant that pretended to be tucked into the Swiss Alps, not on a psychiatrist's sofa. You weren't meant to confess your deepest, darkest secrets on a first date. Hollie hadn't got that memo, and apparently, I didn't mind too much. There was something in those green-blue eyes that made me want to tell her whatever she wanted to know.

"You're not going to meet her tonight," I said. "This is a work thing. We're here to find out which five jewelry houses are through to the finals. You're supposed to be moral support."

"But she's here?" he asked. "In this room?"

God, why did I have to bring Beck? He needed to accept that what he'd found with Stella wasn't for everyone.

"Focus, Beck. Moral support. Remember?"

He snapped his head around. "What? Are you worried or something? Of course you're going to make it to the finals." He looked at me as if I'd just told him I was worried about losing a leg bowling, or crashing my car in an empty car park. He had complete faith in me. That's why he was my brother.

"So how many events like this are there?" he asked. "You seem to have had a lot of man dates recently." Today's reveal of the finalists was a buffet lunch overlooking the Thames.

"A lot," I replied. "They're trying to raise a ton for charity. I said to Primrose I'd much prefer to write a huge check than turn up at all of them but—"

"No, you need to show your face," he said. "You don't

want to piss off the organizers and have them think you think you're too good to mix with your peers."

"It's not that. I'm just antisocial." It wasn't just that. And Beck knew it.

Beck chuckled. "I know. But they don't. Sometimes you've just got to play the game."

He sounded like Primrose. But the people I surrounded myself with all had my best interests at heart and that's why I was here. "That's why I have so many man dates."

I spotted Hollie across the room and the tips of my fingers twitched with a need to touch her. It was difficult to miss her. She was all tumbling pre-Raphaelite curls and pale skin, like she belonged in a different century.

My gaze slid from her to who she was talking to and my stomach began to churn. Charles Ledwin, CEO of Sparkle and a face I'd never forget. He'd aged, but his face young or old was burned into my memory. The first time I saw him he'd dropped into my parents' shop on Hatton Garden as if he were a customer. Only instead of trying to buy a ring, he offered to buy the place. My father had barked out a laugh and sent him on his way, but he'd appeared a couple more times. It was as if he were circling the place, waiting for his prey to weaken. When my parents died, I told my brother we shouldn't accept the offer, that we should run the place together, just as our parents had wanted. But David had been selfish and greedy, and he'd taken Sparkle's money.

Even now, thinking back to what he'd done, the wound was still fresh. How could he have cared so little for me?

A microphone squeaked across the room, catching everyone's attention. The head of the environmental charity being supported by the lunch made a short speech before thanking the room for their donations. Despite each event being voluntary, every jeweler who'd entered the competition had written a check in support of the charity being spotlighted. It was smart of the Finish royal family to design a mutually beneficial arrangement—the jewelers all got publicity and the charities received generous donations.

"And now down to business," the host said. "It's time to announce the five finalists whose designs will be produced ahead of final judgment."

"Wait," Beck said. "There's no actual jewelry been made yet?"

"Not officially. We've submitted the designs." I'd been able to source most of the stones already and the pieces were all but finished. The only thing I didn't have was the emeralds, because of my change of heart from Columbian to Zambian.

"These guys are judging off plan, I see."

"Yeah. It's not like a building though. A piece can be made or broken because of the stones." I understood why the organizers with the Finnish royal family had decided to break the competition down like this. They wanted the maximum number of entrants at the beginning because that would generate the most publicity and money for the charitable causes being supported. And it wouldn't be fair for some of the less-established jewelers to make the pieces unless they were going to have a fair chance at winning. It would be a huge financial outlay to make a collection for a royal wedding. I understood all that. I just didn't agree with it. It was possible to get a feel for a piece when you saw it on paper, but it didn't tell you everything about the final ring or bracelet or tiara.

Someone else took over the lectern—I had no idea who. For years I'd kept my focus on me and my business, not taking too much notice of what was going on in the industry. It worked for me. I hadn't gotten bogged down in gossip and politics. And I'd found a path from which I could honor my parents without hearing the condolences and constant comparisons.

The first name was announced—Garrard. No surprise there. Conservative and steady choice. Then Graff, followed by Cartier.

Two slots left.

I glanced over at Hollie. I'd never seen her anything but smiling, but now her jaw was tense and her expression steady, as if beneath the soft curls and wide smile a layer of steel hid.

"The fourth finalist to go through is Van Cleef and Arples," the emcee said.

Hollie turned toward me and gave me a forlorn look that conveyed a mutual understanding—at least one of us would leave this room disappointed. I had no idea she'd seen me.

"And the last finalist is . . . Daniels & Co."

I took a deep breath as Beck clapped me on the back. "Knew you had it."

I glanced over at Hollie, who looked back with an expression of shock and dismay. I really wanted to go over and comfort her but didn't want to risk bumping into any of the people from Sparkle. Besides, I'd sworn I'd not greet her in public.

Shit. I pulled out my phone.

"You are a shitty date," Beck said. "Aren't you going to get me drunk?"

"Hang on a minute," I replied, typing out a short message to say I was sorry to Hollie.

I stuffed my phone back in my pocket and watched as she read my message.

She looked up and gave me a forced smile.

I should be delighted that Daniels & Co was in this final without Sparkle. But I had no sense of victory.

TEN

Hollie

And the hits just kept on coming.

I stepped out of the Sparkle office and onto the rain-drop-splattered pavement, and glanced up into the sky. Of course it was raining. When I'd first arrived in London, the rain was comforting and familiar, but now it just reminded me I'd be home sooner than I wanted to be.

I'd known this internship was too good to be true. I didn't fit in this kind of life. I'd been stupid for thinking I could exist outside the Sunshine Trailer Park.

How was I going to tell Autumn I'd been fired? She'd believed in me, wanted the win for me almost as much as I wanted it for myself. I was letting my sister down on top of having all my dreams come tumbling down on top of me all at once.

I'd never lost a job in my life before. And now the only job that could lead to something, could lead to a life I wanted, had been ripped away from me. How was this fair? I tipped my head back, letting the rain fall on my face as if it could wash away the despair rising in my chest.

All that money on flights and renting my studio—all gone. My stomach churned at the thought of how many thousands of dollars I had wasted on a couple of weeks in England. I didn't have enough experience for it to count on my resume, I hadn't secured a letter of recommendation, and I wouldn't have any savings left once I'd paid to get back to Oregon early.

I'd had my shot and it was over.

At least Pauly had kept my job open at the factory so I had something to go back to.

And Dexter? I'd never see him again, never get to feel the scrape of his chin against my thigh. We'd had one dinner, but I'd never had such a perfect date. He was meant to be the icing on top of the London cake. My fun. My spa in male form. He'd been the first man who made me laugh out loud, the first man who I looked forward to kissing, the first man I ever wanted to have a second date with. Now none of that would happen.

What a disastrous mess.

I slumped on a bench and my phone buzzed in my hand.

Shit, I was meant to leave the phone. That would be Sparkle's office manager, demanding it back.

I turned the phone over in my hand to reveal the caller. Dexter.

I slid the green button across. "Come and get drunk with me?"

"You going to help me celebrate?" he asked and despite my cloud of misery, I could still picture his relaxed smile. I knew he hadn't called to crow. It wasn't his style.

"Yes. And you can help me commiserate."

"Sparkle will let you go early? I was going to suggest dinner."

"Yeah, Sparkle let me go early. That's what you're going to help me commiserate about."

"What? They let you go early today . . .?" He elongated the question like he knew the answer but didn't want to put it into words.

"I got fired," I coughed out. It hadn't occurred to me they'd just get rid of me if they didn't make the finals of the competition. They said they needed the desk space now they weren't in the competition, which made no sense to me but I guess it didn't need to. I'd been so excited about this opportunity. I'd talked incessantly to Autumn about it, as if this was me going to Harvard or something. But this was *my* Harvard. My chance to focus on me, to have a career, a different life. *Jiminy Cricket.*

Now I was going to have to spend money to change my flight and go home to . . . what?

"Hollie? Did you hear me?"

"What? Sorry? I was just—"

"Where are you right now?" Dexter asked.

I hadn't taken much notice. I looked up for a sign and just saw the Sparkle awning down the street. I hadn't made it far. "I'm getting to the end of Hatton Garden."

"Which end?" he asked. His voice was muffled. "North or south?"

How should I know? "The end with the guy on the horse." I hadn't even had time to figure out why the statue at the end of the street was there. And the plaque on the wall outside our office. I kept meaning to read it but hadn't gotten the chance. Two weeks in London wasn't enough.

"Holborn Circus end?" he asked.

He'd been drinking already. "Nope. There's no sign of a

circus. Not a clown in sight." Having to deal with a clown would really be the cherry on top of the most darn-awful day. "Just a gazillion traffic lights and cars everywhere."

"Yeah. That's Holborn Circus. Stay right there," he snapped. "I'll be ten minutes. I'm coming to get you."

I'd been joking about him taking me drinking, but if he had the afternoon off to celebrate, I wasn't going to complain if he wanted to help me drown my sorrows at the same time.

I changed direction, headed back to Sparkle, dropped the phone through their letterbox and retraced my steps toward the circus that wasn't a circus. I wandered halfway across the street to the pedestrian island separating the cars going in opposite directions, which was where the statue of the man on the horse was. I might not have had a chance to go to the British Museum, but I could at least check this guy out.

The statue was high above me, mounted on a huge block of granite that made it all the more difficult to see it. Why in the hell was this raised high above the ground, over-looking all the traffic?

A car horn behind me made me jump, and I snapped my head around to find Dexter's head poking out of a car stopped at the lights. "Jump in."

Despite my mood, I couldn't help but smile. He was here. I wasn't sure why or how but I was just pleased he was. It made things a tiny bit better.

"Hey," I said as I climbed in the passenger seat. "You skipped out of class early?"

"I had the head teacher's permission." He paused. "How are you feeling? Those bastards at Sparkle are lower than a snake's belly."

"I feel kinda numb." But being here with Dexter was

nice. More than nice. Just sitting next to him dulled the pain and frustration. More time with Dexter, even if it was just a couple of hours, would make this London trip memorable even if it all ended up being a waste of time and money.

"Did they at least pay you until the end of your internship?" he asked.

"It wasn't a paid thing. I saved—" I didn't want him to think I was bummed about the money. The money was an issue, but it was the lack of experience and opportunity that was the worst of it. My future felt bleak—an endless parade of trailer park living, factory work, and dreaming dreams that would never come true.

Dexter's jaw tightened. He wove through traffic before pulling up sharply by the side of the road. "Come on," he said, opening the door. "Let's get drunk."

ELEVEN

Dexter

"Do we have the same drink?" Hollie asked, holding up her glass and squinting as if she were trying to spot a koi carp swimming in her glass.

"You have vodka," I replied.

She slammed her glass down. "Well that was a bad idea. I'm seeing lots of things . . . everything—there's two of everything."

"Vodka was what you asked for."

"You should never listen to me. Ever," she said, dramatically shaking her head. She was a cute drunk. And cheap. She was only on her third drink, albeit each one had been different. She'd started with whiskey. "I have terrible brain ideas."

"Brain ideas?"

"Like coming to London." More head shaking. "Should have saved my money."

Charles Ledwin was a shit. I hated him for making Hollie wish she'd never come to London. Sparkle hadn't even offered to pay her air fare home. And then it hit me—if she was out of a job, there would be no reason for her to stay. She'd be heading back to the US before we'd even got to know each other properly.

"I thought it was the start of something, you know?" She pinched her brows together, earnest in her drunkenness.

I knew exactly what she meant. If she'd stayed the extra few months, I'd have liked to have hung out with her more. She was sexy and fun and sagely naïve. And I hated that she felt bad.

"You've still had the experience though, right? You'll still get something out of it." I was grasping at straws, trying to say something that would help.

"We shouldn't talk about it." She craned her neck toward the bar. "We should drink more. What's this?" She held up her glass.

"Vodka."

"Right. I think maybe wine would be better."

No amount of wine was going to make this better. But I knew I could help.

"I have an idea," I announced. I was pretty sure Beck would tell me it was a terrible idea if he was here. And probably so would Gabriel. But I didn't care. I couldn't stand by and let Sparkle kill Hollie's dreams. I just couldn't. "You should finish your internship at Daniels & Co."

"Definitely wine," Hollie said, wincing as she swallowed the last gulp of vodka.

I'd expected her to throw her arms around me and tell me I was her hero. But she seemed more focused on her drink. "Did you hear me?" I asked.

She clasped my shoulder. "God, I'm being awful company. I'm sorry. You said you have an idea." She pointed at my head and I couldn't help but grin. I wasn't sure I'd ever seen anyone quite so adorable when they were drunk.

"I have several." I called the waiter over and ordered some soft drinks while Hollie held a conversation with the candle.

I grabbed her around the waist and pulled her toward me.

"Hey, what are you doing?" she asked. "I thought we were going to drink wine?" Dropping her voice to a stage whisper, she asked, "Are we going to have sex?"

"Absolutely not."

She turned to me, the expression on her face as if I'd just insulted her.

"Hollie, you've had far too much to drink . . ." I paused. That wasn't quite true. She hadn't had much to drink at all. She was just drunk. "You're too tipsy to be—I'm just moving you closer so you can hear what I'm saying."

Sex wasn't going to happen. Not tonight. Not when she was in a position to be able to regret it.

"I want to talk business with you," I said.

"You don't want to sleep with you?" Her stage whisper had transformed into a semi-shout. "With me, I mean. You don't want to have sex with me?"

I chuckled. "I think you just proved my point." Our tray of nonalcoholic cocktails arrived.

"Pretty!" Hollie said, bouncing in her chair as the waiter transferred each of them from tray to table. "I like this better than wine."

I should probably wait until tomorrow to talk to her about working for Daniels & Co, but I wanted to cheer her up. And it would stop her booking a flight home.

"So, what do you think about being an intern for me?" I asked.

She turned to me, looking at me over her shoulder. "You want me to dress up? Like role play? That's your thing?"

"Hollie, will you focus?" I took the martini glass out of her hand. "Look at me."

"I'm looking," she replied, staring at me. The blue flecks in her green eyes seemed to have expanded over the course of the afternoon.

"Stay in London and finish your internship at Daniels & Co."

She seemed to be following what I was saying and her eyelids fluttered open and shut a thousand times and she reached for me.

"You would do that?" she asked, stroking the palm of her hand down my cheek.

I swallowed, trying to push down the instinct to scoop her up and take her home. "It makes sense. We need more hands on deck now we're through to the finals. And you need a job."

"You are so sweet." She sighed. "The British."

"So that's agreed. You'll start on Monday."

She picked up her martini glass. "Absolutely not. I shall not work for you."

I groaned. I should have waited until she was sober after all. "We can discuss it again tomorrow."

"You don't have to offer me a job to get into my panties. You are welcome there. There's a little brass band down there, ready to say hi whenever you're ready. They have banners and balloons. There is no job required."

I didn't know whether to laugh or be completely horrified by the idea she thought I was offering her a job in return for sex. And I guess I should also be slightly freaked out by the idea of her vagina band. "I'm not offering to swap you a job for sex. It might surprise you to know that I don't have to pay for it."

"There's no such thing as a free lunch," she said, suddenly completely sober. "Why would you even do such a thing?"

I got it. She was a gorgeous girl and I could imagine that she'd been offered a number of things to sleep with a guy before. "I do not want to have sex with you."

"Rude!" she said. "I thought . . ."

This girl gave me whiplash. "Yes, of course I want to have sex with you—if nothing else so I can meet the tiny brass band in your underwear."

She started to giggle and it was so bloody delightful that I wanted to grab her hand and escape somewhere I could hold her for the rest of the evening in front of a roaring fire, watching the London rain freshen up the city.

"I'm not offering you the job so you'll have sex with me. I'm offering you the job because you need a job and I need the help."

"Really?" she asked. "Tell me the truth."

"Okay. That's the truth. Also I don't like the way Sparkle has treated you, and if I get to right some of their wrongs, that makes me feel good."

"Any other reason?"

No more holding back or skating on the surface. "And I'd like to hang out with you some more and if you fly back to Oregon, I won't ever see you again."

She looked at me, concentration freezing her expression. "The problem is . . . if I'm your intern, I can't sleep with you. Because I want to be taken seriously. I want people to see that I'm hardworking and that I have potential, not that I'm humping the boss."

"Humping?"

I got where she was coming from. Daniels & Co wasn't that kind of organization. The people I worked with were professional. They weren't gossips but she wasn't to know that. "Looks like I won't be getting laid, then. Not if you're back in Oregon and not if you stay in London."

She grinned, as if the thought delighted her. "Are you serious? You want me to intern?"

"I have two conditions. First, I need to be open with my head designer, Primrose, about how I know you. I don't keep anything professional from her. But she's discreet and won't judge either of us."

"And the second condition?" She narrowed her eyes suspiciously at me.

"Everyone who works for Daniels & Co gets paid. So, for the next nine weeks, you'll get a salary. Just above minimum wage, so don't get too excited."

"Are you serious? No, I mean, I couldn't. It wouldn't be right."

I just offered her a minimum-wage salary and she'd reacted as if she'd won the lottery. "Take it or leave it. But you're not working for my organization for free. That's not the way I operate."

"Life is freaking ironic, isn't it?" she asked.

"Why? Because the day you lose a job, you get one so much better?" Sparkle were idiots.

She tilted her head to the side. "No. Because I don't think I've ever wanted to sleep with a man more than I want to get naked with you. And now you're my boss and it's strictly not allowed."

Before I could respond, she called the waiter over and asked for the bill—or "check" as she put it. "I'll get this," she said. "As a thank you." She took the bill from the waiter at the same time as I handed him my card. There was no way I was going to let her pay.

"Hey," she said. "This is my treat." And then her eyes widened at the total. "Okay, well, maybe I'm going to let you get this. But I owe you."

"You don't owe me anything. Be a good intern. That's all you need to do for me."

"I'm going to have to tell the guys in my panties to stand down," she said. "It's disappointing for them. They've never been so . . . animated."

I chuckled. "Animated. Right."

"But," she said, and I could almost see the cogs in her brain whirring, "I'm not technically your intern right at this moment, am I?" She slid off her bar stool and stood, her body slipping between my thighs. "A kiss wouldn't hurt, would it?"

Hollie was an adorable drunk. Adorable and *gorgeous*, particularly when she pouted, drawing my attention to her pillow-like lips. "I think a kiss would be acceptable," I replied, standing and turning so I had her pinned against the bar.

Her hands slid up the lapels of my jacket, and I breathed in the clean scent of sunshine and summer flowers as she looked up at me with those green-blue eyes that I wanted to dive into.

She pushed her fingers into my hair, and I bent, pressing my lips into hers, sinking into her softness, relishing the warmth of her. Instinctively, I groaned at the sensation of relief and satisfaction I got from feeling her, from tasting her, from being this close to her.

She sighed against me as if the feeling was entirely mutual and I pushed into her with my tongue, wanting more, needing to be closer.

When had kissing ever been like this before? It felt so perfect, so intimate, so completely necessary.

A loud cough brought us back into the room and we jumped apart like guilty teenagers.

My heart juddered in my chest and my blood ran thick in my veins as I tried to compose myself.

What would I be missing if I couldn't have more of Hollie Lumen?

She looked up at me, her cheeks flushed, an expression of longing on her face. I had to stop myself from tossing her over my shoulder and sprinting home with her.

I cleared my throat, trying to get a grip of myself before I did something I'd regret. "We'll be friends," I said. But I wanted more.

"Absolutely," she replied. "You're my best friend in London."

Although I knew it was hardly a compliment—she knew almost no one in the city—a warmth gathered in my chest at the thought of being someone important to her. Even if it was temporarily.

TWELVE

Hollie

I chewed on my nail as I huddled under the awnings of an office building two doors up from Daniels & Co. I was trying to stay dry and the rain was as relentless here as it was back home.

"You think I should go in?" I asked Autumn for the fiftieth time. I was calling her from my Daniels & Co phone that Dexter had had couriered to me so he could message me.

"I can't believe you would consider not going in."

"But there's no such thing as a free lunch," I said.

"Tell that to Mom and Dad. They seem to take your money left and right without ever worrying."

"Taking favors can wind up messy." I had learned that lesson the hard way.

"You only ever took a favor from anyone once. And it wasn't your fault that your friend's boyfriend had aspirations to be a loan shark."

Even now my stomach churned as I remembered

borrowing the deposit for our trailer. My friend offered to lend me the money. I was dumb and naive and didn't see the catch until I went to repay it and her boyfriend asked for an additional twenty percent. It took me six months to pay it off because he kept making up reasons why I owed him more. To this day, the sting of all that interest paid was a reminder of how easy it would be to follow in my parents' footsteps—careering from one disaster to another. I had to take control and rely on no one but myself.

"And anyway," Autumn continued, "this is not a favor. He's not just handing out money. You're working for it. You have a job description. And he said he needed more staff."

"He was lying," I said. If Dexter had needed more staff, he wouldn't have waited for me to get fired. There were a million people who would have loved to be interning at Daniels & Co.

"Even if he was, you're not going to be filing your nails all day. You're going to work. You're going to learn. If you don't take this opportunity, I'll be furious with you."

Autumn and I were as close as two sisters could be. We were furious with each other rarely. And when we were, it was usually caused by one of the good-for-nothing guys she was dating. "I'm just trying to protect myself," I said.

"No, you're just uncomfortable with good things happening to you—with someone doing something for you —because normally it's you making sacrifices so other people can be happy. It's you making sure people have a roof over their heads and their bills are paid. You're just not used to the shoe being on the other foot."

I sighed and looked out at the sea of people rushing along the sidewalks, umbrellas askew and shoes squelching. Was I just uncomfortable accepting help? "But we've been on a date. We can't do that again if I'm working for him."

"Usually, you're inventing reasons not to go on a second date. Surely you're relieved to finally have a legitimate reason."

Darn her, she knew me too well. She'd backed me into a corner—I either had to admit that no second date was a relief and so there was no reason not to take the job, or that I liked this guy. "Well, I didn't have any reasons *not* to go on a second date with him. Not until now."

My sister screeching down the line made me pull the phone away from my ear for a couple of seconds. "Wow. London has all your good luck wrapped into one. You must really like him if you're saying you'd go on a second date," she said when she finally calmed down.

I wasn't sure if it was because he was British or so freaking good looking or the way I felt his goodness in his core, but I did like Dexter. The kissing didn't hurt either, and the job offer hardly dented those fresh feelings. But I'd have to bury them deep.

"And anyway, who says you can't date the boss?" Autumn asked.

"It would be a breach of duty or an abuse of power or something."

"Jesus, you're only going to be there a few more weeks. Maybe you should abuse your power with him."

I loved that my sister was so carefree about things but we weren't the same. I had always been careful. It was who I was. Coming to London was a huge risk. Going on a date with Dexter was a bigger one. I needed to de-risk, focus on what I came to London for in the first place. Life wasn't full of second chances, but I was getting mine and I wasn't going to throw it away, not even for another kiss with the best kisser I'd ever known.

"Nope. There's no way I'm fooling around with my

boss. But I am going to take the internship. I came to London for experience and if it's a question of accepting a helping hand or . . ." I didn't dare think about the alternative. "Or not getting that experience, then I'd be a fool to—"

"Well, finally. I'm glad you came around to my way of thinking. You need to jump at life's opportunities."

I hoped she took her own advice. "How's Greg?" I asked.

"Oh, he's a loser," she said. "You know it. I know it. But the sex is okay so he'll do until I graduate."

"Autumn! I can't believe you just said—"

"And don't worry, I'm on the pill and I still make sure he wears a condom. The last thing I need is to get pregnant by him."

Perhaps it was the distance that allowed Autumn to admit the truth, but thank God she was focused on her future as much as I was.

"I thought you really liked Greg?"

"He's fine for now. I've always defended him because you've been so anti-him." I started to object but she shut me down. "Don't try to deny it. And I understood that you didn't want him to hold me back, but I wouldn't let that happen. Especially not now."

"Not now? What's happened? Did something happen with Dad?" I'd warned him not to ask Autumn for money but I knew he wouldn't be able to resist it. Who else would he ask if I wasn't there?

"No, nothing's happened with Dad—he's asked me for money practically every day since you left, but I expected that. I mean seeing you follow your dreams and go to London, even though I know that leaving me was tough— it's inspiring, Hollie. I knew you were strong and responsible and resilient and all of those good things. But to see you be so driven, so freaking determined to get out of this shit hole—well, I'm not wasting the opportunities that I have either."

My ribcage lifted in my body as I listened to my sister say everything I'd ever hoped I'd hear from her. "I love you," I said.

"I love you more. I'm so grateful for everything you've done. Now it's time for you to shift your focus from me to yourself." I didn't want to abandon Autumn and it did feel uncomfortable to accept help from Dexter—a virtual stranger—but if Autumn hadn't accepted help from me, she wouldn't be about to graduate. If my parents hadn't accepted my help they'd be—God knows where. I had to work past my discomfort with receiving help, even if I was way more accustomed to giving it. "You've sacrificed enough. Go start your job with this new fancy jewelry company and grab yourself a life outside Sunshine, Oregon."

"Thank you," I said. I may have paid her college tuition, but having her as my cheerleader was more than enough of a payback.

"I love you," she replied.

I slipped the phone back into my pocket and headed into Daniels & Co.

I HAD no complaints about the people I worked with at Sparkle, who had been creative and energetic, but as I sat on my navy velvet chair alongside the rest of the competition team at Daniels & Co, Sparkle seemed a long way away. Daniels & Co people carried themselves slightly differently. Teresa used to high five everyone on the team every morning and my fellow American on the team, Evan, called everyone "winner" regardless of circumstance. The people at Daniels & Co were far more subdued. It was almost as if making the finals had been a foregone conclusion. They'd expected to excel, and now they expected to win.

People spoke in hushed tones as they joined us around the huge black conference table, though the seat at the top of the table remained empty. Over text, I'd tried to get Dexter to agree to act as if he didn't know me. He'd refused to go that far, but agreed to treat me like any colleague. I just hoped I could do the same thing. The problem was I could feel his rough jaw under my fingertips right now, and he hadn't even entered the room yet.

The subdued chatter settled down as an older lady with hair swept up into an elegant chignon came into the room.

"Good morning, team," she said, smiling as she set her silver pen on her notepad. "I see we're all here." She glanced around the table and her gaze set on me. This must be Primrose, Dexter's head designer. The one Dexter was going to tell about me. "You must be Hollie."

"Yes, Hollie Lumen. I'm so happy to be here."

"Well, we're delighted to have you on the team. I'm Primrose and I'm the head designer at Daniels & Co." She beamed at me, but just as I thought she was going to say something else, she turned back to her pad. "So, I know we are all very pleased to have reached the finals of the competition."

Was Dexter not planning to come to this meeting? I didn't know whether to be relieved or disappointed.

"But we can't celebrate yet," Primrose continued. "Now is when we want to increase our focus and commitment."

Had he stayed away to make me feel more comfortable? I needed to focus. On the meeting. On work. I had to stop thinking about Dexter. This was a second chance and I wasn't going to squander it.

"We want to win this entire thing and bejewel the princess of Finland. We're not at work so we can say on our CV that we were on the team that finalled. That's not who we are."

I glanced around the room. No one was doing Jell-O shots or flashing their boobs. I'm not sure Primrose needed to tell her team to focus. Everyone seemed very serious.

I made notes of almost everything Primrose said—details of deadlines, information on the timing of each piece and who was working on what. If someone needed to know what Primrose had said in this meeting, I was their gal.

"Now we're through to the next stage," Primrose continued, "the gems will all be reexamined to see if there's anything else we can improve. Dexter will want to see everything every day, as you know. Don't expect him to be less demanding, less exacting, or any more forgiving. We must not let him down. But more importantly, we must not let down the princess of Finland."

I'd only been on the Daniels & Co team a couple of hours, but I knew already why they'd finalled and Sparkle hadn't. The contrast between there and here was like being on different planets. One was a kindergarten paddling pool and one was the 100-meter freestyle at the Olympics. If I'd thought I was lucky to be interning at Sparkle, I had to believe some kind of divine intervention brought me to Daniels & Co.

Primrose swept out of the room and I turned to Macey, my boss, who sat beside me and had been designated to show me around. "Can you go grab us coffees?" she asked, handing me what looked like a corporate credit card. "I'll have a double espresso. You'll need to take everyone's order."

"Absolutely," I said. Some interns might have balked at the idea of making a coffee run, but not me. This was an opportunity to get in front of everyone, have a one-on-one interaction, and hopefully make a great first impression. Maybe they'd remember me when they needed something other than coffee.

"Don't forget Dexter," she said over her shoulder.

My stomach flipped at just the mention of his name. And I mentally wrapped myself on the knuckles. I was just getting the guy's coffee order. No. Big. Deal.

I scribbled down orders one by one. People were friendly but there was no small talk, and the chatter I over-heard was strictly business. No one was discussing *Love is Blind* or debating whether or not Mark Ronson was attrac-tive—*compelling viewing* and *I would definitely say yes to dinner* would have been my thoughts, had anyone been interested. But they weren't.

My final stop was Dexter's office, which was down a modern but dimly lit corridor. I knocked on the door, expecting an assistant to answer, but it was Dexter who barked deep and low. "Come."

Tingles rippled across my skin.

I opened the heavy door and took a half step inside. "I'm just collecting coffee orders," I said.

He didn't look up from whatever was preoccupying him on his desk. "Come in and shut the door."

I slipped inside and did as he asked, keeping my ass pressed against the back of the door.

Finally, he looked up. "I'll have a sparkling water."

I scribbled it down on my pad and when I looked up,

he'd silently stalked across the room and was placing his hands either side of my head.

"And a kiss," he added.

I ducked under his arm. "Absolutely not," I said. "I told you—I'm not dating the boss."

"I didn't ask you to dinner. I requested a kiss."

"Kissing is not allowed."

"Said who?" he asked, leaning against the wall, clearly amused.

"Said HR. You're off-limits. It's an abuse of power."

He rolled his eyes and headed back to his desk, and it was as if my stomach had dived off the Angel Falls. Why did he have to be such a darn gentleman? I mean, I liked that about him. A lot. But if he'd kissed me, I wouldn't have complained.

I was flip-flopping like the most flip-flopping flip flopper of all time. "Can I take a seat?" I asked, indicating the chair opposite his desk.

He raised his eyebrows, which I took as a yes.

"Look," I said as I sank into the deep purple, leather chair. "I like you. And okay, it's not exactly an abuse of power because . . ." I sighed. "Well, because whatever." How could I say that I'd already found him close to irre-sistible before he'd gone and rescued my dreams from hurtling toward oblivion? Now? It was hard to think when what I wanted to do was hitch my skirt up, hop onto his desk and have him bury his head between my thighs.

He was annoying. Hot. Kind. Thoughtful. The guy bordered on perfect. He was the worst.

"It's not an abuse of power because I said so." I said it with resolve and hopefully that would be enough. "But I don't want to mess up this opportunity. I want to build rela-tionships with your team and have them respect me. I don't want them to think I'm only here because I'm banging the boss."

"Yeah. You mentioned that already." He grinned. "And I'm not going to force you to kiss me. Or even speak to me. So, it's fine. I get it."

Lead settled in my stomach. The problem was I *wanted* him to kiss me. A lot. I'd never felt this pull, this sensation of someone blowing bubbles in my stomach whenever Dexter was nearby, and I didn't want to give that up. London was meant to be the start of a new life and I'd assumed that meant a new career. But maybe it could be more than that. Autumn might have been right. Perhaps, for once, I could spend time with a man who made me feel special—a guy who gave me goosebumps, who I thought about every spare moment of the day. I'd heard about those kinds of feelings—read about them in romance novels—but I'd never experienced any of it.

Maybe Dexter was my shot at more.

"I have a suggestion," I said.

"Go on," he replied and I leaned back in my chair. I was always so sure of my decisions, but there was something about being in London that made me willing to take risks I'd usually run from. Or maybe it wasn't London at all. Maybe it was the man right in front of me.

"If we were somewhere private, no one would find out about us."

"You want us to sneak around like teenagers trying not to get caught by our parents?"

"Or maybe jewel thieves on the run?" I suggested.

He chuckled. "You should know that I'm not a role-play kind of guy."

The gravelly tone he used had me thinking immediately about what type of guy he was. When he was naked. In bed.

Or in the shower or . . . I needed to leave. "Okay then, maybe not."

"You clearly have a plan. What were you thinking?"

"Maybe just dinner. In private."

"I can work with that. I can get a private room at Le Gavroche."

I was guessing that was some fancy restaurant, which would be nice and everything, but I was fast running out of outfits to wear to those places. "I was thinking maybe I'd come over to your place and cook you a meatloaf. Maybe some pie?"

A beat of silence passed between us and the corners of his mouth twitched. "I can work with that," he replied, looking at me as if he were stripping me naked in his imagination.

I could work with that too.

THIRTEEN

Dexter

I rarely used my kitchen and wasn't territorial about it at all, but it still felt odd as I sat on the bar stool and watched Hollie buzz about, poking her head in cupboards and pulling out bits of equipment I didn't even realize I had.

"Considering you don't cook, you're set up like a world-famous chef or something," she said as she pulled out some kind of device that looked like a sieve gone wrong.

"I used to have a housekeeper who liked to cook," I replied, taking a sip of my wine and pretending to be preoccupied with the emails on my phone. I needed something to take the edge off. Everything about tonight was making me itch. Not because I was uncomfortable, but because the exact opposite was true. I barely knew Hollie, hadn't even slept with her, but here we were in my flat as she cooked for me. No woman had ever made herself at home in my kitchen. Cooking together was the kind of shit married people did. And the only woman I'd ever even imagined marrying was Bridget.

"Have you ever lived with anyone?" I asked and immediately wished I hadn't. It felt too probing, too intimate. And I didn't want the same question back.

She turned to look at me, her hand hovering over the tap as she filled a saucepan with water. "I live with my sister." She paused. "And of course, my parents, back in the day."

"How long have you lived with your sister?"

"Ten years or so," she replied, shutting off the tap and putting the saucepan on the hob.

My creaky brain whirred and did the maths. "How old are you?"

"Twenty-five. But I look twenty-one, right?" She winked at me and turned back to the hob.

I wasn't sure whether or not there was much difference in what a twenty-one-year-old and a twenty-five-year-old looked like, but if it made her feel better . . . "Not a day older. You moved out at fifteen?" I asked.

She had her back to me and seemed to still at the question.

"Yeah. I mean," she said, her voice softer. "We were just a few trailers down. My parents were fighting a lot. And . . . it was just easier to move out."

She kept mentioning trailers. I was pretty sure she meant something other than the thing you towed behind a car to transport camping gear or rubbish. I'd heard of a condo, but I didn't get US real estate. It was true what they said; we were two nations separated by a common language.

"Do you like marionberries? I'm going to make a pie."

Marionberries? Christ, I hoped she was a good cook. I wasn't the best liar—I became an awkward fifteen-year-old and might as well have a neon sign above my head with an arrow pointing down that flashed *liar liar,* and I really didn't want to upset her. "I have no idea. What are they?"

"You have *no idea?*" She skated across to my fridge and threw the door open. I was half expecting her to pull out a selection of sea slugs but instead she held up a bag of blackberries.

"Oh, blackberries," I said, relieved that it was something I actually liked. "Jesus, I wish you Americans would learn English."

"You like them?" she asked, her eyes shiny and wide as if she were showing a child the ocean for the first time.

"Sure. Only a monster doesn't like blackberries."

She tipped her head back and laughed. "Maybe. My sister and I used to pick them wild when we were kids."

"Me too," I said. Bridget and I used to go down to a wild patch outside her parents' village. "Funny," I said. Those long lazy summers together had felt impossibly long and impossibly hot. I thought they would last our entire lives.

"Funny?" she asked.

"Not ha ha funny," I replied. "Just . . . you know, we live on different sides of the planet and have that in common."

"I bet you didn't grow up in a trailer though," she said. "I'm not sure we have so much in common."

"I have to confess, I don't know what you mean by 'trailer.' Do I need to consult my Anglo-American dictionary?"

"You're too funny." She pulled out her phone from a pocket in jeans that hugged her rather perfect bottom. "There," she said, showing me a picture of her and a girl, their arms around each other.

"You look lovely. Is that your sister?"

"Yes, Autumn. But behind us. That's a trailer." She pointed at the static caravan behind her and her sister.

"Oh, I see. Like a holiday park or something?"

"I guess," she said. "Except we're not on vacation. It's a

cheap way to live. Maybe you don't have them in England. My parents have never been able to keep a job longer than three weeks at a time, so cheap was what we needed if I was going to pay rent on two places." Her tone was very matter-of-fact. She clearly wasn't looking for sympathy but she'd obviously not grown up with much. Coming to London must have taken a lot—not just money, but vision. Drive.

"You still live there?" I asked. Living so far away, in a different country, and in many ways, a different world, it was difficult to picture her in her natural environment. And I found myself wanting to know who she was—before London, back in America—who she was right at the core of herself.

Her mouth twitched a little, almost as if she was considering what answer to give. She shrugged. "Doesn't make me a bad person." Her voice faded as she turned away and headed back to the fridge.

I hadn't meant for her to feel judged. I pushed my stool back and followed her. Why would she think that's what I meant? I stood behind her and wrapped my arms around her waist. "I think something got lost in translation. I wasn't suggesting it was a bad thing."

She froze. "I'm not after your money, if that's what you think."

I couldn't help but laugh. "What are you talking about? I have about fifty quid in my wallet and you're welcome to it. But it hadn't crossed my mind that you were after it." It was as if we were having two entirely separate conversations. She was clearly worked up about something. "Did I say something wrong? I've offended you but I don't know how."

She relaxed into my arms and tipped her head back

onto my chest. "I don't know what's got me so worked up—defensive and acting crazy. I've never dated a guy with money—no, that's not it . . . I've just never met someone like you. I like you and I'm not used to feeling this way. It's making me edgy." She twisted out of my arms and began scraping the potatoes she'd just taken from the fridge.

I wanted to make her feel better. "You're edgy because you like me?"

"Okay, Mr. Gigantic Ego—"

"Hey," I said, leaning against the counter as she focused on the vegetables. "We broke through the surface, remember. I'm asking so I understand, not so I can poke fun at you." I paused. I hadn't had a conversation like this with a woman for a long time—about feelings and emotions. And it wasn't because the women in my life hadn't tried. One by one they had come at my ice with a pickaxe and one by one, I'd managed to hold my defenses in place. Eventually they'd given up or I'd shifted away from them in every sense. But here I was with Hollie, handing her the axe and hoping we might melt in each other's sunshine.

"Everything is different here in London. Probably because I'm so far away from home in so many ways. This isn't a normal situation. You're not normally the kind of guy I date . . . I don't know how to explain it. I'm used to dating men who I'm not that into." She abandoned the potato on the work surface and came over to the island.

"So why do you date them? Are you bored?"

She tossed the blackberries into a normal looking sieve and held them under the tap before transferring them to a bowl. "On paper we look like we should fit, you know? Similar backgrounds and families. But it's like where I am physically and where I am in my head are two different places. So, we match in terms of geography but mentally . . ." She shook her head. "I'm not making any sense. But you and me, we're the opposite. You're this super successful guy, you live in London, you certainly didn't grow up in a trailer park. But in here—" She knocked the potato on her head. "In here, it's like, not that we're in the same place but . . . you're where I want to get to."

She pulled out a rolling pin from a drawer as I tried to digest what she was saying. What she was talking about was connection. Fit.

And I understood because I felt the same.

"I'm not confessing my undying love, don't worry," she said, maybe to fill the silence I'd left.

"I didn't think you were. I have a suggestion." I wanted to make her feel more comfortable—less edgy. "I think we should just spend some time deliberately trying not to analyze what's going on. Just enjoy it."

She nodded her head. "You're right. I need to relax."

I wasn't sure what I was saying but it seemed right. I didn't want to worry about what I was feeling for me or what I was feeling for her. I liked her—that was enough. I wanted to hang out with her. I wanted to taste her cooking. And at some point—like every minute I was with her—I wanted to get her naked.

"You know what's good to empty your mind?" I asked.

She gave me a sideways glance. "Kissing?"

I slid my arms around her waist and buried myself into her neck. "Yup. Very relaxing."

She let go of the rolling pin and swiveled to face me. "Show me."

"Wait," I said, as she grabbed my arse. "Did you just surreptitiously dry your hands on my bottom and pretend you were feeling me up?"

She tried to bite back a smile. "You know all my

secrets."

I didn't, but I wanted to. I dipped my head and pressed a kiss to her lips, tension easing from my muscles as I did. I hadn't been lying, at least from my perspective—kissing Hollie was like meditation. And it was addictive.

Her breathy sighs made me want to get closer to her, and I pressed my hand into her back, drawing us together.

"Do you have anything in the oven? Anything likely to burn that I'm going to get the blame for?" I asked.

She shook her head, her eyes sleepy with desire. "Nope. Wanna meet the band?"

I chuckled and lifted her up and over my shoulder. "I just hope there's a French horn player. A brass band is nothing without a French horn."

I strode out of the kitchen and down the hall to my bedroom, where I tipped her onto my bed.

"Wow. This bedroom is ridiculous."

I glanced over my shoulder before grabbing Hollie's hips and pulling her to the edge of the bed.

"It's got an entire living room in it. Two sofas and—Our entire trailer isn't as big as just this one room."

I pulled her top from her jeans and dragged it over her head. I inhaled as I took in her smooth, creamy skin. I wanted to rip her bra off but knew I had to be patient.

"Are you the richest man in England?" she asked as if it were a serious question.

"Don't be crazy," I said, unfastening her jeans. She wiggled, helping me as I peeled them off her. I took a step back as she lay on my bed in her underwear. "But I feel like the luckiest."

She groaned. "Cheese alert!"

"Is it cheesy if it's true?" I asked. I crawled over her and stole a kiss.

"Absolutely," she replied, her fingers undoing the buttons on my shirt. "Especially if it's pre-sex. It sounds like you're persuading me to get naked. And I don't need persuading. Not by you."

"Oh yes," I replied, kneeling as I stripped off my open shirt. "The band." I hooked my thumbs into her underwear and pulled them down. "Now, where are they?"

"They are quite small. You might have to look really hard."

I chuckled. I don't think even Tristan made me laugh as often as Hollie did. I kneeled on the floor, my thumbs pressed against her hips, my eyes level with her pussy. "Nope, can't see a thing. I hope you weren't lying, Hollie. I'll be very disappointed if I don't get a warm welcome."

She moaned and her hips shifted. "Closer. You have to look very close," she whispered.

I don't know who I was torturing more—her or me. I wanted to taste her more than I wanted most things, but knowing she wanted me? Knowing she was wet just at the thought of my tongue on her was doing things to my cock that felt illegal but oh-so-good.

"Still nothing," I said, the edges of my lips almost touching hers, my breath warming her skin.

She moved her legs a fraction, rubbing the inside of her thigh against my jaw. She moaned. I was toast. I couldn't hold back any longer. I pressed my tongue over her clit and almost dissolved at the warm slide of her.

Her fingers in my hair urged me on, and all I wanted to do was make her happy, make her come, show her that what we were doing wasn't banging, whether or not I was her boss. I circled over and over, one way and then the other, feeling her clit unfurl beneath me. I pressed hard and began to flick up and down, reaching up for her hands, linking her fingers with mine. She fought me a little—no doubt unwilling to relinquish control. But I wanted to touch her, make her come—I just wanted her to lie back and enjoy it. From what I could read between the lines of how she described her life back in Oregon, she was all too used to taking responsibility and looking after people, all while feeling like an outsider. I wanted her to see how she could relax with me, how she belonged under my tongue.

She'd confessed to me that I made her edgy. Well I was going to smooth all her edges away.

Her fingers tightened in mine and her hips lifted. "Dexter," she cried out, almost in disbelief. She made to shift away from me, to escape her pleasure, but I pressed my elbows down onto her thighs, keeping her in place. As I pushed my tongue through her folds, she began to pulse—her entire body juddered as she cried out. I stilled my tongue and watched as her orgasm coursed through her, her eyes opening to mine as she reached the peak and floated down back to me.

"You're gorgeous," I said, skirting my thumbs up her palms and then releasing her hands.

She shook her head as she tried to push to her elbows. "You're . . . I mean. Wow. I'm in trouble."

I chuckled and crawled over her and she swept her thumbs over my cheekbones and pulled me to her, kissing herself from my lips and then reaching down to undo my jeans. With fast fingers and a weird maneuver with her feet, my jeans and boxers were pushed to my ankles and I shook them off as she unclasped her bra.

"So, I met the band," I said, lying on top of her as I pushed her hair off her face.

She giggled and squeezed her eyes shut. "How were they?"

"You taste fucking amazing," I replied. "And watching you come is . . ."

She covered her eyes with her hand and I pulled it down.

"Look at me."

Slowly she opened her eyes.

"Watching you come is like seeing a cut stone for the first time." God, what was it with this woman and how corny she had me sounding? But I couldn't explain it any other way—she was at her most beautiful when she climaxed.

"And it got me rock fucking hard," I said, moving against her.

"I feel that." She brought her legs up and I rested against her mound, the throb that had started in my dick spreading down my legs, up my torso. She began to rock under me, just tiny movements, that connected my dick and her clit.

"Are you dry humping me?" I asked.

"I wouldn't say dry," she replied.

I groaned just at the thought of driving into her wetness.

"You have a condom?" she asked.

I grabbed the one I'd left on the bedside table before I got undressed and covered my cock in record time. "You ready?"

She took a deep breath as if she were preparing herself for my dick inside her—as if she was slightly concerned it would be too much. Too big. Too hard. It felt like someone had cut the tie on my self-control—I couldn't wait a moment longer.

I kneeled up, instinctively wanting to take in her reaction when I plunged into her. It wasn't enough just to fuck her or taste her pussy—I wanted to possess this woman. I positioned her legs over my shoulders and for just a second before I pushed in, I paused, teasing—her or me, I wasn't sure.

"Please," she whimpered.

Had this girl burrowed into my subconscious and figured out the exact thing that would press my buttons, send me over the edge, and cause me to lose myself in the moment? Apparently, Hollie Lumen was my kryptonite.

I tensed my body, bracing myself for sensation, and thrust in as deep as I could go. A guttural roar ripped through my throat at being connected to this woman. The feeling was primal, as if what we were doing was necessary for our survival—like if we didn't fuck, something would be desperately wrong in the world.

She shifted her hips and I turned to press a kiss against the delicate, soft skin of her leg and slid my hand down to press gently on her lower belly before pulling out softly and ramming back in.

Her hand covered mine. "That feels . . ."

I thrust in again and felt the ripples under my palm before she finished her sentence.

"Dexter, I'm going to come again. Wait—"

But I wasn't going to wait. I couldn't. Didn't want to. I wanted to fuck. I wanted her to come and I wanted to do it all night.

I thrust and thrust and my jaw tensed so powerfully I thought it would shatter as her orgasm squeezed me oh-so-tightly. But I didn't stop—wasn't going to give her time to recover, make me laugh, make me want her more. No. I was just going to concentrate on fucking her. She was going to see that she should never have joked that she didn't want to have dinner with me, never questioned whether or not we should date, or whether she should take the job. I was going to convince her that questioning anything to do with us was entirely ridiculous.

"What are you doing?" she asked, her words pushed out in a breathy fog.

"I'm fucking you. We're fucking." Sweat sheeted my skin and my lungs filled and emptied as if I was approaching the finishing line on a marathon. But I didn't care. All I could focus on was this woman beneath me who had me so wound up.

I pulled out and moved her leg from one side to the other so she was on her side and then I pushed in again. The blood sang in my veins as it pumped around my body, pulsing in my wrists, neck and cock. I positioned her leg further up so I could get deeper. I wanted to crawl into her and become one person.

Her hand clamped around the arm that was holding her leg in place and she looked at me, her gaze full of vulnerability and desperation. "Oh god, oh god, oh god, oh god, oh god." Her head tipped back and her entire body began to convulse. From this angle, as she clamped around my cock, I couldn't hold back any longer, didn't want to. We should have this moment together.

I cried out, ramming myself into her one final time before collapsing behind her.

I wanted to stay like this forever.

Spent.

Floating.

Exhausted but so fucking happy.

Her body sprawled half on mine, and the rise and fall of her rib cage had me mesmerized.

Had sex ever been so all-consuming? So intense?

She made to roll away from me and I circled my arms around her waist, shifted and pulled her toward me so we were spooning. She smelled good, like vanilla and flowers. Sliding her hand back, she grasped my thigh, as if she wanted to actively hold me, like it wasn't enough for me to be holding her. It was as if she couldn't take without giving at the same time.

"That was . . ." She paused but I wasn't going to make a suggestion to end her sentence. "What would you say that was?" she asked, and I tried to push down the belly laugh she elicited.

"Sex?" I suggested.

"What kind of sex?" she asked. "Like, normal first-time sex?"

"You want me to mark it out of ten?" I didn't think she'd object if it confirmed what she suspected—that nothing about that had been normal first-time sex.

She elbowed me in the ribs. "I just . . . that wasn't normal first-time sex for me," she confessed. "Not normal anytime sex."

My chest expanded at the thought that I'd been able to fuck her properly for the first time. But perhaps I was looking at this wrong; perhaps she was fucking *me* properly for the first time.

"We're still doing the sex," I replied. "It's not finished yet." I leaned across the bed with one hand and grabbed another condom.

I'd gotten hard again almost immediately. No, nothing about tonight was normal first-time sex.

"I'm not going to have time to make the pie," she said as I slid into her.

"You want my dick or the pie?" I thrust into her again, and she placed my hands on her breasts.

"Is it wrong to want both?" she asked, twisting her hips.

I picked up my pace. "So greedy." Truth was, I was the greedy one. I just couldn't get enough of her.

After too short a time, our orgasms collided and we lay tangled and sweaty, breaths choppy, limbs heavy.

She shifted and I pulled her closer. I wanted to keep her beside me, entwined with me. I didn't want her going anywhere.

"I need to use the restroom," she said.

Reluctantly, I released my grip and watched as she didn't even attempt to cover up as she strode to the loo. Fuck, I liked everything about this woman. "Hey, Gabriel's having a birthday party on Saturday. Want to come?"

No answer.

Maybe it was too much too soon—meeting the friends.

"Who's Gabriel?"

I turned and found her leaning, completely naked, on the door jamb. Her hair hung over her shoulders, almost covering up the perfectly sharp nipples that managed to jut out from beneath the treacle-colored hair.

"You're beautiful," I said, tucking my hands under my head.

"You too. Who's Gabriel? One of your pack?"

"Yeah. The best looking one of us if you ask me."

Her lips curled into a grin as she approached the bed. "Where do you rank? Because if you're not the best looking one, I can't wait to meet Gabriel."

I grabbed her and pulled her on top of me. "Sorry to disappoint. He's married." Separated, technically, but he wasn't dating.

She sighed melodramatically. "Darn," she said as she pressed a kiss against my cheek. Rearranging herself, she sat astride me. "You want to go to a party together?" she asked. "I thought we agreed that this was just between us. I was serious when I said I didn't want anyone at work to find out."

"No one from work will be there. Come on. It will be fun. It's a fancy-dress party. I get to channel my inner geek, which I'm sure you'll take every opportunity to exploit. And if you're with me, I don't have to wonder about what you're doing."

She reached over me, her breasts pressing against my torso, and I slid my hands down her back to her arse. When she straightened up, she presented me with condom from the bedside table.

"Make me come again and I'll go with you."

I chuckled. "You're bargaining with me?"

She scrunched up her nose. "Am I?" She shrugged. "I don't think so. I think no matter what, you're going to make me come again, given—" She slid her pussy down my cock and gasped. "Given past experience. And as for your party, I'm not sure I'm capable of saying no to you."

"Fuck, Hollie." A couple of weeks ago, I'd never laid eyes on this woman. How was that even possible? The things she was saying, the way she was making me feel. Whenever I was with her, it was as if the concept of time was different. Just during the course of this evening, it was as if months had gone by and she knew me in a way few others did.

I ripped open the condom, slid it on and then reached for the base of my cock, ready to have her sit on me.

She lifted up and slid her hands down her thighs, throwing her head back as she lowered herself onto me. I was wrong—we might be floating in space, but this wasn't a black hole we were nearing. We were lying firmly in heaven.

I deliberately never looked forward when I was in a

relationship with a woman. I operated in the present—I liked her. The sex was good—that's all I needed to know. But with Hollie, I couldn't help but think of what was next—the way I was going to cook her eggs tomorrow morning, the party on Saturday, the fact that I was certain another few weeks wasn't going to be enough with this woman.

"What are you thinking about?" she asked as she sat still, my cock inside of her.

"How much I like you sitting on my dick," I replied.

She laughed and pressed her palms onto my chest, the shift creating a wave of pleasure. "Well, I like sitting on your dick, so I guess we're the perfect pair."

I dug my fingertips into her arse and pulled her deep onto me. She swiveled her hips as we both groaned. "I guess we are," I said. "Oh, and no, I've never had sex this spectacular either."

She rolled her lips back, trying to fight a grin. "Lay off the fondue," she said. It wasn't a line. Suddenly she paused. "You got to promise me something?"

"Anything," I replied without even thinking about it.

"I know this is just . . . I'm not in London long and you're . . . Well you're you and I'm just some girl from Nowhere, Oregon—"

The six thousand miles between where we'd each built our lives was an obstacle to a future together, but where exactly she'd come from was completely immaterial "Hey, Hollie—you're you and I'm me. I don't care if you live in a castle or—"

She placed her fingers over my lips. "All I'm saying is, don't say things you don't mean. Don't make promises you won't keep, and don't pretend to be anything you're not. Let's just enjoy these weeks together."

It was an easy deal to agree to. Except weeks didn't seem long enough. Even now.

FOURTEEN

Dexter

I pulled up my collar against the biting wind and out of the corner of my eye, saw the familiar blue-green of Hollie's eyes. I turned my head to see a scarf in the window of Hermes, stretched as if it were a canvas in a museum.

As I stepped closer, I could see the colors were a swirl of feathers, each one a different shade of blue or green doing its best to block out the black image of a panther hiding beneath. Hollie would love this. The colors were her completely—the blue and green would bring out her eyes and her black hair echoed the big cat. The combination of soft and fierce would suit her too.

I pulled out my phone to take a picture, to show Primrose how the colors worked together and how the flat image managed to produce a sense of movement. She could take inspiration from this for the collection that we'd begin work on after the competition was over.

I took a snap on my phone and shoved it back in my pocket.

Yeah, it would really suit Hollie. I could imagine it bunched around her neck or draped over her naked body.

I checked my watch. I had ten minutes before I was to meet Beck and Stella for lunch. I headed inside the shop and it took less than half that time to purchase the scarf. The assistant folded it intricately then covered it with ribbons, tissue and a box.

With my orange gift bag, I headed south onto Piccadilly, which is when the realization of what I'd done hit me full force. A Hermes scarf wasn't the same as picking up the bill for dinner. A gift like this was a big deal, wasn't it? And Hollie and I had made a deal—not to make promises I wouldn't keep, say things I didn't mean or be anything I wasn't.

That scarf was breaking every part of that deal. I wasn't a man who bought expensive gifts for his girlfriend, was I? And what did that expensive gift silently promise? More than I had to give.

I could just give the scarf to Primrose to use as inspiration. Or I could return it. Or I could just sling it in my wardrobe and not think about it again. There were several solutions that didn't involve giving it to Hollie. I didn't want to mislead her or let her down. She'd been through enough. I wasn't going to be another thing on the list of rubbish things that happened to her.

I pulled open the heavy oak and brass doors of Fortnum and Mason, resolving not to think about it.

This was most definitely a lunch arranged by Stella. Left to our own devices, Beck and I would have picked up a sandwich and found a bench. Although, in this wind, I was pleased we would be indoors. Dodging the tourists, I made my way across the lobby, with its tables, cabinets and shelves filled with jams, teas, confectionary and everything quintessentially English. I should bring Hollie here—perhaps we could come for afternoon tea. As I was making mental plans in my head, I realized she'd never agree to go out in public with me. Perhaps when the competition was over and she wasn't an intern anymore. There I was again, thinking about Hollie when my head was supposed to be elsewhere. It was as if she'd permeated every thought.

I took a clearing breath and climbed the few stairs on the far side of the store. I spotted Stella waving from a window seat, nodded and headed toward her and Beck. Stella pulled me into a half hug before I pulled off my scarf and put it on the back of the seat beside her.

"Hermes. Someone's been shopping. Next time can you take Beck?" She peered in the corner of the bag. "What is it?"

"A scarf." I should have picked it up on the way back to the office to avoid attracting Stella's attention.

"What kind of scarf?" she asked.

"Have we got menus?" I asked, looking around for a waiter.

"What kind of scarf," Stella repeated. "Can I see?"

"You know what a Hermes scarf looks like. I want to show Primrose the color. It's design inspiration." That would throw Stella off the scent. I didn't want her to put two and two together and come up with eight, which is what would happen if I told her I'd bought the scarf for Hollie. Because it *was* also design inspiration. I beckoned over a waiter, who gave us menus and offered us drinks. Just as I thought Stella had forgotten about the scarf, she got a second wind.

"How's Hollie?" Stella asked and it was all I could do not to groan. Instead I focused my energy on glaring at Beck.

"What?" he asked, not even trying to pretend he wasn't delighted that his fiancée was giving me a load of grief. "It's not like I could keep news like that to myself."

"Why would you want to hide that you've got a new girlfriend, Dexter?" Stella asked. "I was hoping you'd bring her today. When do we get to meet her?"

This time I couldn't contain a groan at their pestering questions. "You've got all the disadvantages of parents without the advantage of me being able to borrow money from you."

Stella fumbled in her wallet and pulled out a twenty-pound note. "Here you go. Now tell Auntie Stella exactly what's going on in your love life."

"Love?" Beck interrupted.

"Okay," Stella said, taking the drink the waiter just brought over. "If it's not love, what is it? Just sex?"

"Stella, we're not going to talk in detail about my sex life," I said. "Beck is a very good friend of mine and I really don't want to make him look bad."

She laughed. "Throw a girl a bone. Beck said you like this girl. I want to know more about her. At least tell me, is the scarf for her?"

"Christ, I thought you had a successful career and happy relationship. Why do you have time to stick your nose into my life?"

She slung her arm around my shoulder. "We're family. I make time for family."

I chuckled. "She's a lot," I said to Beck.

"Right?" he said, grinning as if he were completely proud of it.

"What if the scarf is for her?" I wouldn't mind Stella's take on me giving Hollie the scarf. Would it be inappropriate? Too much? "It doesn't mean anything. Does it? It's not like I planned it. I didn't make a special trip—I was just on my way here and saw it in the window."

Stella's eyes widened. "So, you were passing Hermes, saw a scarf in the window that you thought would suit Hollie, and decided to get it for her? You're making me swoon."

Did I want to make Hollie swoon? Yes. *Should* I want to? I couldn't decide.

"Seriously, is it a big deal? I don't want to be a dick to this girl." I glanced at Beck because he knew my history better than Stella did. He'd met Bridget and knew how I'd felt about her. "Shall I take it back?"

"How could giving Hollie the scarf be a dick move?" Stella asked.

"He doesn't want to give her the wrong message," Beck explained. "Because you know . . . Bridget."

The silence of what wasn't being said filled the space between us. I knew Beck thought I needed to get over Bridget, but he also knew *I* knew that wasn't possible. There was no point going through it again.

"But you like Hollie, or you wouldn't have bought the scarf?" Stella asked.

"Yes of course I like her," I replied.

Stella wriggled in her seat and threw some very unsubtle *I told you so* looks at Beck.

"This is not the first time I've liked a woman, Stella. I'm not some kind of man-whore who can only handle one-night stands. I've liked women before. I liked all my girlfriends." Stella was reading too much into a very small word.

"Do something for me?" she asked.

"Stella," Beck warned.

"It's okay," I said to Beck. "I can handle your fiancée. I think."

"Have Hollie be a new book—a fresh page if you like," she said. "It's almost as if you have a script to follow with a girlfriend. You know how things are going to turn out before the first kiss. Don't look ahead too far and be open to what-ever happens." She lifted her chin in Beck's direction. "Sometimes life can surprise you. Don't second-guess giving her the scarf. It's thoughtful and caring and you felt the desire to buy it for her. It's generous, and that's part of who you are. That's not a bad thing, Dexter."

The way Stella put it made sense. Maybe I wouldn't be saying anything I didn't mean if I gave Hollie the scarf. I wouldn't be being anyone but me. But what, if anything, did a gift like this promise?

"It doesn't have to be a big deal," Stella said, answering the question before I could ask it. "It is what it is. You saw it, you thought of her, you bought it. It doesn't mean anything beyond that."

Our food arrived and that gave me a chance for Stella's words to settle. She was right—I was second-guessing myself when I didn't need to. I'd had the urge to buy Hollie the scarf because it reminded me of her, simple as that.

"I'm going to give her the scarf."

FIFTEEN

Hollie

Today was going to be another day jammed full of firsts. And not the kind of firsts that I experienced back in Oregon. I wouldn't be running out of gas at the end of the week, unclogging a septic line, or having Billy from the arcade hitting on me, which was a rite of passage for all the girls in Sunshine, Oregon. I was going to see the earrings that would be submitted to the competition by Daniels & Co for the first time. I was going to help out on the photo shoot where the earrings were going to be modelled. And I was going to assist Jeremy, who was presenting to Dexter the different ways we could display the jewelry for the competition.

I would also be face-to-face with Dexter at work for the first time since we'd had sex.

I wasn't in Kansas anymore. Or Oregon. Sometimes I wondered if it was even the same solar system.

"Everyone in the conference room, please," Primrose said. I'd already fetched coffee for everyone and had just finished rearranging the furniture so we could fit in a podium for the earrings that would be submitted for the competition. We'd all seen the drawings, and obviously some of the team had been involved in production, but this was the first time they would be seen by everyone.

I couldn't wait. The drawings were beautiful and I knew they would be even more so in real life. The energy in the office was buzzing, ready for the reveal of the first finished works.

People began to file in when Frank, the chief jewelry engineer, came from the other end of the corridor carrying a big white box. Everyone paused so he could go ahead and he set the cube on top of the podium.

"Okay, everyone, please take your seats. Hollie," Primrose said, turning to me. "Can you take the stand around and show everyone while they're seated so we don't have a crowd around the podium?"

Holy Hercules, I couldn't be trusted to handle something so precious. I was guaranteed to trip and send one of the earrings hurtling down a drain that would magically appear in the floor. Frank handed me a pair of white gloves and I put them on, trying to hide my trembling hands as he took the lid off the box.

I tried to act nonchalant, as if holding diamonds meant for the princess of Finland was an everyday occurrence for me. I took the stand from the box, which was like a six-inch high tree with just two branches, each one displaying a cacophony of diamonds. I wanted to remark on how freaking sparkly they looked and ask whether diamonds always looked that way, because, for the record, cubic zirconia definitely didn't.

Primrose stood up. "As you know, this was the option Dexter picked out of the three earring designs we had.

Our theme, the Finnish landscape, comes through strongly in these pieces. The loop here," she said, indicating the row of diamonds that formed an unfinished almond-shaped loop, "represent the lakes of Finland. There's a great deal of skill to make this chandelier earring asymmetrical while still ensuring a symmetrical hang. Frank and his team have had to come up with some creative solutions to bring the design to fruition and they've done a great job."

The chairs were arranged around the edge of the room. I started at one end and very slowly moved along the line.

Along the edge of the lake hung different-sized diamonds that represented falling snow. Each was a slightly different cut, echoing the way each snowflake was unique. They were the most beautiful earrings I'd ever seen.

People's reactions ranged from scribbling down notes, to trying to get so close I was concerned the earrings might get inhaled. Most seemed excited, in the subdued way people at Daniels & Co did, and remarked on how beautifully they'd turned out.

"I know everyone is working really hard on this," Primrose said. "And although some of you haven't worked on the earrings, none of this collection works without all the components. So, thank you to everyone in this room. You all contributed and we wouldn't be here without your talent and creativity."

"You think we'll win?" Jamie, one of the guys who did a lot of work on the computer—I just wasn't sure what, exactly—asked.

Primrose frowned. "There are lots of things that I don't know. But I'm sure we will all have done our best."

The door opened and Dexter swept in. I hadn't been expecting him until Jeremy's presentation. I clung to the stand with the earrings, and tried to pretend my life was no big deal.

"What does everyone think?" he asked, scanning the faces of his employees. He glanced at the earrings and then up at me. "Hollie?"

I tried to ignore the heat crawling up my neck. "I think they're beautiful. And a little daring."

A smile curled the corner of his lips. "I like that. Daring. Anyone else?"

"The design is modern," Sarah said. "I think most other houses will go much more traditional—"

"I don't want us comparing ourselves to other houses," he said, cutting Sarah off. "We are competing against ourselves. I want us to give everything we have—to know we've left it all on the field and if we had our time again, we wouldn't do anything differently. If we win, that's great. If we don't? Well fuck them for not choosing us because we know we're the best."

The room dissolved into laughter, and I tried hard not to toss the earrings at Jeremy, jump into Dexter's arms and kiss his face off.

"Judging takes place at the end of the week," Primrose said. "But we won't have results until all the pieces are in."

Everyone groaned and chatter started to rise about how we wouldn't know the score before the bracelet was submitted. But Dexter was right, knowing wouldn't change anything.

"Did no one hear what I said earlier?" Dexter asked. "The score doesn't matter. It doesn't affect our output. Come on guys—be your own competition. Push yourself. Now get back to work. Jeremy, Frank, Hollie, Primrose, stay behind."

Everyone filed out and Jeremy's cheeks began to flush.

Was he nervous because he'd come up with the presentation concepts or because he was presenting to Dexter, who looked even more completely fuckable than usual? His skin seemed bronzer than normal, his hair a deeper black if that was even possible, and there was a lightness about him I didn't usually see at the office.

"Frank," he said, beckoning to the chief engineer. "Two of those settings need to be redone." He spoke so quietly I could barely make out what he was saying.

"Two?" he asked, approaching me to stare intently at the earrings I still held.

I put them down on the plinth and the two men bent to look at the stand as if they were watching a flea circus.

"I knew about that one," Frank said, pointing at one of the solitaire diamonds that hung from the lake. "I told you about it."

"And there," Dexter said.

Frank looked closer then pulled out his loupe to inspect it more thoroughly. "Bloody hell. How did I miss that?" he asked. "I'm pissed off with myself."

"Frank," Primrose said. "You know what an eagle eye Dexter has. Don't beat yourself up."

"This is my job, Frank. If you were perfect, I wouldn't have anything to do." Dexter patted Frank on the back. "But you know, it's good you're pissed off. Keep those standards high."

Frank huffed as he left the room, mumbling under his breath. Dexter turned to Jeremy. "So, what are the options on presentation?"

I pulled out my Daniels & Co phone, ready to take a note of everything everyone said. Jeremy had just asked me to attend to make sure he remembered Dexter's and Primrose's comments, and to help out if he needed an extra pair of hands. I'd only seen one of the concepts, but I knew he'd worked on several ideas.

Jeremy flipped open his laptop. "I have three options." He launched a video. "I've put together a film of the Finnish landscape," he explained. "The idea is to have the landscape in the backdrop, but add subtle, dynamic movement. Then in the front"—he pointed to three rocks that looked like they'd been fished out of the sea—"I've picked out pieces of stone—"

"Rocks," Primrose said to herself.

"We place the jewelry on the rocks," Jeremy continued. "And they really stand out. Look, I've used some place-holder jewelry in the next bit."

Jeremy's gaze flitted between Primrose and Dexter as the video played. "The advantage of this is that it under-lines the concept of the collection and it's the most innova-tive. I think it will really capture the judges' attention."

From where I sat, the presentation just didn't work. It was pretty and everything, and Jeremy had clearly worked hard on it. But the jewelry was lost in everything going on. There was too much to look at, and the concept didn't reflect the Daniels & Co brand, which was all about under-statement. But what did I know? Perhaps it would be exactly what Dexter and Primrose had envisioned.

Dexter pinched the bridge of his nose. He didn't like it. I knew I shouldn't be mentally high-fiving myself because I liked Jeremy and wanted him to impress his boss, but at the same time Finlandian fairies danced about in my stomach because I agreed with Dexter, the most successful jewelry designer in the business.

"What else?" Dexter asked, clearly not wanting to spend more time on the first concept.

Jeremy pressed play on the video of a glass case that

reminded me of an ornament Mrs. Daugherty, the woman two trailers down from my parents, had in her living room window. She'd inherited it from her mother—a red rose preserved in a sort-of snow globe, except there was no snow or liquid. It always made me think that if Mrs. Daugherty had the space for it, her trailer would be full of stuffed beavers and animal heads. In Jeremy's concept, each item of jewelry was encased in a glass dome set on a mirrored stand. It felt old and staid. I glanced at Dexter to see if I was going to be two for two. His face was completely blank.

"I think this is better," Primrose said. "Less going on. But I wonder if you had a third option?" From what Dexter had said, he'd known Primrose so long, she knew what he wanted almost before he did. The fairies in my stomach were partying like it was 1999 at the thought that I, too, had anticipated Dexter's reaction. It felt like a victory to be in agreement with Dexter and Primrose, but at the same time I felt bad for Jeremy.

"I don't have anything else fully developed," Jeremy confessed, his shoulders hunched and his gaze focused on the computer screen. He looked defeated.

"Why don't you tell them about what you were telling me earlier," I chimed in. "You know—about 'back to basics.'" Jeremy mentioned he'd played around with plain black velvet in a traditional display case, and I was surprised he hadn't worked that up into a third concept. Dexter and Primrose both turned to me and I stepped back. I was just the intern. I shouldn't have said anything.

"What's back to basics?" Dexter asked.

Jeremy shrugged. "That was a very straightforward display on black velvet."

Dexter nodded. "I was just thinking that might be the way to go."

"I have some images," Jeremy said, clicking through to a new file. "I didn't do a video though." He brought up some images of a traditional set up with jewelry mounted at different levels on a swath of black velvet. "I also did this," he said, flicking to what looked like pebbles covered in black velvet.

"It's simple," Jeremy said, almost anticipating Dexter and Primrose's rejection.

"Regal," I countered, unable to stop myself. "The shapes of the pebbles are elemental. And the black is classic Daniels & Co coloring while still representing the earth, the land of Finland," I said. I wanted to save Jeremy's ass and sell the concept to Dexter and Primrose, but also, I believed in it. I thought it was the best option—not just of the three we'd seen. I was a big believer in keeping things simple. I glanced at Jeremy to see if he was preparing to wrestle me to the ground and gag me, but he just winked.

"It shows confidence," Primrose said.

"That's agreed then," Dexter said and turned toward the door. "Work up several set-ups for each piece on its own and for the collection together. Different sizes." I couldn't wait for Dexter and Primrose to leave so I could high-five Jeremy. "Oh," he said as he reached the door. "Work with Hollie. I want to see what you two create together." He swept out and Primrose followed him.

"You saved me back there," Jeremy said, collapsing back in his chair. "I felt so sure they would go with the first one. I assumed they'd love all the technology and the way it played into the theme." I understood why he thought that, but Dexter wasn't ever going to go with a presentation that didn't focus on the jewelry. "I worked so bloody hard on it."

"I know but just think—at least you don't have to worry

about setting up computers and screens and all that technical stuff before the judging."

He nodded. "And we're back to jewelry on velvet. Not very innovative."

"But it's classic. And very Daniels & Co—understated elegance," I said. Jeremy had been trying to impress Dexter and Primrose, but he should have focused on the jewelry. "The pebble shapes add something unique, give a little bit of edge."

"I guess," he said. "Thank God you were here or I would have been sacked. You understood what they wanted more than I did and I've been here two years."

"Lucky, I guess," I said. Of course, I hoped it wasn't luck. I hoped I was on track to see stones and design jewelry in the way Dexter and Primrose did. If I had only a tiny fraction of their vision, I might be able to create a new future for myself.

Every day spent in London felt like a step taken in the opposite direction of my life in Oregon. The only problem was I didn't know what I was walking toward.

SIXTEEN

Hollie

"You saved Jeremy's arse today," Dexter said as we sat cross-legged in his bed, me in one of Dexter's shirts, eating the cheese and crackers I'd brought over. I wasn't sure how it happened but we'd gotten into a little routine. Most nights, I would arrive at Dexter's flat about eight with some food, and he'd just be arriving home from work. I'd cook while he showered and finished up some emails. Today we'd gotten distracted and I'd ended up in the shower with him.

I was enjoying having a salary, and I'd splurged on some expensive cheese I was sure Dexter would love. I'd assumed men like Dexter lived on caviar and champagne, but he loved my grilled cheese and told me my chicken pie was the best thing he'd ever tasted. And then he'd said something dirty and I thwacked him with a tea towel.

"I just went with my gut," I replied.

"What did it say?" he asked.

"That whatever the display was, it had to be all about the jewelry."

"Exactly." He sighed. "I was disappointed he didn't get it."

"We shouldn't talk about this," I said. I didn't want to know what Dexter thought about his staff—didn't want the responsibility of insider information in case it changed the way I looked at my colleagues, who I liked a lot. "Work is work and this is," I said, pointing at the cheese, "delicious."

"You're delicious. Are you sure I can't just have you for dinner?"

My insides shimmied at his words. "You're going to need your strength for what I have planned for you later," I replied.

"I can't wait. Oh, that reminds me. I have something for you," he said. He reached over the side of the bed and produced one of those thick paper bags with rope handles that you get from expensive stores.

"What is it?" I asked, eyeing up the orange bag with a big H on it. It looked a bit like the Hermes logo, but of course it couldn't be. "My birthday isn't for weeks."

"Well, why don't you open it and find out," Dexter replied.

I wasn't sure why, but suddenly I felt out of place, sitting on this bed, opposite the most handsome man I'd ever seen. If I was reading the room right, Dexter had bought me a gift. But why would he do that?

I fingered the corner of the bag.

"It won't bite," he said.

He was asking me to open a bag—not exactly a demanding request. I wasn't sure why I was hesitating but if I'd thought I was on a different planet earlier in the day, now we'd rocketed to a different universe. I just felt uncomfortable.

Stop being ridiculous. I pulled the light package onto

my lap and picked at the brown, monogrammed tape that sealed it shut. Inside I found a square, shallow box that felt lightweight when I balanced it on my lap. The game was up —the box had *Hermes* written on it, and I was pretty sure this wasn't a knock-off. Regardless of what the box held, it was too much for me.

"Can I ask you something?" I said. "Did you buy me this? Like as a gift or something?"

Dexter frowned before putting a piece of cheese on his cracker. "Yeah. I said that before. That I got you a gift."

Those hadn't been his exact words. He'd said he *had something* for me—slightly more ambiguous, and a lot less overwhelming. I wanted to know for sure when I opened the box on my lap what it was for and why. "You don't need to give me presents," I said, staring at the box, half itching to open it, half scared to see what was inside.

"It's not a big deal," he said. "You want me to open it?" He reached for the box and I held it out of his way.

I pulled at the thin brown ribbon then lifted the lid. I wasn't sure what I was expecting to see but what I got was white tissue paper.

I pulled open the tissue to find fabric that looked like silk—proper silk, not the rayon imitators in my wardrobe. It was printed in the most beautiful colors—every blue and green that had ever been. "What is it?"

"You keep asking me the same questions and I'm going to keep giving you the same answers," he said. "Pull it out, for goodness sake." This time he got hold of a corner and pulled the silk from its box, letting it float in a canopy over our heads. The peacock colors swirled above us like the most gorgeous indoor parachute.

"Careful," I said, jumping up and catching it as it floated down toward our cheese picnic.

"It's a scarf," he said as I held the fabric in front of me like it was a picture I was deciding where to hang.

"It's beautiful." It was more than that. It was breathtaking. Stunning. It was the kind of scarf that let you know immediately who someone was—sophisticated, well-travelled and college-educated.

Disappointment roiled in my stomach.

I was none of those things.

I glanced over at him and he shrugged. "I saw it in the window and it reminded me of you—your eyes. Your hair. I thought you'd like it."

Someone cut the cable in my ribcage and my heart landed with a thud in a pool of mixed emotion. I didn't know if I should laugh or cry. And then a voice inside my head whispered, *Go home. You don't belong here.*

"You okay?" he asked. "Shouldn't I have bought it?"

"It's just not . . ." How could I explain what I was feeling when I didn't know myself? He bought me a gift. I should be giddy. Instead I wanted to throw some clothes on and get on the next plane back to Oregon. I'd never felt so far away from home.

"Hey," he said and pulled me onto his lap. "Did I do something wrong?"

I wanted to push off his lap, get away, but I didn't want to be ungrateful. "It was really nice of you," I said, my fingers fiddling with the buttons on the shirt I was wearing.

"Do you hate it?" he asked.

I shook my head. No one could have hated something so beautiful.

"Was it inappropriate? I thought it might be but Stella convinced me to go with my gut. It doesn't have to be a big deal. I can take it back, even."

Inappropriate wasn't quite the right word, but it was in

the neighborhood. "Maybe not inappropriate but . . . it wouldn't be right on me."

Dexter cupped my face in his hands. "Tell me what you're thinking, Hollie Lumen. Because I know it would suit you."

If I'd learned anything about Dexter over these weeks, it was that he was like a dog with a bone—determined and driven. I wasn't going to get him to change the subject unless the building was on fire. "I wasn't thinking about whether or not it would suit me."

"Then I hope it's not because you don't think you're worth it."

It was as if the lights went out and someone had sucked all the oxygen from the room. Five minutes ago, we'd been eating cheese and quoting our favorite films. Why had things suddenly gotten so deep?

Why was Dexter wondering what I thought I was worth? I'd been thinking I would never wear a silk scarf once I went back to Oregon, that it would sit in its box the rest of its life. And that led to a thousand more questions. After spending time in London, how could I go back? Would I be successful in getting a job at a jewelers in New York? And even if I did, wherever I was, whatever job I was doing, would I always be Hollie Lumen from the trailer park?

Of course I would.

I'd never have a reason to wear a scarf so expensive and beautiful. My die was cast.

The scarf represented a life I'd never have and a woman I'd never be.

"Hey," Dexter said, pulling me closer. "It wasn't meant to make you sad."

It wasn't his fault. He'd done something nice for me. Something wonderful.

"I'm not sad," I replied, the hitch in my voice telling a different story. "It's just too much." For me. "Too expensive," I corrected myself.

"It's just money, Hollie. And given the jewelry we're surrounded by every day, it's not that much money."

I rolled my eyes and pushed off his lap. He had no clue. Only people with money could afford to say that anything was *just money*.

"We come from very different worlds, Dexter. I have no idea what a Hermes scarf would cost, but I can guarantee it's way too much money. I'm guessing that's a month's grocery shopping right there." I lifted my chin to the silk strewn on the bed next to us.

He scowled at me. "You're right. We do come from different worlds. But I don't see why that means I can't use my money to buy you something nice."

"I don't need your money."

"I know you don't." His tone had changed to the one I was used to hearing in the office but never here. Never when it was just us. "I don't know what the hell I've done. Maybe you're only happy when people are bleeding you dry."

His words were like a physical blow.

"You're saying my family are leeches now?" I stood on the bed, waiting for his reply. "I've never said anything that would make you think that."

He didn't reply and when I glanced at him, he was pinching the bridge of his nose. I'd learned now that Dexter did this when he didn't like what was happening or what someone was telling him. "I can put two and two together and come up with four. You pay your sister's tuition, your parents' rent. Does anyone in your family do anything for themselves?"

I was so angry I was rooted to the spot, not knowing if I should punch him in the mouth or flee. "They're my family. Are you telling me if your parents were alive, you wouldn't help them out if they needed something?"

Dexter abandoned his cheese plate and tried to grab my arm. But I scooted away and jumped off the bed. I'd had enough of this conversation. I was ready to go back to my apartment. I'd call my sister, who was sure to agree with me that Dexter was a complete nutjob.

"Hey," he said, following me into the bathroom. "I wasn't trying to upset you. I was just trying to make sense of why giving you the scarf made you look like you were going to vomit all over my duvet. I could take offense, you know."

I ignored him, fastening my bra and slipping on my shirt. "You're ridiculous," I said, my anger simmering, ready to boil over. He clearly wasn't taking offense. He was far more interested in pissing me off. Leeches? "Not everyone who doesn't have money is a leech. Some people in this world don't have the opportunities, the talent or gene pool you did." I pulled on my underwear and jeans, my anger giving way to a wave of grief over all those lives I could have led if things were different—all those opportunities I hadn't had. I worked hard to make sure my sister could go to college and my parents always had a roof over their heads. But it was hard. There wasn't anything left for me after everyone else was taken care of and sometimes, I could admit, it felt thankless. All Dexter was doing was reminding me of my responsibilities, and of how much I'd sacrificed to fulfill them.

I had to leave. A rumble of self-pity sounded in the distance and clouds of sadness gathered in my ribcage. If I didn't get out of here, I was going to cry until I ran out of tears. And Jiminy Cricket, that was the last thing I wanted Dexter to see.

He came up behind me. "I'm sorry," he said. "I shouldn't have said that about your family. But it sounds like you go unappreciated. That's all."

His words were coaxing out my tears. "I have to go." I scanned the floor, pretending to be looking for something so he wouldn't see how upset I was.

"Seriously," he said, grabbing my hand as I went past him. I tried to shake him off but he gripped my wrist tighter.

"I won't have you—"

Before I had the chance to finish my sentence, he'd scooped me up, carried me to the bedroom and tossed me on the bed, capturing my wrists on either side of my head. "I need you to listen to me. Because this is getting out of hand. You're overreacting. I'm clearly being insensitive—I'm pushing every one of your buttons, and I have no clue what's really going on."

"Just get off me," I said, squirming underneath him. Anger would be easier. Tears would be far more difficult to explain.

"I want to talk," he said as he released me. "I don't want you running out when we're having an argument I don't understand. I was trying to do something nice and you're upset and angry and I want to resolve this."

I didn't move from where he'd left me. He was a jerk for calling my family leeches, even if sometimes it felt like my parents could do more to help themselves.

On a sigh, he grabbed the scarf and tossed it in the trash. "Sod the fucking scarf. I wish I'd never listened to Stella."

My skin seemed to shrivel as if I'd been dunked in an ice-cold lake. I'd hurt his feelings, been rude to the one person who had my back. Dexter probably thought I was being spoiled. He couldn't know that a kind and thoughtful gift would stir up so much in me. "It just felt a bit weird," I said, my voice small. I slid my gaze sideways, barely able to look at him.

He was sitting on the edge of the bed, his back to me, raking his fingers through his hair. He was too gorgeous. Too kind. Too good to me. "I'm sorry," I said, reaching for him and then pulling my hand away, concerned he'd flinch if I touched him. "Maybe I'm scared I'm going to get used to . . ." Him? Anyone other than Autumn being so good to me? A life that I knew I was going to have to walk away from? "You're just really nice to me."

"And you're really nice to me. Normally."

How could he even think that? What had I done for him? "I am not."

"What do you mean you're not?" He turned toward me, shaking his head. "Really, Hollie, you are. Otherwise I wouldn't be here with you."

"Come on, Dexter. Look at everything you've done for me. The job, the salary, now the scarf. It's a lot. And maybe you're right, maybe I'm not used to some billionaire saving my ass all the time. It's not something many girls at the Sunshine Trailer Park are used to."

"Don't you see that you do nice things for me too? You make food for me most nights and you're the most amazing cook. When you've been here, I always find a vase of flowers on the kitchen side or—"

"Dexter, the roses I buy cost me five pounds from Tesco and I've only done it twice."

"The money doesn't matter, Hollie. You're being kind. You're giving. I might buy you a Hermes scarf, but I have more money than you. It's the thought behind it—the inten- tion." He sighed. "Maybe I shouldn't have . . ."

I hadn't thought about how the cooking and the flowers could be thought of as giving. It seemed like nothing in comparison to what he'd given me, though I supposed it was. But it wasn't a big deal. I was happy to do it—I enjoyed it. "I like cooking. I like that you like it. And I didn't even realize you noticed the flowers," I replied. His flat was gorgeous, like something you'd see in a magazine. Cheap flowers probably made it look worse, not better.

"I don't want you to freak out, but you just said yourself that you don't even realize when you're giving, when you're doing nice things for people. It's ingrained in you. You're so used to it that you don't even see it. Usually between people, it's a two-way street—both parties are nice to each other. I'm just not sure that's your normal."

"Maybe that's true," I said. "And maybe the reason I was so upset is that I can't be anyone other than who I am. I'm always going to be the girl from Nowheresville, Oregon. I'm never going to be some sophisticated city girl who went to college, majored in marketing and then got a job in New York City. Even if I got out of Sunshine someday, it wouldn't erase who I am. For me, a Hermes scarf will never not be a big deal."

"I think who you are is kind of wonderful," he said and my heart lifted a little, trying to find a foothold to burst out of my chest and give itself to this man in front of me.

How had I found him?

"I'm really sorry for acting crazy." I slipped my fingers into the waistband of his jeans and pulled him toward the bed. I didn't want to fight anymore.

"You're a good person, Hollie. And *I'm* really sorry. I wasn't trying to cast aspersions on your parents—"

I couldn't help but laugh despite feeling as if I were in a heap of limbs at the end of a fairground ride. "'Cast aspersions?' You're so British."

"I can't help that." He circled his arms around my waist. "But seriously, I wasn't trying to make you feel bad. Quite the opposite." We sat for what felt like ages, Dexter's arms around me and our breaths the only sound surrounding us. "Don't leave tonight." He buried his head in my neck.

I was dressed now, and I would normally leave before midnight anyway. "I should go home."

"You could stay the night, you know. Go home tomorrow morning if it makes you feel better not to go straight to the office from here."

Despite my initial instinct to run, right now I wanted to spend the night in his arms.

"You promise not to return the scarf?" I said, a small smile curling around my mouth.

"With what I've got planned to do to you with it, I'm not sure Hermes would take it."

There was no way I was going to let him ruin such a beautiful thing. I pushed away from him and retrieved the scarf, folded it quickly, slipped it back in the box and put it on the seat under the window. "Well, that's not going to work for me. No one's ever given me anything quite so beautiful and I'm not going to let you ruin it." Even if I never had an opportunity to wear the scarf, I'd keep it. I'd take it home and put it in my memory box. If I ended up retiring at the Sunshine Trailer Park, I could bring it out and remember that one summer in London when the most amazing guy in the world thought I had peacock-colored eyes.

SEVENTEEN

Dexter

I didn't argue with women. I didn't have the energy or the will. I'd never cared enough.

Hollie was different.

"Are we good?" I asked, following her into the kitchen where she was checking she hadn't left anything on. I wanted to make things better for her. I hated the idea that she felt she wouldn't ever get to be the kind of woman who wore a Hermes scarf. There were plenty of women who didn't have half her heart or soul that wore head-to-toe Hermes.

It had been a confounding evening, but there was nowhere I'd rather be. The last time I fought with a woman had to have been the last time Bridget and I argued. I'd had things thrown at me a couple of times but I just didn't engage. And some women would sometimes go completely silent on me. I just ignored it. I never cajoled them into talking about it or told them I didn't want them to leave. I hadn't meant to be cruel. I just thought it was better if they cooled off in their own time. And if they were so annoyed they didn't want to hang out anymore—well, we lived in a free country. That was their choice.

"Yeah, we're good," she replied, looking at me over her shoulder from where she stood by the hob.

"Then can I kiss you?" I asked. I needed to *know* she was okay, not just hear her say it.

I didn't want to lose her.

The realization hit me like a tree trunk to the forehead —I liked this woman. Really liked her. Liked her more than I could ever remember liking anyone.

Except Bridget of course. Although it had been such a long time since Bridget and I had been together. Such a long time since I fell in love with her. And although I would always love her, I wasn't sure I was actually *in love* with her. I wasn't sure it was possible to be in love with a woman I hadn't seen for fifteen years.

Not that I was in love with Hollie. I just really liked her, more than I'd liked anyone in a long time. I hadn't been looking for it. I hadn't been looking for anything. I'd just thought she was beautiful from the very moment I'd laid eyes on her. And I wanted to make her laugh, buy her dinner, sleep with her. But all those things had been true for other women who had been in my life since Bridget. There was something different about Hollie from the start, but there hadn't been any seismic shifting of tectonic plates under my feet until tonight. Until I realized I didn't want her to leave. That I'd miss her if she did go. That I wanted us to talk through whatever was bothering her about the scarf because I didn't want her to be upset—but more because I wanted to know her better. I wanted to know how to soothe her, how to avoid upsetting her the next time.

It was as if I was standing under a waterfall of new feelings cascading over me.

"The answer to that question is always yes," she replied. Streetlights shining in from the window lit her up, a halo of yellow light making her look even more beautiful than usual.

For how long would that be her answer? I wondered. At the moment it was always yes but what if we had another argument and she made it out of the door that time? What about when she went back to Oregon?

Before I could think too much, she came over to me and hiked herself up onto the kitchen island, sliding her hands up my arms. I sighed, instantly soothed by her, her touch some kind of hypnotic balm.

I cupped her face in my hands. She really did have the most astonishing eyes. And I pressed my lips to hers.

"Thank you for not leaving," I said as I pulled away.

"Thank you for convincing me to stay," she replied, slipping her fingers into the waistband of my trousers.

"We have some making up to do," I said, undoing the shirt she'd just buttoned.

"Is that a promise?" she asked.

I unpeeled the white cotton and pulled off her bra to reveal her soft skin. Just like I'd wanted to know her mind and what she was thinking earlier in the evening, now I wanted to map her body with my tongue.

I wanted to know every part of her, inside and out.

I pushed her back onto the marble, smoothing my hands down her stomach, over the peaks and dips of her hips and down to her thighs.

"You're touching me like you think I might not really be here," she whispered.

I sighed and pressed a kiss just above her ankle bone

and another on the inside of her knee. Maybe she was on to something. Perhaps the woman in my bed wasn't the one I'd been expecting all those weeks ago when I'd first spotted her at the launch of the competition. She was now the woman I fought with. The woman I didn't want to go home. The woman I was going to bury myself in so she'd never leave.

I pressed open her legs and placed my tongue flat against her clit. Christ, she was delicious. She was almost instantly wet and I wanted to be surrounded by it. I slid my fingers inside her, and she began to twist away.

"Too much. I'll come too soon," she panted.

I placed my hand on her stomach, keeping her in place. Yes, she'd come quickly. That's what I wanted. I wanted her to lose count of the number of times I made her climax tonight. I wanted to leave a mark on her mind and body—make tonight unforgettable—not because we'd fought. But because we'd made up.

As I licked, Hollie gave a little wiggle of her hips as if trying to get my fingers deeper and my tongue harder. I growled at the realization she wanted to belong to me as much as I wanted to possess her. I pulled back, not to punish her for being so greedy but because she tasted so fucking delicious I wasn't ready to give it up.

She moaned and I put my mouth on her again, this time letting my tongue trace her up and down, through her folds over and over. Her back arched off the stone, and I pressed my fingers into her again, grinning as I watch the calm sedation pass over her—like she'd given up whatever she was holding back. Like she had surrendered.

To me. To us.

I used my fingers to explore and twist while my tongue just tasted and tasted and tasted. She flopped her arms over her head and spread her legs wider. She was mine. To do with what I pleased.

Her bulging clit began to pulse and my hardened cock reared in response. Fuck, being able to bring her to the edge so quickly made me feel like a fucking king.

"Dexter," she cried out and reached for me. I grabbed her hand, pressing my lips onto her stomach, feeling the ripple of her orgasm against my skin as she came.

Her eyes still closed, my impatience to be inside her took over. I wanted my cock coated in her wetness and my fingers digging into her flesh. Just the thought had me as hard as wood, sweat starting to prickle at my neck. I gathered her in my arms and took her over to the sofa, bending her over the back cushions and pulling a condom from my trouser pocket.

I stripped out of my clothes, rolled on the condom and rested my cock at her entrance. "Are you ready?" I asked. I was rushing. She rid me of the unflappable detachment that I had. I needed more of her. And each time she gave me what I craved, I got greedy and took more still.

I needed to take a moment. To breathe her in. To enjoy every second. But she undid my self-control.

"For you? Always." I groaned and drove my cock into her, long, slow and deep. It was so good—so hot, tight and wet. I slid my hands under her arms and cupped her breasts. Her hard nipples pressed against my palms and she reached behind me, urging me deeper still.

I wanted to stay there, buried inside her until sunrise, but she shifted, and the pleasure that bloomed in my chest at the drag against my cock was nearly too much.

"Fuck, Hollie," I said as I started to draw out and push back in, eeking out the pleasure, wanting to make each stroke last as long as possible. Being here was so good. So fucking perfect. Thank fuck she hadn't left tonight. Thank fuck we had this. All night. How lucky was I to have found this woman who could make me feel so fucking right? It was as if for years I'd had a piece of my soul missing and she'd found it. I felt more alive when I was fucking Hollie than I could ever remember. I felt like I belonged. Like I could do anything as long as I could be with this woman.

Her hand coaxed mine from her breast and she interlaced my fingers with hers as I almost roared at the perfection of it. How such a nonsexual movement could make my cock ache as much as it did. But it was the intensity of the connection—the purity of it—that really got me. It represented her and us and how I felt about her.

She began to tremble beneath me. Her legs started to shake, her entire body consumed by her climax. She pushed down further on my cock and the shift in position had me driving deeper into her. Her climax pulsed around me, squeezing my cock, making me pant and grunt and fuck harder and harder until I was almost blind with effort. All I could do was feel. And all I felt was Hollie.

I exploded into her on a moan and pulled my arms tighter around her.

"You're going to ruin me," she whispered.

If I'd had any energy left, I'd have asked her what she meant. I'd have questioned whether she was talking about the scarf. But I'd given her every last drop of effort I had.

And I'd do it all again if she asked me.

At some point we made it to the bedroom, though it was long past dark when Hollie shifted out of my arms and crossed my room into the bathroom.

"Have I told you you're beautiful?" I asked.

She turned and looked at me over her shoulder as if I'd just said the most ridiculous thing. She shouldn't be shocked. If she was, that was my fault. There should be no doubt in her mind that I thought she was the most beautiful woman on the planet. Because that was the truth.

"Let me go to *the loo*," she said and I grinned at her anglicization. She suited London. And she had a natural eye for what showed off stones, which was important if she was going to be in this business.

"You never told me if you actually liked the earrings," I called out to her. She reappeared at the bathroom door, smiling as if she'd been waiting for me to bring it up. We weren't supposed to talk about the office, but I wanted to know what she thought.

"Okay, let's have a five minute time-out so we can talk about work." She grabbed her mobile from beside the bed. "We have until six minutes to the hour."

I grinned, enjoying her rules as much as her disapplication of them.

"You know what I thought?" she asked, tucking her hands under her cheek as we lay on our sides, facing each other.

"No," I said, rolling my eyes as if I found her exasperating instead of sexy and completely fascinating.

She ignored me. "I thought they would go perfectly with your parents' tiara."

Her statement left me slightly winded. It wasn't at all what I'd expected her to say. I'd thought she'd comment on the theme or technical innovation. What did my parents have to do with those earrings?

"You know," she continued, "modern but classic. Innovative but still regal. And of course, they were beautiful," she said. "The theme is amazing and there's the technical thing of getting them to hang straight without it looking too obvious that you're using the snowflakes as the counterbalance. I loved every part of them. It's clear you're the son of two incredibly talented people."

I didn't have a response to that. It wasn't sadness I felt when Hollie mentioned my parents, as it was when most people spoke of them. I didn't rush to quieten her or quickly change the subject. I liked that she respected my connection to them still, fifteen years later. And I wasn't sure anyone had paid me such an incredible compliment. I reached for her and pulled her toward me, needing her heat against me. Enjoying the closeness of her.

Whatever was between us wasn't about easy company and regular, outstanding sex—although it was those things. It was more than that. It was about hanging out with someone I found endlessly fascinating, feeling cared for and wanting to care for someone else. It was wanting her to love what Daniels & Co produced. And it was so much more than I'd ever felt in such a long time.

EIGHTEEN

Hollie

I only had thirty minutes before I had to leave for Gabriel's party, but I hadn't spoken to Autumn for two days. I'd mastered video calling on my Daniels & Co smartphone, far quicker than I'd mastered the design software—though I was improving on that front—so Autumn and I could chat while I got ready to meet Dexter.

"What's Dexter going as?" Autumn asked as I pulled out my onesie from the pile of clean laundry.

Dexter had blindsided me, telling me Gabriel's birthday party wasn't fancy dress as in we had to dress fancy, but the British version of a costume party. I'd had two days and zero dollars to find the perfect outfit.

"Maverick."

"Top Gun?"

"Yeah. You know what guys are like. They all think they have a Navy fighter pilot on the inside waiting to get out." Though Dexter was always Mr. Cool and Above It All, I actually thought it was refreshingly human that he had an inner child wanting to be Tom Cruise.

"And you're not going as Kelly McGillis?"

I groaned. Autumn was usually a little more creative. "I have at least five reasons why that's a bad idea."

"I have enough patience for your top three."

"One, it's boring. It's the first time I'm meeting his friends. I don't want them to think I have zero imagination. Two, why should my costume be dependent on his? Maverick was Maverick. You can't even remember Kelly McGillis' character's name."

"Okay, so you could have gone as Goose. And anyway, that was only two reasons."

"No," I said. "I'm steering away from anything with a Simpson-Bruckheimer vibe."

"But you want your costumes to interrelate, right?"

"No. Absolutely not," I confessed.

"I'm totally confused," she said. "Why not?"

I didn't want to talk to my sister about something I didn't want to even think about. But as usual, what I wanted really didn't matter. "Because, you know, it's not like we're engaged."

"But you're a couple, right?"

It felt like we were a couple. It had been creeping up on me for a while, but it wasn't a feeling I was used to, so it was difficult to recognize. Ever since our fight, things had been different. Something had shifted. He'd given his doorman my name so I could go up to his apartment without him in case he got tied up at work. He kissed me differently—his eyes were more searching before his lips touched mine. We were interconnected in a way we weren't before, but there'd been no discussion or labelling and that was completely fine. "I don't know what we are," I confessed. "It's going to look a little stalkersville if I dress in a complementary costume and he wasn't expecting it. Anyway, I go back to my previous argument—I should have my own cool costume. My decision about what I wear shouldn't be dictated by what Dexter's wearing."

"Oh my God, Hollie," Autumn said. "I've never heard you so ruffled by a guy."

"I'm not ruffled," I said. "I'm saying the opposite—that I don't want to be dressing a certain way because of his costume."

"I call ruffled," she said. "I can count on one hand the number of second dates you've ever been on, and with any of those guys, you wouldn't even consider what they were wearing to a costume party. You'd just wear whatever you wanted."

She was exasperating and a bad listener. "That's exactly what I just said I was going to do."

"Hmmm, maybe. But you're not picking a complementary costume because you don't want to freak him out, not because you don't give a shit. It's an important distinction." I could almost hear her grin. "You like this guy, Hollie."

This wasn't news to me but hearing it out loud was kind of weird. "Yeah, maybe I do."

Autumn squealed. "This is amazing. Why didn't you choose to go as Princess Leia in the gold bikini? Guys love that and your hair would be perfect—"

"Absolutely not. It's a complete cliché and . . ." I'd like to think Dexter was a little bit above the whole female objectification/Leia fantasy, but of course he wasn't. He was a guy. With a pulse. "Just absolutely and completely not. My idea is cool. I don't care what you say."

"I want to meet this guy," Autumn said. "He must be special to finally get my sister to fall in love."

"Autumn! I am not in love with him. He's a great guy to hang out with in London, but it's not like it's going to work out between us." The soon-to-be five thousand miles between us ensured what we had was a short-term thing. Even if I did end up with a job in New York, we'd still be an ocean apart. "I haven't even told you about the fight we had. He bought me a gift, and I had a meltdown that led to the world's biggest argument."

"What was the gift? A butt plug?"

I wasn't sure if she was trying to be funny or if she just assumed the gift must have been inappropriate to spark a fight. She could only go on past history of the men I'd dated. And if I had been talking about any of them, she'd wouldn't have been so off base with a butt plug. But Dexter would never do that. If he wanted anal sex, he'd just suggest it—not pretend it was a gift. Autumn was going to think I was an idiot when I told her what had sparked our disagreement. "No, he bought me a scarf. It's really beautiful."

"And you freaked out because . . .?"

She was going to think I was a maniac. I took a deep breath and exhaled slow. "There were a lot of reasons. But he had a theory about me. He thinks I'm not used to accepting presents, receiving stuff."

"Did he mean gifts or is this an oral sex issue?"

I laughed, relieved she'd lightened the moment. I never had a problem receiving Dexter's tongue. That's where his argument failed completely—a point I'd be sure to make if we ever argued about this again. "He thinks because I pay Mom and Dad's rent that I'm not used to . . ." It was a little awkward to talk about this with Autumn, since she was someone in my life that I helped out. But she was younger. And my parents weren't stepping up to help her, so what did he expect? That I would just leave her high and dry? If I could help, of course I was going to.

"He's right." She sighed. "I like this guy and I've never even met him."

"Wait, what do you mean he's right? I haven't even told you what he's said."

"Well, you've said bits and it doesn't take a genius to fill in the rest. You're not used to a two-way relationship. You're used to being the giver, the caretaker. And everyone else takes from you."

"Life isn't perfect. If it was, there'd be zero calories in fried chicken and I'd wake up looking like Irina Shayk."

My sister grinned and her smile filled the entire phone screen. I wish I was there. Or that she was here. I wanted us to grab the duvet from the bed, snuggle under it and watch *America's Got Talent* while eating ice cream straight from the carton. "I didn't say anything about perfect. But you're a natural giver. And you've never been in a relationship with a guy you really like. Ever. He could really take advantage."

She was sweet to be concerned. I was usually the protective one with her boyfriends. I shook my head. "Dexter's not like that."

"Bet you cook for him. Go down on him."

"Well, I like to do both, so we're good."

"Just remember—it's a two-way street. I like the fact that he bought you something. It's nice. And you should let him. It's what good boyfriends should do. I read it somewhere. And one of these days, I'll be treating you. I think you can rule Mom and Dad out on that score."

I snorted. As if I was banking on that. Neither of them ever had more than five dollars in the bank and they weren't particularly practical. If they were stopped by the police for a broken tail light, left to their own devices they'd end up in jail. And it would never be because they'd ever done anything terrible—they'd just piss people off, forget dates and not turn up when and where they were supposed to. It was easier for me to step in to pay the fine for the broken tail light, and then there wasn't a danger of me having to pay lawyers' fees for a jury trial. That was just life with our parents.

"Exactly. It's totally natural that you'd have a warped idea of what your role is in a relationship. Let him do nice stuff for you. And if he doesn't, dump him. Kindness goes both ways."

It was simple the way she said it. And it was pretty much what Dexter had said. I didn't know if it was because I was hearing it from Autumn or because I'd had a couple of days to think about the fight, but the accusation that I wasn't used to getting what I should in a relationship seemed to make more sense today.

"How do you know when they're doing too much?" I asked. "Should I keep a list? Make sure I only do something nice for him when he does something nice for me?" That seemed a little over the top, but I was a novice, apparently. Surely a Hermes scarf was too much. How could I ever repay him?

"No, Hollie, you don't keep a tally. You're just caring for each other—him for you, you for him. Equal doesn't mean identical."

She paused and I tried to read her expression but the screen froze. "It probably wasn't that much to him. You said he has money. And you're not prone to exaggerate. I'm thinking this guy could buy and sell the whole trailer park."

"Right. That's what he said. Not about the trailer park. About the scarf."

"So, let him do what he wants to do for you. And you do

what you want for him. If you make each other happy, that's when shit gets serious."

That made sense. I should just do what was in my heart and he should do the same. As long as we were both happy.

"When did you get so wise?" I asked.

"Grew up this way. It was the way my sister raised me."

I was suddenly so homesick I could barely stand. Not for Oregon. Not for the Sunshine Trailer Park or my parents, but for Autumn. "I miss you," I said.

"Don't you dare miss me. You're chasing your dreams and hanging out with Sexy Dexter. You don't have time to miss me."

I might have paid Autumn's tuition, but that girl gave me the strength and courage to try to carve out a life for myself outside of the trailer park.

"Although I'm going to miss you like crazy on your birthday."

"It's the first one I won't spend with you."

"You'll just have to make Dexter sit in bed, eat ice cream and watch reruns of the *Housewives*."

If he was capable of that, the man was worth marrying.

"Is that a glue gun?" Autumn asked, frowning at me as I stuck together the blue felt.

"I just spotted a hole in the hat."

"Well, if he has sex with you after seeing you in that outfit, you'll be engaged by Christmas."

NINETEEN

Dexter

I'd offered to pick Hollie up but, she said she'd meet me outside Gabriel's place and made me promise not to go inside without her. I leaned against the car, trying to see if I could spot her. I didn't know what I should be looking for, given we were going to a fancy-dress party. I'd asked her a couple of times about her costume but she'd refused to tell me anything. When I suggested Kelly McGillis, Hollie had challenged me to remember the character's name, and when I couldn't, she told me she wasn't going to go as my nameless appendage. Then I made a crude joke about my dick being my best appendage, and she thwacked me with a towel.

I transferred my fighter pilot helmet from one hand to the other. My assistant had done a good job with the costume. The red and black striped helmet even had the word *Maverick* painted on it in white. My green jumpsuit had all the requisite patches, including the American flag, Top Gun school crest, and Tom Cat. But I felt a bit of a dick. Costumes weren't really my thing.

I checked my watch. She'd said she'd be here ten minutes ago, but it was difficult to know whether she was normally late. Our relationship had been conducted entirely behind closed doors in my apartment. We'd had that one dinner when we first met, but since then we'd been banished from going outside together.

"Hey, wanna be my wingman?" Hollie called from behind me.

I turned to find her grinning at me. And then her face dropped. "You guys have Dr. Seuss, right?"

I chuckled, taking in her red flannel outfit and the white circular label on her chest that read *Thing 1*. "You're adorable. And yes, we do. Where's Thing 2?"

She pulled out her keys and dangled a miniature version of herself in front of me. "Autumn bought it for me. She has another." Then she slipped her red-gloved hands around my waist and put her head on my chest. "I like you as a pilot. Maybe I should have gone for something a little more feminine, Sexy Dexter."

Her blue felt hat, shaped like an upside-down octopus, smacked me in the face.

"You're the sexiest I've ever seen you," I replied.

"You're a terrible liar," she said.

"I mean it. Are you wearing anything under that—what is that—is it all-in-one? Does this zip work?" I reached for the neck of her costume to see if I could reveal what was underneath.

She batted my hand away. "I'm wearing pajamas," she said. "I got a bunch of felt online and with hand stitching and glue, this is what I came up with. And yes, I have underwear on, you pervert."

She looked completely cute. I was relieved she'd gone to some effort and not bunged on a suit and said she was a

CIA agent or something. Gabriel would appreciate her commitment. All the boys would.

"You look phenomenal," I replied, kissing her on her forehead. No one would be dressed like her.

"You're sure you don't wish I'd come as Princess Leia in the gold bikini?" she asked, looking up at me.

I'd be lying if I confessed that the image she'd conjured up wasn't appealing. "Was that an option? Do you have the bikini back at your place?" I asked. "We could have our own private party later if you insist."

She rolled her eyes. "So predictable. But this," she said, pulling away and sweeping an arm down her soft, crimson body, "is as sexy as you can handle."

I grabbed her hand and pulled her toward Gabriel's drive. "If we stay here in the dark a moment longer, I'll have you unzipped and naked in the back of the Sentinel."

"If I'm completely honest, I'm not feeling hugely sexy," she said, holding on to her hat as we crossed the road.

"My jumpsuit is chafing if it makes you feel any better."

"It does. It's good to know it's not just women who suffer for their fashion choices. I'm a fire hazard most of the time given the materials in my clothes."

"Well, at least tonight, no one will miss you in a fire."

I knocked on the door and went in. The hallway led into the open-plan kitchen area where Gabriel and his daughter spent most of their time. The glass doors into the garden had been opened and the party had spilled out onto the patio.

I didn't see anyone I knew. Probably due to the fact that we were all dressed up and pretending to be someone else. Then Stella, in a gold helmet and blue cloak, came toward us, her gaze pinned on Hollie.

"Hey!" she said, brandishing a spear. "You must be

Hollie. I fucking love your outfit. Just my type of girl. I thought you might turn up in a Princess Leia bikini and I'd have had to take off your head," she said, wiggling her spear.

"What the fuck is with the spear?" I asked, kissing her on both cheeks.

"I'm Boudica, you walking cliché. You know that film is full of homoerotic imagery?" she asked.

"I like fast planes and good-looking guys," I replied. "Shoot me."

"You're ridiculous," Hollie said, laughing.

"He *is*," Stella said, grinning as if she finally had a partner in crime. "I'm so pleased I don't have to break it to you. Come and get a drink. You have to see what Beck has come as. He's even more ridiculous. The testosterone is exhausting. Gabriel's the only normal friend they have."

Hollie looked at me and smiled, her blue hat wobbling to one side. "Thank you," she said.

I wasn't sure what she meant, and I didn't have time to ask her before we found Tristan, Gabriel and Beck. I couldn't help but laugh at how predictable Tristan's outfit was. "Han Solo?" I asked.

"Yeah, I'm hoping there'll be a few women here dressed as Leia. You know," he said, making a cupping gesture in front of him. "In the bikini."

"You know I'm carrying a spear," Stella said. "And you're just asking to have me target your balls."

Tristan just shrugged.

I turned to Gabriel. "Happy birthday." I looked him up and down. "Did you two come as a couple?" I asked, taking in his Darth Vader costume. The five-year-old in me was dying to know if the mask pushed to the top of his head did the voice.

"No. And I have to say, I think Han Solo is a weak

costume. It's too conventional. Tristan's basically rummaged at the back of his wardrobe and found what he wore to university and picked up a plastic gun. Unlike me. Or you." He held his hand out to Hollie. "I'm Darth," he said.

"Thing 1. Happy birthday," she said. They shook hands as if this was any old introduction in the pub.

"Very good," he said. "I read Dr. Seuss to my daughter. She's three so I'm not sure she appreciates all the nuances, but I do."

"How's it going?" I asked. It was his first birthday since his wife had left.

He nodded and took a large swig of wine. I didn't press him. It was his birthday, and I was sure he didn't want to get into it.

"Why are you so pissed off at Beck?" I asked Stella, taking in Beck's Hulk costume.

"I'm just irritated. He's greener than I ordinarily like a man. I wanted him to come as Batman," she said. "That's a manly costume. And much less green."

"Yeah but too Vader-y," he said, indicating Gabriel's billowing cloak.

"It was thoughtful not to upstage the host," Hollie muttered beside me.

Stella leaned toward us both. "I know. It's very sweet that he didn't want to overshadow Gabriel, but I'm hoping he's going to put on the costume I got him when we get home so I'm pretending to sulk."

Hollie laughed and her blue hair fell off, revealing her own dark tendrils. "Oh, this thing is so hard to keep on," she said. "Where's your restroom? I'll go reattach it. I have some bobby pins with me."

Gabriel pointed over to the door by the stairs. I tried to catch Hollie's eye to see if she wanted me to go with her, but she'd already turned to go. She'd been so adamant she didn't want me going into the party before her, I wasn't sure if she was okay to be on her own. "You think I should go?" I asked Stella.

She frowned. "No. She would have asked you to help her with her hat if she hadn't wanted to go by herself."

I nodded. "Yeah, hadn't thought of that."

"But it's very sweet that you're considering her feelings. You're very . . . touchy with each other," she said.

"We're not," I said. Yes, I was holding her hand when we came in, and perhaps I'd given her a reassuring back stroke. But I wanted Hollie to feel comfortable. And it was rare for there to be so many people surrounding us. I just wanted her to know that I was . . . here. "No more than you and Beck."

"Yeah, Beck and I are very touchy. It's not a criticism. It's nice to see you like that with a woman."

I was about to defend myself and say how it was no different from any other girlfriend, but there was no point. I'd never had the same desire to touch a woman every moment the way I did with Hollie, and although I'd not thought about it consciously before, no doubt that was obvious from someone like Stella's point of view.

"But you know the thing that makes me sure she's a winner?" Stella asked.

"Go on," I said, making clear from my tone that I didn't want to know.

"Her costume."

I laughed. "You think Hollie is my perfect match because she's dressed as a Dr. Seuss character?"

"Absolutely. She could have come as Wonder Woman or Catgirl. Or Princess Leia in that bloody gold bikini. But she came in a onesie. I like the lack of vanity. She'd be completely entitled to come as some super-sexy character, but I like that she didn't. It proves there's more to her than the pretty face. She's quirky."

"She's not that quirky," I said defensively. I didn't want Stella to think Hollie was some kind of novelty. "She's just . . ."

I couldn't find the right word because Hollie deserved more than a throwaway phrase to describe her. She was more interesting than that.

"You like her."

"Of course I like her or I wouldn't be hanging out with her." I could feel myself falling into the same old argument I had with all my friends—how yes, she was a nice girl but how she wasn't Bridget. Only this time, I stopped myself. "But yes, I really like her."

Beck interrupted us. "What are you two gossiping about? Hollie? I like her outfit. Thank God she didn't wear that Princess Leia bikini or you would be competing with Tristan."

Women who flirted with my friends to get my attention didn't last long. "No, I don't think I would," I said. "Hollie's not like that."

I didn't miss the nudge Stella gave Beck. It was to be expected, I guessed. I liked Hollie a lot, and it was only in the context of the outside world that it was so obvious.

"I like her outfit," Beck said. "Shows she's a woman with her own mind."

"That's what I said," Stella replied.

And that was what Hollie was for me—unlike anyone else I'd ever met. She was just . . . Hollie.

TWENTY

Hollie

"Today is Friday," Dexter announced from where he was lying in his bed, watching me scrabble about, collecting bits of clothing from where they were strewn last night.

"Honestly, Dexter, I think we need to get you in for some lab tests. You're beyond smart," I replied. "What other nuggets of wisdom do you have? Grass is green? I'm American?"

I glanced up to find him grinning at me.

"I really like you," he said, sliding one hand behind his head. The sheets shifted to reveal more of that hard torso that felt so very, very good under my hands. Darn, he was distracting.

"I'm naturally very charming," I replied, trying to stay focused.

"And now, you're picking up all your stuff so you can go back to your place after work before turning right back around and coming here tonight. Just like you did yesterday, and the day before. Only today is Friday."

I was going to be late if I didn't get a move on. "Do you have a point or are you just running through what my day is going to look like? My boss is a real asshole, and if I'm late, there's no telling what he might do."

"I'm serious, Hollie," he said, swinging his legs over the side of the bed and padding into the bathroom. He was acting like he made any kind of sense. "What's the point in you going home every morning? Like now, for example. Why don't you have a shower here? If you don't want to drive into work with me, fine, but there's no point in leaving at six just so you can shower on the other side of town. It's crazy."

He was right. Getting up this early wasn't doing anything for the bags underneath my eyes. "Okay, so maybe I'll bring an overnight bag sometimes." If I went by tube and Dexter drove, there was no way anyone would ever know about us. Dexter was true to his word, keeping our interactions professional at the office. No one had the slightest clue —if some of the mundane tasks I was given were anything to go by.

"Yeah that's one option," he said as he swept past me and grabbed his toothbrush.

I couldn't stay today. I didn't have any clothes here, and I wasn't about to wear the same outfit as I wore yesterday. "Okay, well, we can talk about it again later." There was never any discussion about whether or not I was going to come over. Only what time and what we were going to do. Sometimes it was easy to forget that a couple of months ago, we'd never met.

"Things are going to get busier and busier in the office," he said before brushing his teeth.

I pushed my wallet into my purse and paused. What was he trying to say? Was he giving me the brush-off? I'd heard my girlfriends complain about this excuse men made when they wanted to end things but were too scared to actually say the words. *Oh, I'm going to be away for most of August,* or, *my car is getting fixed up in the next couple of weeks and I won't be able to come over*. Well if that was Dexter's game, I was going to make him say the words.

"Spit it out, Dexter. What are you trying to say?"

On cue he spat his toothpaste, rinsed his mouth and turned to me. "I think we should go over to your place tomorrow and collect all your stuff and bring it back here. I want you to stay with me."

I stared at him, my brain trying to work through what he'd just said. I took a deep breath, trying to even out my whiplash. I didn't know why I'd just jumped to the conclusion he might be trying to end things when there hadn't been any signs. I supposed I was just used to disappointment. But move in here? That seemed like a lot, but the corners of my mouth were twitching as if I was about to break into a grin. "All of it?" was all I could come up with at first.

"Sure. You came over from the US. It's not like you have a lot." He froze. "Right?"

I shrugged. "As much as I could fit in two suitcases."

"Exactly. So, we could go and get it," he said again. "You spend almost all of your free time here anyway. And as we get closer to the finals, there will be less time to spend together. We should make the most of it."

It made sense, but at the same time, this was more than practicality. This guy was asking me to move in with him, even if it was only for a few weeks. "Isn't this a big decision? Don't we have to discuss it and come up with pros and cons, and shouldn't I ask you questions or something?" My logical brain told me this was fast and reckless. I would be putting my faith in this guy to keep a roof over my head—not something I could even trust my parents to do for me when I was a child. So why wasn't I freaking out and telling him no?

Dexter turned on the shower, slid out of his boxers and stepped in, the steam quickly obstructing my view of his perfect body. "Well we could analyze it to death or we could simply see it as convenient. If you decide to stay in London, then we can have another discussion."

Stay in London? Now the elevator of anxiety started to clunk into gear and hurtle skywards. That wasn't even on my radar. "Who said anything about staying in London?"

"Well, aren't you applying for jobs?"

Should I have been? My palms started to sweat and I wrestled off my cardigan. I'd assumed I'd go back to Oregon when this was all over, go to my sister's graduation and polish up my resume before starting to apply for things. "I haven't so far."

"You want me to see if Primrose knows anyone who might have a vacancy?"

This morning I'd expected to collect my things and haul my butt over to the other side of town just like I did every morning, but instead, I'd woken up on the freaking yellow brick road. "Just hold your white horses, there," I replied. "A fast second ago we were talking about bringing my two suitcases over this weekend and now you have me immigrating to London. We might want to slow down a second because I'm starting to feel the pull of the g-force."

He pushed the soap and water back over his head. My mind went entirely blank for a split second as I imagined stripping naked and joining him. That would cool me off, stop me thinking too far ahead. I turned away, intent on clearing my head.

I loved London. There was no doubt about that. It felt

like this city was the world and Oregon had been some kind of waiting room. I knew it would be difficult to go back when now my eyes had been opened to what was out here in the world. But while my sister was still in Oregon, that was home. "I appreciate that you're thinking of me," I replied, turning back toward Dexter but keeping my gaze trained on the floor. "But there are a lot of things I need to consider. You know Autumn hasn't graduated yet. She needs me."

"She's a grown woman. Surely she wants you to live your life," he said.

"You don't understand," I replied. "I've always looked after her."

"No, you're right. I don't understand. My brother couldn't wait to disappoint me."

I hated hearing him talk about his brother, because he was still so obviously upset about it. I just didn't understand why David hadn't protected him from Sparkle, hadn't fought for the family business. "Yeah, I know, I'm sorry. I can't imagine what it would be like if I didn't have Autumn. Were you and your brother close before your parents died?"

"Very. The four of us were . . . unbreakable."

I couldn't imagine it was possible for the bond between Autumn and I to be broken. Devastated wouldn't even begin to describe my feelings if we were suddenly estranged. "And you haven't spoken since your parents died?"

"Since after I found out what he'd done." He stood directly under the water as if he were trying to wash away the memories.

"It's unthinkable to me that he did that even though he knew it would have been the last thing your parents wanted and you were so set against it." I would do anything to make my sister happy. Perhaps it was because I saw my parents fail to make sacrifices for either of us, but I just wanted her to have what I never did—someone who would put me first.

"The difference is you're a good person, Hollie."

"But you would have said the same thing about your brother," I replied. There must have been a reason for David to do what he did, but Dexter clearly didn't think so. "What changed?"

He yanked the lever to turn off the shower and his mood shifted. "So, you moving in or what?" he asked, obviously not wanting to dwell on his broken relationship with his brother. "If you think it's too much then it's not a big deal. We can keep things as they are."

I liked things as they were. A lot. I liked Dexter *a lot*. I glanced around his bedroom. I only went back to my studio to shower and change these days. It was two hundred and twenty square feet I wouldn't miss. "You'd have to clear out some closet space," I said as Dexter stepped out of the shower, completely naked. "And you're going to have to keep away from me in the morning when you're naked."

He tilted his head. "Can't resist me, huh?" He grinned, wrapped a towel around his waist and swept past me. "Follow me."

I glanced at the clock on my watch. I was going to have to get moving or I was going to be really late. And I needed time away from Dexter so I could think clearly. "Can this wait?" I said, padding after him. "I really have to get out of here."

I followed him into one of his guest rooms. "So, this wardrobe is totally free. But I put some of my old suits into the other bedroom so there's a couple of rails in the master as well. Up to you how you want to distribute stuff."

He must know that everything I owned would fit in half

of one of the units in his closet, but it was super sweet of him not to banish me to the guest room. He really wanted me here. And I wanted to be here. What was there to analyze? Dexter had done nothing that deserved anything but my complete trust.

"I can get on board with the suitcase thing," I conceded. "But on the condition that we park any talk about future jobs and moving to London."

"Deal," he said, turning to kiss me.

"You're wet," I said. "And I need to leave." He kissed me again and I headed toward the door, trying to bite back a smile. I knew it was only for a few weeks, but I'd never lived with a guy before if you didn't count my father. I'd never even considered it.

Dexter, just like everything in London, was a whole new world.

"Move in this weekend," he said. "And at some point, we'll talk about what happens after the competition ends."

I pretended not to hear him and headed out. Being with Dexter had me thinking about things in new ways, had me living a different life to the one I thought I was destined for. But the pull of home—of my sister—was a bond welded in hardship and struggle and wasn't easily dismissed. Dexter was a dream come true, but at some point, I knew I would have to wake up and get back to the real world.

TWENTY-ONE

Dexter

I prided myself on having laser focus at work, but today I was distracted. I had to approve the final bracelet for the competition, yet I was mulling over the brief conversation about my brother I'd had with Hollie this morning.

Hollie and Autumn were as close as two sisters could be. I wasn't sure if it was because their parents didn't seem capable of looking after themselves, let alone two children, that Hollie had taken on more of a mother role to Autumn. Maybe it was just Hollie's intrinsically good nature. But listening to Hollie talk to her sister on the phone or talk about Autumn and how proud she was—I couldn't help but think about David. Since he'd sold the business to Sparkle, I'd not only cut him out of my life but cut him out of my memories, out of my brain. I had done my best not to even think about him. But over the last few weeks, the unanswered questions I had for him were all clamoring for attention in my mind.

"Come in," I called to the knock at the door.

Primrose came in together with Frank. I could tell by their expressions that the bracelet would be fine. If they'd not believed it to be perfect, they would be downcast and miserable. These two lived for their work just as I did. "You two look happy," I said.

"Satisfied," Primrose said. Frank just mumbled under his breath because Frank was never satisfied.

I sat back in my chair and Primrose set a black velvet tray in front of me that contained the fruits of all our labor. I took a breath in relief. The one thing I'd been worried about was the clasp on the bracelet, but I could see without touching it, it was perfect. I pulled out a pair of white gloves from my desk drawer and picked it up. "Very nice," I said, seeing the changes we'd made to the setting of the diamonds. "It looks much cleaner."

"I agree. This setting is the better option. But I thought we might put the original setting on the retail version." If we won, we'd planned to do some limited-edition pieces inspired by the collection. We'd need to make them different but similar enough that people thought they were wearing something fit for a princess.

"Yes, that would work," I said. "And we should bring in a different stone. Given that we've just gone with the diamonds and the Zambian emerald, we should steer away from that scheme and do sapphires and rubies with diamonds." I checked over the bracelet—turning it in my hands, looking at it through my loupe—despite the fact I knew that Frank and Primrose wouldn't have brought it to me unless it was perfect.

"I'm happy," I announced.

Frank's expression didn't change. I swear if I told him he'd just won the lottery he would remain dour and serious.

He was always focused on what wasn't right and determined to make it better. That's why I employed him.

"Good," Primrose said. "Shall we go through our normal agenda?"

Frank stood and took the tray and bracelet from in front of me before leaving me with Primrose.

"I got your email," she said as she closed the door.

"I can talk directly to the design consultants if that's easier," I said. I was surprised I hadn't gotten a call from Primrose as soon as I'd sent her the email asking her to go and see a Knightsbridge property with some design consultants.

"No, I'm happy to go with Beck. From the brief, you want to know a rough outline of display space. To see if it's financially viable . . . right?"

"Exactly," I said, sitting back in my chair. I was waiting for the question Primrose would be dying to ask me.

"So come on, Dexter, why the sudden change of heart? Now you want to open in London? After all these years?"

"It's time," I said. I'd spent long enough trying to erase painful memories of my parents, and avoiding the city where they'd grown their business. "Being in this competition and seeing people my parents used to work with or compete against has been . . . Well, it's not been as difficult as I expected." I'd enjoyed hearing people's stories about my parents. It was good to see familiar, if now older, faces.

"I'm so very glad to hear it," Primrose said, shuffling forward in her seat. "You would make them so proud. Everything you've built—it's quite extraordinary."

"I did it for them," I said.

Silence settled between us. Their death had been so raw at the beginning, the only thing I could do to survive was to push it away. But the edges had softened, and although I still missed them and wished I'd spent the last fifteen years being able to seek their advice and see their smiles, now I could just be grateful for what they'd given me.

"I want to ask you something and I want you to tell me the truth," I said. When Primrose and I first started working together, she'd made a number of attempts to try to talk to me about my brother. I'd been very clear if she ever brought him up to me again, not only could she no longer work for me, but I couldn't have anything to do with her. I hadn't wanted to hear any excuses about what he'd done. The actions he'd taken were unforgivable. Nothing could be said or done that could undo his betrayal, or even justify it. She'd agreed and from that day, had never mentioned him. From time to time I did wonder if she'd stayed in touch with him, whether they swapped Christmas cards or saw each other at all. "Are you in touch with my brother?"

She sat back in her chair as if I'd hit her.

My heart began to thud as I waited for her reply. I wasn't sure what I wanted her to say. Did I want her to have stayed in touch with David? What did it mean if she had? Would I be pleased he still had a connection to our parents through Primrose?

Primrose's gaze was in her lap. "Dexter, I don't want this to be an issue between us."

"It won't be," I snapped. Primrose could make her own decisions. "I never asked you not to see him. It's none of my business. I just specified that you were never to speak to me about him. I was wondering whether you saw him— whether you see him still."

She cleared her throat. "I do."

I wanted her to elaborate but she stayed silent, no doubt honoring the request I'd made of her. It said something that

Primrose had maintained a connection. I couldn't help being curious as to what kept her in contact with David. "Okay," I said, changing the subject. "I'm not in a rush to open in London, but if the Knightsbridge property works, we should be ready. Let's work up what Daniels & Co would look like in London. Are you okay to liaise with the team?"

"Certainly," she replied. "I'm really happy you're—"

"It makes good business sense," I said, shattering any kind of emotional lens she wanted to see this through.

"How are you and Hollie?" she asked. "She's getting on very well in the role. She's got a real eye—an instinct."

I tried not to grin and agree too readily. "I'm pleased. No special treatment though. She'd hate that." Hollie never expected anything she didn't work for, and it was one of the things I liked most about her.

"No, she gets treated like an intern. But I like her. That's all."

"Good," I said. "I like her too. In fact, she's going to be staying with me for the rest of her time in London." We'd not talked too much about the future, but I couldn't see a time when I didn't want to be with Hollie. "It makes sense."

"I think that's wonderful, Dexter. You deserve someone worthy of you."

It was an interesting phrase to use. "I surround myself with good people, Primrose. Same as you do." I just wasn't sure how her relationship with my brother fitted.

"I just wonder if historically, there's been a gap," she replied. "Things have shifted for you in recent months, Dexter. You're thinking about opening in London. You're facing things from your past and investing in your future."

I'd opened the door to this conversation but it was

getting drafty. I wanted to put my shoulder to the wood and press it closed.

"I'm pleased for you," she continued. "You might want to consider whether it's time to hear the whys of the past." That was cryptic. "Good people don't suddenly turn bad, Dexter, but sometimes they're put in a position where they have to make a choice and every option is dreadful." Without saying his name, she was talking about David, trying to make excuses for his betrayal. She stood, leaned across the table and pressed her hand over mine before heading out.

I wasn't about to accept he was a good person, but lately I'd become more curious about the why.

TWENTY-TWO

Dexter

I'd thought Hollie was underestimating how much stuff she had. But she was true to her word when she said she had two suitcases.

"Can you put it in a guest room?" she asked me as I pulled the large suitcase into my hallway. She'd insisted on towing the smaller one.

"You're not going to put things in the master bedroom?" I asked.

"Yeah, I just don't want to mess it up in there. You're always so . . . neat with everything."

I'd left her a gift in the second bedroom, so I supposed now was as good a time as any to give it to her. "If you say so."

"You know that girls fart, right?"

She'd been hitting me with all these stupid bits of information since we woke up. "Will you stop trying to sabotage you moving in?" I said as I set her suitcase in the walk-in wardrobe.

"Why do you need all these bedrooms, anyway?" she asked. "Oh," she said, looking at the rails where I set out her gifts, still wrapped in garment bags. "Do you want me to put my things somewhere else?"

"Yes, I want your things in the master bedroom," I said. "But you insisted on me bringing the suitcases in here."

"To unpack and put things I don't use so much. Am I still okay in here or shall I use another closet?" she asked, nodding at the rail that had been empty.

"You're okay. And these," I said, running my hand along the four hangers, "are for you. Well, for you to pick between. Moving-in gift."

You'd have thought I'd told her it was time to pull her fingernails from her hands, given the expression on her face. "For me? Dexter? You've got to stop doing that."

"No, I really don't." I found I quite enjoyed treating her. Although I had hoped the gesture would elicit a smile rather than the grimace I was actually faced with.

She rose from the floor, abandoning her suitcase, and moved toward the rail. "What are they?"

"Dresses. For the final ceremony of the competition. I picked out four so you can choose one. Or if you want to keep all four, that works." I shoved my hands in my pockets, hoping she wasn't going to be pissed off.

"You bought me dresses?" she asked, glancing between me and the rail. "Dexter," she whispered, then stepped toward me and slid her hand around my waist. "You really shouldn't have. It's too sweet."

"You've not seen them yet. You might hate them."

She squeezed me tighter. "Impossible. I know your taste. And anyway, I don't even care. I just can't believe you would do that for me."

"You deserve it."

The sound of her deep breath filled the space between us. "I don't think—"

"Let me do this, Hollie. I enjoy it. I like seeing you happy."

"I don't need gifts to make me happy," she said. "You've already done so much for me."

"I keep saying this—it's a two-way street. You make me happy and I want to do the same for you."

She reached up on her tiptoes and pressed a kiss to my neck. "I actually have a little something for you."

"Hollie, I don't need—"

"Hey," she replied. "You don't get to give me stuff and then complain when I do the same. This is a two-way street, remember?" She grinned at me as if she had me bang to rights.

She dived into her suitcase and pulled out an envelope. "I haven't had time to wrap it. I had Autumn send it because it was something I was experimenting with back in Oregon." She produced a woven, brown leather bracelet with a silver clasp.

"Wow, that's beautiful," I said, examining the silver.

"It's meant to be like the trunk of a tree or a log or something. Like I said, it was a bit of an experiment."

I didn't wear jewelry. Ever. I always thought there was something very wrong with men who ran out of ways to spend their money so decided that jewelry was the way to show off. But this I'd make an exception for. It was gorgeous, and there was nothing Hollie could give me that I wouldn't wear. I loved that her hands had crafted this, and she wanted me to have it.

She opened it and put it around my wrist. "You don't have to wear it, of course. But it's yours anyway. The clasp reminded me of you. You know—solid. Steadfast."

I caught her by the waist and pulled her against me. "Thank you."

She shrugged. "Less about you, let's move on to my gift!" She grinned and pulled out of my arms. "No one's bought me clothes since I was about twelve."

I didn't like to pry into Hollie's upbringing, but it clearly wasn't a privileged one. She seemed to have raised herself and her sister. I loved to treat her.

"If you don't like any of them, we can send them back and start again. I didn't think you'd picked a dress for the finals yet."

"This is crazy," she said, moving the hangers on the rail.

"You know you have to unzip the bags to see what's inside, right?"

She glanced at me, then started to undo the first bag.

There were lots of *Oh wows, This is gorgeous*-es and *Jiminy Crickets* as she unpacked and examined all four dresses.

"Which is your favorite?" she asked. They all seemed nice to me, and Hollie would make anything look gorgeous.

"I like them all. You could video call your sister and ask her opinion."

She held the navy-blue sequined dress against her body and swung her hips. "I don't think so."

"She doesn't have good taste?" She and her sister shared everything. I would have thought that trying on clothes would be a classic sister bonding activity.

"I don't want to make her feel bad."

"Feel bad? Why would she feel bad because you have something nice?"

She hung the dress back on the hanger and took down the black halter-neck Tom Ford. "She'd be completely happy for me. But the Sunshine Trailer Park is a long way away from your Knightsbridge apartment. And I would hate it if she felt a little sorry for herself when we got off the phone. This is . . . a lot." She swept her hand around, so I wasn't sure if she meant the gift was a lot or my apartment or London . . . or our relationship.

"Too much?"

She shook her head and slid her hands around my waist. "Of course not. You're amazing. I'm bursting at the seams to show her these dresses and your apartment, where I'm actually staying. My life is like some kind of fairytale at the moment. But hers isn't, and she doesn't need to be reminded of that."

Hollie was such a beautiful human being that she was prepared to put a lid on her own happiness just in case it created a shadow over her sister. "You're a good sister."

"It's my job," she said.

I wish David had felt that way. I'd found him with just a Google search, still working back office at a bank. I didn't know if he was married or if he had children. Maybe if he had, he'd regret what he'd done to me. Maybe he understood the value of family now.

"But you know I've made plenty of wrong decisions in my time," she said. "When I first got the trailer and moved out of my parents' place, I left Autumn with Mom and Dad." She shook her head and a curtain of shame fell across her face.

"You were fifteen and your sister was eleven. You were a kid, even if you were old enough to forge your parents' signature on a lease, from what you've told me. There's nothing to feel bad about."

"I know. I try to make up for it. And Autumn didn't hold it against me, which I'm grateful for."

"Have you ever fallen out?" I asked. Their situation wasn't enviable, but their relationship certainly was.

"Yeah. We argue a lot when we're living together." She took the red Valentino dress off the rack—it had a big, floaty skirt and she twirled around, the fabric lifting as she turned. "I mean, there's not much space and she's so messy she drives me crazy. But our differences have only almost broken us once." She turned away from me and put the dress back on the rail. "I told her I wasn't going to pay tuition for her if she went to some community college in Idaho." Her shoulders lifted and her head bowed. "She hated me. But I knew she'd picked the place because her boyfriend was going there. And she had an offer from Oregon State, which is a really good school. And she could still live at home and commute, which would save so much money."

I nodded, trying to be encouraging. She was clearly just trying to do the best for her sister. "I'm sure she gets it now."

"I hope. She still brings it up every now and then." Her voice rose an octave as she said, "It was hard because my parents took her side. I wanted to cave in so many times but I knew that guy would end up dumping her and she'd end up dropping out and she'd have lost her place at Oregon State . . . but I couldn't say that to her." She pulled the next dress from the rail. "That red one was really pretty," she said, sounding like her dog had just been run over.

I didn't know how to make her feel better. I knew a pretty dress wasn't going to cut it. "What can I do? I hate to see you sad."

She sucked in a breath and unhooked the final dress from the rail. "It's fine. I was looking out for her, trying to do the best I could by her. So, I have to live with that. And this is really pretty," she said, holding up a long black one.

I chuckled. "It is pretty. But I think I like the Tom Ford one best."

"Tom freaking Ford? Are you serious? That's ridiculous, Dexter. I don't belong in a Tom Ford dress."

I'd never bought a woman a dress before, but if I had, I couldn't think that any one of them would belong in these dresses more than Hollie did. "Then take the Valentino," I said, grinning at her.

She turned to me. "Valent—You need to take this back. I'm fine with Zara."

"I think you should keep all four."

"You're just saying that because I'm upset about Autumn. But nothing's going to stop the hurt of her thinking I wasn't trying to do my best for her. I hope she knows by now I'd do anything to make her happy."

"That's why you're such a great sister," I said, pulling her toward me and kissing the top of her head. "I wish my brother had the same instinct to protect me that you have for Autumn."

She sighed against my chest. "You said you haven't spoken since your parents died."

"No, not since I found out what he'd done."

"Maybe he's sorry." She slid her arms around my waist.

"Doesn't undo what he did."

"True. But if he regrets it, wouldn't it make it easier? Or if he had a reason? Don't you want to ask him to justify what he did?"

After my parents' death, it was as if I'd been sucked into a black hole of despair. I couldn't remember the details; I just remembered finding out he'd sold my parents' business and feeling as if I'd lost them all over again. "He was always the back-office guy—all about the money and profits. He never got the beauty of the jewelry. Never felt it in his soul like I did. I guess he saw the chance to get a pile of cash for not doing much and he took it."

"But he didn't say that to you, did he? He didn't tell you that was the reason why."

I sighed. I understood that Hollie would see it from David's perspective but it was different. "I was always the one interested in the gems and spent my summers working in the shop. He wasn't ever going to be that guy. He was always the one at the till, counting the coins. We're not made the same way."

"But you don't know whether that's the reason he sold the business," she said, gazing up at me with those hypno-tizing eyes.

"What other reason could there possibly be?"

"The only person who knows that is your brother."

Or Primrose, I thought. But she'd honored her word and never mentioned my brother or the sale of the business. No doubt they'd talked about it. "I don't want to dredge it all up again. They say the definition of madness is to keep doing the same thing and expecting a different result."

"It's not worth a conversation? He's your only family, Dexter."

My body went rigid. Beck, Gabriel, Joshua, Andrew and Tristan were my family. They were more my brothers than David had ever been. "He is not." I twisted to pull away from Hollie but she locked her arms around me.

"I'm sorry," she said. "I know you have a very close circle of friends, and I know your brother upset you deeply."

"Hollie," I said. "You have no idea. After my parents died, my friends showed me it's not your DNA or your blood that counts, it's who you're prepared to bleed for. If it hadn't been for those guys, I might not have survived. I couldn't function. I was driven half mad by guilt and grief and anger. I didn't sleep for weeks, couldn't hold a conversation for much longer. Part of me died with them. You don't know how it was."

I sucked in a breath, trying not to be overwhelmed at the memories of that time in my life. Trying to forget the darkness that settled in me and grew and grew until it nearly took me over. At nineteen, I'd been a legal adult, but it wasn't until my parents died that I grew up.

"You're right. I can't begin to imagine how awful things must have been for you, Dexter. Nothing's going to take that away. But you've got nothing to lose by asking him the question. And maybe it would help in a small way if you heard it from him, and he was apologetic and regretful. Maybe it would be closure."

"I don't need closure. I don't need David. I need a time machine that will let me go back and change history."

"Well, if I could, I would build you one with my bare hands. But take it from an older sister who has to parent a younger sister—it's freaking hard. And you get it wrong all the time. All I can hope for is that she forgives me my mistakes and gives me a chance to explain myself."

Her words came out like rain, soaking through to my core. I saw Hollie's point of view so clearly when she talked about making decisions that impacted her sister's life. That was because I knew Hollie's heart. She was always trying to do her best.

It was exactly who I'd thought my brother was until he'd betrayed me so badly.

"It's different," I said, thinking back to the photograph of my brother that I'd found online. He looked older—even had a few gray hairs at his temples. A lot of time had passed since I'd last seen him.

"Is it though?" Hollie said. "You'll never know unless you ask him."

Hollie made it sound simple. "A conversation can't just wash away years of pain and hurt, Hollie. That's not how life works."

"But it might," she said. "Until I got the internship at Sparkle, I didn't believe in miracles. And then meeting you and working at Daniels & Co—the strangest, most magical things can happen. What have you got to lose by picking up the phone? It might be the best thing you ever did."

Being with Hollie made music a little sweeter, the sea air a little fresher and the sun a little brighter. And all those things added up to making my life a whole lot richer.

She was beautiful. Creative. Talented. Sweet. Funny. Caring. Innocent and wise in the same breath. But she couldn't perform miracles. Not even she could reconcile my brother and me.

TWENTY-THREE

Hollie

I wasn't the only one to gasp as Jeremy removed the velvet from the stand to reveal the Daniels & Co entry for the princess of Finland's tiara. There was no doubt it was beautiful. Nothing created drama like diamonds. The peaks and valleys on the band, representing the mountains of Finland, were breathtaking. But despite feeling a little disloyal and a lot ridiculous, I couldn't shake the feeling that something was missing.

What did I know? I was just the intern.

"Does everyone love it?" I turned to see Dexter scanning the faces of everyone in the conference room. We locked eyes. He frowned, looked away, then whispered to Primrose.

She nodded and turned back to the room. "It would be good to hear each of your voices. Let's go around the room. Lauren, what's your reaction?"

"It's mesmerizing. Even better than the picture. And

the way that emerald hangs in the center, it's—" Lauren looked like she was about to tear up, so Primrose moved swiftly to the next person, who said similar things. Shit, what was I going to do? They were right, it was beautiful and amazing. There was no doubt about that. But that wasn't my only thought. Should I be honest and risk embarrassing myself and upsetting Dexter and Primrose, who had both been so good to me?

"Hollie?" Primrose asked. How was it my turn already?

"I mean, just what they said. I've never seen anything like it. It's gorgeous."

"But?" Dexter asked. I felt all the eyes in the room slide to him before following his gaze to me.

I sucked in a breath and nodded. "I mean, I think it's a winner."

"But you have a comment," Dexter said. Dexter had never spoken to me in front of the team before. Even though Primrose knew we were dating, she'd never singled me out for anything other than tasks strictly within the remit of an intern. Dexter shining the spotlight on me like this was going to make people suspicious, and he needed to quit it. "Hollie, I've asked everyone to speak freely."

He could make his own dinner tonight.

"I think it's beautiful. But I think . . . if it was my design, I would have been tempted to create some kind of link between the future and the past."

"But that's not the theme," Dexter said. "The theme is the Finnish landscape."

"I agree. I wasn't thinking it would have to be anything particularly extreme—just a subtle hint at the link between the generations." Every time I saw the design of this tiara, I couldn't help being brought back to that night I'd met

Dexter, the night I'd seen the tiara his parents had made for the queen of Finland.

"And how exactly," Dexter said, "would you do that?"

I briefly glanced to my right, where the rest of the team glared back at me, horrified, as if I'd just told a convent full of nuns I didn't believe in God.

But I believed in Dexter. If he'd been entirely happy, he wouldn't want to hear what I had to say. "The tiara the queen wore on her wedding day was designed by your parents. That's an advantage your competitors don't have. If you just whispered that connection in this piece, I think it might give you the edge." I stood and took a step toward the tiara. If I was going to tell him what I thought, I wasn't going to half do it—I was all in. "The way your parents' tiara links these points with the twisted rope of diamonds," I said as I looked up at Dexter and Primrose, who had both stepped forward. "You could do something similar with these smaller peaks at the back. The rope would be too much, but a single swath of diamonds might work. I think it would give emphasis to the larger peaks, which would enhance this design while incorporating a technique from her mother's tiara that the princess might appreciate."

Dexter glanced at Primrose, who was looking at the tiara intently.

"It's a sentimental touch without taking away from the theme."

"You mean here?" Primrose asked, pointing to the sides of the tiara. I nodded. "Create that bunting feel—that was what we were trying to do when we designed the queen's tiara—make it a celebration."

I shrugged. "But it's beautiful as it is, too," I said.

Dexter chuckled. "You need to have more faith in yourself," he said. "Thank you for sharing your thoughts. Primrose, Frank, let's discuss in my office." And he swept out, leaving me unsure of whether I'd embarrassed myself with my naïve ideas, or doubled my money by giving away to the entire team that Dexter and I were in a relationship.

TWENTY-FOUR

Hollie

It had been a tough week and I was looking forward to the weekend, but I'd never thought I could enjoy a job before working at Daniels & Co. I pushed through the doors to Dexter's apartment building to find him pacing in front of the concierge desk in the lobby.

"Hey," I said. "What are you doing home and what are you doing down here?" He normally didn't get back until around eight.

He beamed at me and raced over, grabbing my hand and pulling me toward the elevators. "It's your birthday tomorrow," he said.

"Did I tell you that?" I asked. I was sure I hadn't mentioned it. The last thing I needed was to give Dexter an excuse to buy more expensive gifts.

"Sort of. You told me it was in a few weeks and I did some detective work."

The doors to the elevator slid open and Dexter ushered me inside.

"Are we in a hurry?" I asked, and he grinned as wide as the ocean.

"So, I've been wondering what I could get you for your birthday. I realize you're not a Chanel bag kind of girl."

"More a pint of Rocky Road and Netflix."

He leaned and placed a kiss on my lips. It started off as a peck before he slid his tongue between my lips and I slipped my hands up his chest. He groaned and pulled away.

Something must be wrong. Usually, I'd be half undressed by the time the elevator reached the penthouse.

"We were talking about your birthday. I've arranged an early gift. I hope you like it," he said as we stepped out of the lift.

Oh gosh. I hoped he hadn't bought me anything too extravagant. I really would have liked to just spend the day in bed, watching movies with Autumn on FaceTime. It was our long-standing birthday tradition, and while I was in no way sad to spend my birthday with Dexter, a part of me felt a pang of longing for my sister. "I'm sure whatever it is, it will be lovely," I said.

When we got to his front door, instead of pulling out his key, he stood behind me and moved me onto the mat, so I was facing the door. Then he knocked. On his own front door.

"What are you doing?" I asked, turning my head.

He pointed ahead of me as I heard rustling at the door. Who was in there?

The door flew open and *Autumn* was standing opposite me. Before I had a chance to react, she leapt into my arms, circling her arms and legs around me like she used to when she was a toddler. "I've missed you so much."

She slid down my body as I started to cry. I couldn't

believe she was here. I turned to Dexter to see him grinning at the pair of us.

"Dexter," I said, standing up on tiptoes and reaching up for a kiss. "I can't believe—how did you—"

"I can explain the logistics later. Let's get inside."

"It gets better," Autumn said, linking her arm into mine as we clattered into the hallway.

How was she here? How did Dexter know that Autumn being here was the only thing I really wanted for my birthday? How was it possible that I was in London with my two favorite people in the world?

"I'm in here," Autumn said, pointing to one of the guest bedrooms.

"But I've set up a little something in here," Dexter said, showing us into another of the guest bedrooms.

I gasped as we went in. The ceiling was covered in balloons of every color, and there was a huge Happy Birthday banner stretched across one wall.

"I know it's not until tomorrow but I thought you might want to get a head start. Seeing as Autumn is here."

Why had he set this up in the guest bedroom? I squinted at a weird-looking piece of new furniture in the corner. "Is that a fridge?"

"Holy shit, you're going to love this," Autumn said. She sprang across the room and opened the door, revealing a hundred tubs of ice cream.

"I got a few flavors," Dexter said, nodding to the window. "And the TV is set up. You can watch Netflix, the *Housewives*. Anything you want."

There hadn't been a TV in here before. He must have set this up especially. "Are you serious?" I said, sliding my arm around Dexter's waist. "This is insane."

"I thought this was what you'd want to do on your birthday? Stay in bed all day, eat ice cream and watch TV with your sister."

Dexter's thoughtfulness was off the scale. It would have been easy, and very generous for him to buy me a Chanel bag. But this? This was a thousand times better.

"Oh," he said, pulling away from me and putting his head into the walk-in closet. "There are matching pajamas, slippers and robes in the wardrobe," he said. "If you get sick of ice cream, we can order in tonight. Tomorrow, I've arranged a chef for the day to make you anything you want. I figured you wouldn't want to go out if Autumn was here."

The last thing I wanted to do was go to a fancy restaurant. But having the fancy restaurant come to me? Who was I to complain?

"You are a very special man, Dexter Daniels," I said, grabbing his hand and kissing him.

"I'm going to leave you two to it. Gabriel's going to stop by any minute on his way to a charity thing. He needs to borrow a bowtie."

"Is he single and as handsome as you?" Autumn asked.

"He's red hot," Dexter said with a wink.

I turned to her as Dexter left us in the guest room. "I can't believe you're here. When did you get in?"

"Around lunchtime. Dexter arranged everything, Hollie. That man is gold, let me tell you."

We headed into the closet and found matching silk pajamas, gorgeous robes and the most beautiful fluffy slippers.

"How did he even know how to get in contact with you?" I asked, kicking off my shoes and trying on the slippers. Of course they fit perfectly.

"He emailed me. Got my address from HR. You put me down as your emergency contact."

"Sneaky," I said, as I began to undress. I couldn't wait to change into my jammies and catch up with Autumn face-to-face.

"But amazing."

That was a good way to describe Dexter Daniels —amazing.

"How's school?" I asked, slipping the pajamas on. Autumn was an adult, but part of me was a little concerned that once I'd taken off, she'd stop studying quite so hard or she'd get distracted by some worthless guy. Or even more likely, she'd end up spending her time sorting out Mom and Dad.

"Are these silk?" she asked. "Oh, and I made the Dean's list this semester."

I scrambled to grab her in a hug and ended up half falling over, tangled in lengths of silk. "Are you serious? That's completely amazing."

"Yeah, I'm pretty happy about it," she replied.

"When did this happen? Why didn't you tell me?" Now properly pajamaed, I held her at arm's length as if I were inspecting her to see if she looked more intelligent since the last time I'd seen her.

"Because I wanted to tell you in person. I've nearly let the cat out of the bag a thousand times. It's been hard to keep it from you."

"I'm just so happy for you. Sounds like you've been studying extra hard this semester. I was obviously a distraction." I was so proud of her. Dexter was right—she was a grown woman. Perhaps she didn't need as much taking care of as I thought. And that was great, obviously, but also . . . unbalancing.

"I didn't want you to feel any more guilty about leaving than you already did." She crouched on the floor and slid on a pair of slippers. "What can I say? Seeing you chase after what you wanted made me want to do the same. I haven't found what I'm passionate about yet, but I will, and when I do, I want to be in the best shape," she said. She couldn't have said anything that would have made me any happier. The fact I could be some kind of role model for my sister was all I could ever want. "And honestly, Mom still has that job at Trader Bob's, which means they've had money and they haven't been bothering me."

I couldn't remember the last time my mom held down a job for three months. "I can't believe she's still there. What happened?" We pulled the robes off their hangers and headed back into the bedroom.

Autumn shook her head. "I don't know. I think Jenny working there helps because she has someone she can ask if she doesn't know what to do, rather than just quitting like she normally would. A group of them from the store went out for breakfast last weekend."

I couldn't ever remember a time when my mom had money for waffles. "She's holding down a job, has money in her pocket and is socializing? What is happening to the world?" Both my sister and my mom were doing better than they ever had since I'd left.

"I know. I wouldn't believe it if I hadn't seen it with my own eyes. Honestly, I thought she was lying to me when she told me she was still working. But I was in there the other day to pick up some groceries and saw it for myself. She was showing a customer where the almonds were."

No one could think this was anything but good news, but there was a drag at the pit of my stomach that made me feel uneasy. "And she hasn't been talking back to her boss or missing shifts because she can't work the alarm on her phone?" I collapsed on the bed while Autumn went to inspect the ice cream fridge.

"Apparently she loves her boss. Honestly, I was over at their place earlier in the week and she made lasagna for dinner."

"She did not," I said. "She can barely boil water." What was happening? I'd half expected to go back to Oregon to find both my parents in prison.

"I know. She said Jenny showed her what to do."

All the years I'd cooked for the four of us. Even when we moved out, twice a week, I'd take food around for my parents. "I can't believe it," I said. "It would have been nice if she could have made a lasagna once in a while when we were kids." Of course I wanted her to be more capable, more focused, but I hadn't *expected* it actually to happen. Especially not when I was five thousand miles away. "How's dad?" I asked. "I bet he thinks aliens have invaded."

"Well, he's getting a home-cooked meal so he's happy. And he's been helping Kenny over at the bike shop."

"What do you mean helping? Is he doing something he shouldn't be doing?" My jaw tensed as I waited for the bad news that was going to inevitably follow Autumn's cascade of good news.

"Nope." She decided on a tub and picked up two spoons and brought it over to the bed. "Kenny's apprentice walked out and left Kenny short so Dad offered to help. Was only meant to be for a few days but that was four weeks ago."

Why hadn't she said something before? I'd just assumed they were sitting watching *Wheel of Fortune* and complaining about not having enough money—because why would anything have changed? Would this have happened if I'd still been around, or had they gotten off their asses to spite me? To show me that they didn't need me. "I guess that's great."

"I don't think he gets paid much, but he said he likes learning about the bikes. And honestly, I figure helping for free is still better than sitting at home, thinking up trouble."

"Yeah, I agree. Sounds like you're all better off without me." I said it with a smile but I wasn't joking. It kind of hurt that as soon as I'd left, things got better, as if I'd been the problem all along.

"Oh, I bet you by Friday, Mom will ask me for a loan."

"Well, I told you that if she does, you have to get her to call me. You don't have enough as it is."

"None of us has enough," she replied. "Except maybe Dexter."

"Dexter definitely has enough." I took the tub from Autumn and dug in to the Rocky Road. I'd never even seen it on sale in London. "A lot of people in London do. I can't wait to show you around. When do you have to go home?"

"I have class on Monday. I'm flying home Sunday. Can you believe he flew me out here for two nights?"

I wanted Autumn to make her classes, but I also wanted her to stay. I shouldn't be greedy. Having her here on my birthday was more than I could ever dream of.

"I saw the final tiara the other day and guess what?" I asked. "You'll have to strap yourself in before I tell you this."

"Dexter gave it to you?" she guessed.

I laughed. "I know you think Dexter is the perfect guy, but no, he did not give me a tiara."

"A ring? Are you engaged?"

"What the hell is wrong with you?" I handed her back

the ice cream. "As if I'm going to get engaged to a guy who lives five thousand miles away."

"You're living with him," she challenged.

"Until I come back to Oregon. And it's just logistics. It means we can see a little more of each other as the competition gets more demanding. No, they asked everyone to give feedback on the tiara and everyone said how amazing it was —and it was totally amazing. You've never seen anything like it—"

"Can I see it? I'm dying to."

I shook my head, half saying no to her request, half trying to get rid of the brain freeze. "It's all top secret until the finals next week. Don't you want to hear what happened?" She nodded. "Well when everyone was saying how great the tiara was, I couldn't help but think there was something missing. So, I made a suggestion. And they decided to incorporate it. Can you believe it? An idea I had about the design for a freaking tiara is going to be made." Even saying those words gave me the chills. I'd made Dexter promise he wasn't taking up the idea just because it was mine, and he basically told me I was an idiot if I thought that was possible.

"That's amazing. But not really because you're so talented." She would say that. "Don't you just pinch yourself? To think that a few months ago you were sitting here." She slapped her hands down on the bed. "And now you're designing royal stuff. And you're in London with a hot, British boyfriend."

My life was very different from how it had been up until a few months ago. But by the sounds of it, my mom and dad's lives had changed almost beyond recognition as well. Why had it taken me leaving the country for them to get jobs and put their lives in something like order? Perhaps they would be able to manage without me if I wanted to extend my stay. Dexter had been true to his word and not brought up the idea of me applying for jobs again. Maybe I should be the one to restart the conversation.

"Are you two decent? Can we come in?" Dexter called from the corridor.

I slid off the bed as the two hottest guys on the planet walked in.

"Happy nearly birthday, Hollie," Gabriel said. "I brought you a card. Handmade by a three-year-old, so don't judge." I lifted up on my toes to hug him and he said "Hi" over my shoulder.

"This is my sister, Autumn."

He nodded and my sister stood and extended her arm. I swear she'd never shaken hands with anyone in her life. "Dexter was right," she muttered.

"All the way from Oregon," Gabriel said, smiling at Autumn as Autumn smiled back at him. There were lots of smiles. "Well, I don't want to interrupt. You two look very cozy."

Maybe it was me but it seemed like Gabriel was having a hard time looking away from my baby sister.

"Are you staying in London long, Autumn?"

"Just two nights," I interrupted.

It was as if I'd broken some kind of spell he was under. Gabriel cleared his throat and nodded again. "Well, happy birthday. Very good to meet you, Autumn. I hope to see you again." And with that both of them swept out, leaving Autumn fake fanning herself with her hand.

"What is it with the men in this town? Are they all like this? No wonder you fell in love here."

I dissolved into laughter. "I'm not in love."

"Of course you are," Autumn replied, her eyebrows

pulled together as if I'd just told her there were twenty-six hours in the day.

"Don't be crazy." I wasn't in love. Dexter was just the first man I'd dated who didn't want me to be his mother. Yes, I cooked for him, but he bought me scarves and dresses, flew my sister over for my birthday and told me I was beautiful, like all the time. Yes, I listened as he told me about the frustrations of his day but he did the same for me. And yes, I wanted to make things better for him, just as I did with my family, but he wanted to do the same for me. "It's a stupid thing to say because he's Dexter Daniels and he has everything anyone could ever want, but it feels like we're a team, you know?"

"Well, like I told you, that makes a change for you."

"Yeah, remember when I dated Pauly for those few weeks and he asked me how to use the washer and it turned out his mom was out of town seeing his aunt? I swear he was hoping I'd offer to do his laundry for him."

"He was ridiculous. But I don't mean it's a change in the men you date. What I mean is, in Oregon you're out front, trying to lead everyone out of the woods. While behind you, people are getting distracted swimming in the lake, eating marionberries, or just looking up at the sun. It's good to have someone who goes at the same speed as you, someone who's working with you rather than against you."

Dexter and I were at completely different points in our careers. We weren't going at the same speed. He was in the New York marathon and I was doing a charity five-mile fun run. And it sounded like my family had all put their names down for the same run as me now I'd left for London. "Sounds like everyone's making their way out of the woods just fine without me."

"Maybe Mom and Dad have realized that they've got to stand on their own two feet."

It sounded great in theory—just what I'd always wanted. Except, if I wasn't looking after them, I didn't know who I was leading out of the woods anymore. If they all had their own paths, where did that leave me? Wandering around, and maybe a little lost.

TWENTY-FIVE

Dexter

It had only taken three words—sixteen letters—to get me to this place. This café. On this day. Sixteen letters and fifteen years and now I was about to see my brother.

The email from me had been short and to the point. I had questions. I wanted answers. I named the time and place. He replied in three words—*I'll be there*.

I slowed my gait and glanced into the coffee shop. I saw him a half second before my eyes landed on him. Still the same—the height, the short hair, the starched collar. But at the same time, a stranger to me. I didn't even know if he was married.

He picked up his coffee cup and then, without taking a sip, put it down again. Was it nerves? Irritation? I pushed open the door, heading straight for the table. I wasn't interested in coffee.

I pulled out the chair opposite him. His head shot up and he stood.

"Dexter."

I sat quickly to avoid the shaking of hands or any other greeting that might or might not be appropriate.

"David," I replied as he sat down. For a long time, I'd told myself I didn't need to know anything more than I already did. I'd buried my past along with my parents and moved on, just wanting to create a legacy that was worthy of them. But now . . .? I blew out a breath. Why now? What had changed? Yes, the competition and seeing so many people who knew and loved my parents had started unpicking the locks on the door I'd shut so firmly behind me, but there was something about Hollie—something about seeing my future so clearly with her that I needed to understand where I'd come from. "I need to hear in your own words why you—" I'd told myself to stay unemotional. I just wanted the facts. He didn't need to hear the hurt in my voice. Now we were both men rather than boys pretending, I wanted to hear what possible excuse he had to have betrayed me and my parents so fundamentally and completely. "I want to understand the circumstances that led up to you selling the business to Sparkle."

The gray suit jacket my brother was wearing seemed to deflate like a balloon with a slow puncture. For a moment, he looked as if he'd expected me to come here and ask him how he thought Frank Lampard was doing at Chelsea. Had he really thought I was going to offer him my hand and suggest we let bygones be bygones?

He shook his head, took a sip of his coffee and leaned back in his chair. "I was twenty-three. Our parents had just died. And then I'd found out—"

I waited for him to finish his sentence.

"You have to be sure you want to hear this," he continued.

"Hear what?" I asked. "I've been quite clear in telling you what I want."

He glanced around as if to check no one was listening in on our conversation. "Sometimes, it's best to remember the best about something. Or someone. Sometimes it's good not to know everything."

What was he talking about? "I want to know everything. I'm a grown man. I want the truth."

"I get it," he replied, nodding. "I just—Our parents were good people. And they gave us a good life before theirs were cut short." His voice faltered as he finished his sentence.

Ice trailed down my spine. I wasn't sure if it was a reaction to thinking about my parents' death, hearing the upset in my brother's voice or the anticipation of getting to know something I'd been missing for fifteen years.

"I know that," I said, my tone curt, trying to cover up the emotions simmering just beneath the surface.

"Primrose and the solicitor called me in for a meeting just after the funeral. They told me the business had taken on a lot of debt over the years. There was always just enough to keep everything going—to pay all the bills and cover all the staff costs, but only just."

"What sort of debts? For the shop?"

"Yes, there were several mortgages taken out on the property on Hatton Garden, and there were also personal loans."

"But there was plenty of stock. Dad always had a full safe."

David nodded. "Yes, they were keeping their heads above water. Remember, Dexter, I was twenty-three. I didn't know anything much about business at the time."

Looking back, David had always seemed so much older than me, but it was only a few years—the kind of time that dissolves to nothing as you get older. We'd both been kids when our parents had died. We knew nothing of the world.

"Primrose and the solicitor took me through the options but really there was only one."

My skin heated and I fisted my hands. "There's always more than one option."

He shrugged. "Maybe in the circles you move in," he said. "But for a twenty-three-year-old who just found out his parents' business wasn't the thriving, moneymaking place he'd thought it was, it didn't seem that way."

I unclenched my fists. "Go on." I needed to hear him out. It was my one chance.

"The debts were piling up—already by the funeral we'd missed a mortgage payment because the shop had closed. People's jobs were at stake. And the business couldn't take on another designer and cutter."

"Primrose could have done the design," I said, instinctively trying to find a hole in his theory.

"Maybe, but trying to find a gem cutter? And someone who could actually run the business? I know you wanted to be that person but, Dexter, you were . . ."

I was young. I knew that. But I was a fast learner.

"You were broken," he said. It wasn't what I'd expected. "You were inconsolable in your grief."

"My parents had just died," I snapped.

"Our parents, Dexter. Our parents. I lost them too." He sighed and shook his head. "You weren't in a position to take on a failing business and neither was I. The offer Sparkle presented paid off all the debts and gave us both a little money—"

"The money wasn't important. I didn't give a shit about having money."

"I thought it would give you a start if you wanted to

launch a business yourself. The last thing I wanted was you to start off in life with a concrete block chained to your legs. It would have pulled you under."

"I'm a fighter," I said. "You knew that."

He sighed and nodded. "I know but then? You were drinking. You wouldn't—couldn't engage. You wouldn't even talk about the funeral plans."

I thought back to that time. It was just a dark pit of horror I thought I would drown in. If it hadn't been for Beck. And Gabriel. And all the guys. I'd forgotten, but they'd taken shifts and stayed by my side, drunk with me, listened as I ranted. But my real blood brother hadn't been there.

"The funeral wasn't important," I replied. "Their business, their legacy was important."

"I agree," he replied. "But what was their business? It was their work ethic, their love for what they did, their talent." He paused and glanced out of the window. "You're their legacy."

His words were like a sucker punch to my gut. All I'd wanted my entire life was to be the son they would have wanted me to be. To have the business they should have had. I'd wanted to honor them. "Why didn't you talk to me about it? You could have told me about the debts and—"

"I tried, Dexter. You were just . . . you were grieving. And you didn't want to hear about the possibility of selling the business."

"Of course I didn't. Mum and Dad were gone. I didn't want to lose their business as well."

"Which is completely understandable. Neither did I. You think I didn't want you to run that business? To carry on their name? To do what you'd always dreamed of? Of course I did. But it was impossible. The business was teetering on the brink, and without Mum and Dad it would have gone under. There was no doubt about that. I had to think of the jobs that would have been lost when the business collapsed. Sparkle agreed to keep everyone on. And I had to think about you. How would you have felt if I'd let you go into that business and it had failed? How much guilt would you have felt? I know you're angry, but I wanted you to have a good life—not one marred by a huge failure right at the outset. And the way you were consumed by your grief— I was afraid. Afraid for you. Afraid of the consequences of whatever decision I made."

What he was saying sounded completely . . . right. Not just true or accurate, but *right,* like finding the perfect uncut stone after seeing hundreds and hundreds of not-quite-perfect alternatives. My instinct always knew instantly that it was just right. I'd created explanations for David's behavior that never felt like an exact fit. But what he was telling me now was the entire truth.

I'd felt angry at my brother for so long, I didn't know how to feel any other way. But the anger was no longer directed at him. Instead, as he spoke, I turned that anger around and pointed it back at myself. There was no wild conspiracy to cheat me of my legacy, no selfish, quick decision that made life easy for David.

Why had I thought so badly of him for so long? I'd held on to so much futile fury. So much bitterness. For too many wasted years.

I swallowed, trying to clear the regret from my throat. "Why Sparkle?" I asked. "Of all the people."

"That was . . . tough. I asked the solicitor to see if anyone else was interested. But realistically, Sparkle was willing to pay far more than the business was worth. They were guaranteeing the jobs of the people who had worked for Mum and Dad. And it left some money for you to use to start again. I asked myself time and time again what our parents would have wanted me to do, and to this day I still think they would have told me to take the money."

It was as if someone had wrapped a belt around my chest and was pulling it tighter and tighter. My brother had done everything he could. He'd made the best decision—the decision I would have made if I'd been brave enough or cognizant enough to have been involved.

"And you got to start your own business. I know they would have been so proud of you."

"I still miss them," I said, wincing at the constriction around my chest. "All these years later, the pain is still there."

"I don't think it will ever go away," he replied.

He had it too—we both shared their loss. Over the years I'd been able to convince myself that *my pain* was deeper, stronger, harder somehow. I thought the fact that I'd been denied their legacy meant I loved them more. But that wasn't true.

"I blamed you," I said. "For a lot of years." The wall of rancor I'd placed between me and my brother slowly crumbled as I looked at him through fresh eyes.

"I blamed myself. I still do."

"You did nothing wrong." All these years I'd pushed him away when I'd needed him. He'd just been trying to do his best.

"I wanted to save the business so badly," he said. "For you. For us. For them. I wanted to keep them close."

"It wouldn't have worked," I said. "Nothing would have brought them back." By hating my brother, I'd just punished myself even more.

"I'm sorry," he whispered. "I failed you when you needed me most."

"Don't say that. If I hadn't been so bloody minded. So blinkered." I paused, trying to take it all in. Hollie had been right. "If I'd just remembered who you were, I would never have assumed the worst of you."

"I should have made you see somehow. Made you listen to me."

I managed to let out a small laugh. "No one other than Mum and Dad ever made me do anything I didn't want to."

He grinned at me. "I guess that's true." He sighed. "But I wish over the years I had tried more. I thought if I gave you a little space, you might come around."

"I guess I did. But it shouldn't have taken so long. *I'm* sorry, brother." I took a steadying breath. "They would hate that we haven't spoken in so long."

He nodded, his glassy eyes giving way to tears. He pulled out a handkerchief and blew his nose, clearing away the signs of grief. "I think that's why I pushed for the bank to sponsor the competition."

"That's why you were on the list of attendees at the launch?" I'd thought he was there with Sparkle. Again, I'd made assumptions I had no right to.

"I heard you were entering and I got the bank to sponsor. I wanted . . . some kind of connection. I didn't dare to hope we'd talk, but I just wanted to be a part of your life in some small way. I couldn't face attending in the end. Didn't want to risk coming face-to-face with you and it going badly."

I'd spent the last fifteen years thinking David had been plotting against me. All that futile anger I'd felt toward him. All that pointless fury.

Too much time had been wasted.

Too much lost that neither of us would get back.

We had to make things right.

Most importantly, I had to learn my lesson. I had to seize opportunities. I had to make the most of everything and everybody in my life.

TWENTY-SIX

Dexter

"Gosh darn it, Dexter Daniels. This is all your fault," Hollie called from the bedroom.

"Hollie's furious because she can't decide what to wear tomorrow night," I explained to my brother, who had just called.

"We do have it lucky just throwing on a dinner jacket and combing our hair," David replied.

"Thank God," I replied. "Is Layla having the same issue?"

"I think she picked something. She's excited to meet you. Won't stop going on about it."

It was weird I hadn't met my brother's wife. Fifteen years may have passed, but we'd spoken every day since we'd met in the café. It felt as if the time we hadn't been speaking had collapsed to a mere moment. It was like it had always been between us when our parents were alive.

"Hollie's the same. You'll like her. She's different to Bridget but she's great."

"Different to who?" he asked.

Hadn't he heard me? "Bridget. You know, who I was going to marry."

"The girl you dated at uni?"

Who else could he think I was talking about? "Yeah. You don't remember her?"

"Vaguely. The one with the curly hair and the tiny feet."

"No, that was Paula." I'd forgotten about her. I'd gone out with her before Bridget. "Bridget was the girl on the same course as me."

"The one with that insane laugh? With the button nose and hips."

"Well as far as I can recall, every woman I've ever dated has had hips." David was just as he always had been, focused on the details. "But no, that was Verity. Bridget was blond."

"Did she have a nose ring?"

Finally, he remembered. "That's the one."

"Oh, I vaguely remember her. You got *engaged* to her?" Why did he sound so incredulous? It must have been obvious that Bridget wasn't Verity or Paula. That she was the one. David must have met her countless times. He would have known we were serious.

"No, but I would have asked her." I hadn't had a chance before I'd ended things after a stupid argument.

He chuckled. "Well Mum wouldn't have been happy. You know how she hated nose rings."

"But she liked Bridget?" I wasn't sure if it was a question or a statement. It was so hard to remember back then.

"God knows, Dexter. You went through women like most students go through pints of beer." Why hadn't Bridget stood out to him? "I don't think any of us thought you were close to getting serious with someone, let alone married. You were young. Having fun. If Mum and Dad thought you were going to marry any of those girls from uni, they would have had something to say. And it wouldn't have been good."

I wanted to press him on what he remembered about Bridget, because it was clearly different from what I remembered, when I heard Hollie in the hallway.

"Yes, I'll just get him," she said as she came into the sitting room, her phone clamped to her ear. "It's Primrose. Was trying to get you but you're on the phone. It sounds urgent."

It was getting late. What would Primrose have to speak to me about that wouldn't wait until the morning?

"David, I've got to go, I've got Primrose on the other line. I'm sending a car for you tomorrow so I'll see you at the venue."

Hollie handed me her phone.

"Dexter, we have a problem," Primrose said. "One of the pieces was dropped while we were packing up for transport to the venue."

My jaw clenched and I tried to take a deep breath, steeling myself for more bad news.

"It's the tiara. One of the emeralds came out and when they tried to force it back into the setting it . . . the stone cracked."

I didn't know where to start. I stood and strode to the kitchen to find my car keys. "Who the hell tried to replace it? Was it Frank?" I knew without asking it hadn't been because he didn't go around cracking emeralds. Whoever was stupid enough to drop the tiara was stupid enough to try to cover up the damage.

"Dexter, you know I'm not going to tell you. But it could

be worse. It was one of the smaller stones."

I didn't give a shit if it was the smaller stones. A crack was a crack. I had to contain my anger and focus on what mattered, which was making sure that tiara was ready for the final round of judging tomorrow morning. The ceremony to announce the winner would happen later in the evening.

"Get Frank in. I'm on my way," I said and hung up. I'd chosen every stone for every setting for this competition. We had some Zambian emeralds I'd sourced for the earrings until we'd chosen to go only with diamonds. I'd have to hope one of them worked for the tiara.

As I got to the doorway, I spun around to find Hollie running up behind me.

"You okay? What happened? Can I help?"

I pinched the bridge of my nose. "One of the stones in the tiara has cracked. I have to go and sort it out. I'll be back later."

She slid her hands up to my face and cupped my jaw. "Oh gosh, Dexter, I'm sorry. Is it fixable?"

I shrugged. I wasn't sure the extent of the damage or which exact stone had cracked. I just needed to see it for myself and then figure out what to do.

"Shall I come with you?"

I shook my head. There was no point in neither of us getting any sleep. "I need to focus. I'll call and tell you what's happening, but you stay here." I kissed her on the head and headed out.

Up until five minutes ago, Daniels & Co was perfectly positioned to win the competition and carry on the Daniels family legacy.

But no one would win with cracked stones and a broken tiara as the centerpiece to their entry—not even me.

TWENTY-SEVEN

Hollie

Arms folded, I looked at the four dresses hanging in the closet. Should I even be worrying about what I was going to wear to the finals when Dexter was back at the office trying to salvage the tiara? It felt wrong, but at the same time, I knew Dexter would handle things. That's what he did.

My phone buzzed and I slid it open, expecting it to be Dexter. But it was Autumn calling.

"Hey, lovely, how are you?"

No answer.

"Autumn?"

"Hey," she replied in a small voice.

"Hey yourself. What's up?" I headed back in the kitchen to figure out what to cook for dinner. Something that would be good cold if Dexter came in late.

"Hollie, I fucked up."

I closed my eyes, willing down the fear rising through my body. This was it. This was the conversation I'd been dreading for years now. "You're pregnant," I said.

"God, no."

I collapsed onto the couch. I didn't care what came next, as long as Autumn's future was still waiting for her.

"But it might be worse," she said. "I ended things with Greg. And he didn't take it well."

No surprises there, and as far as I was concerned, the fact that Autumn was single was only a good thing. "Okay. Well he'll get over it. Or he won't." Did it matter?

"Except that he's out for revenge. I'm really fucking sorry." Her voice faltered as she spoke. What in the hell had happened?

"Mind your manners," I replied. "What are you sorry about? What's the worst he could do?" He'd probably spread all sorts of gossip about Autumn, but people who knew us would know the truth. It wasn't like Greg was the type to get violent.

"You got a letter today. Mom and Dad got one too. From the park."

"And . . .?" My stomach squeezed into a ball, winding my breath tighter and tighter.

"His dad has tripled the rent on our trailer and Mom and Dad's starting next month."

"Tripled? But that's impossible. We weren't getting a great deal to start off with because Mom and Dad have been late with payments so often. How can they just triple our rent?"

"I don't know. I'm so sorry."

I needed a solution. Something to make it right. "Can you make up with Greg? Apologize?"

"He saw some messages between me and some guy at the college. He got all bent out of shape and there's no talking him down. I've tried, believe me. There's nothing I wouldn't have done to set this straight."

I dreaded to think what Autumn had offered Greg.

Just when I thought things had moved on in Oregon. My last conversation with Autumn had unsettled me. I'd questioned whether I should have left years ago to leave everyone to fend for themselves, seeing as they seemed to be doing so much better without me. But now? There was no way we could afford triple the rent on two trailers. We'd have to find an apartment in town. It would be more expensive, but likely not triple what we were paying now. I wouldn't be able to walk to work. I'd have to get a car, plus insurance . . . Costs were adding up in my head.

What a mess. "At least we've got a month to figure things out." Hopefully, I'd win the lottery.

"What do you mean a month?" Autumn asked. "It's three days until the rent's due."

The bitter taste of diesel fumes coated my tongue and all at once I was transported back to Oregon.

Ten minutes ago, my biggest problem was which dress I was going to wear tomorrow night. Now it didn't matter because I wasn't going to make it. I switched the phone to speaker and started to look up flights.

"I'll come home," I said, defeated.

My time in London had come to an end. I'd been stupid to think I could have a new life just because my sister was graduating. Life just wasn't that easy. I'd thought that with some experience, I'd be able to get a job and leave Oregon with Autumn. That wasn't going to happen now. I was going to be trapped paying expensive rent.

"No, don't do that," Autumn said. "I'll try to talk to him again."

It wouldn't work. I knew it in my heart. I'd go back to Oregon and figure something out. Because that's what I did.

I should have saved more while I'd been in London. I'd

been frivolous buying flowers and fancy cheese for Dexter's place.

I scanned the flights online. There was one I could afford in three hours. I'd have to Usain Bolt it, but I could just make it. In just a few clicks my future was sealed.

I needed to accept my fate. I wasn't getting out of Oregon. By tomorrow night I'd be back at the Sunshine Trailer Park and everything in London, including Dexter, would be five thousand miles and a million lifetimes away.

At least I'd had this time, this experience—Dexter. Even if it had been so temporary. I'd hold these memories close for the rest of my life.

TWENTY-EIGHT

Dexter

Three missed calls. Three voicemails. I hung up on the last one just as I stepped into my apartment after working through most of the night. My phone had been on silent at the office as we'd been focused on saving Daniels & Co's place in the competition.

One crisis bled into another. The new stone was in place on the tiara but Hollie was thirty thousand feet up on her way back to Oregon.

Her messages were garbled and muffled. All I could glean was that she had to go back because her parents and her sister were threatened with eviction. What I didn't understand was why it took Hollie to fly five thousand miles to sort it out. Her parents and Autumn were adults.

Instinctively, I pressed call, even though I knew she'd be in the air. A phone rang in the kitchen. I followed the sound and found Hollie's Daniels & Co phone on the counter. Locked.

I didn't even have her US mobile number.

I scrolled through my phone, looking for Autumn's number then realized we'd only communicated by email about Hollie's birthday. We'd never actually spoken.

I wandered through my apartment, looking for signs that she was coming back, but her mobile and four still-covered dresses for tonight's event told a different story.

There was nothing left of Hollie in London.

TWENTY-NINE

Dexter

I stepped out of the cab with the feeling I'd left something vital behind at home. But Hollie wasn't back at my flat. I checked my watch. She'd have landed by now and I still hadn't heard anything.

This evening was meant to be different. I'd thought I was going to introduce her to my brother.

I tried to shake it off, put on my best poker face, as I pushed the revolving door into the lobby. Near the check-in desk stood a woman whose profile looked familiar. Her hair was a chestnut brown bob and she was a little taller than Hollie. And then she turned in my direction.

Bridget.

My heart began to pound as if I'd been searching for buried treasure for a decade and my spade had just hit gold.

She looked at me with no recognition in her eyes, turned and started toward the bank of lifts.

"Bridget," I called after her. I couldn't let her walk away without saying something.

She stopped and turned around. Narrowing her eyes, she took two steps toward me. "Dexter? Oh my God, how are you?"

"Hi," I said, bending to kiss her on both cheeks, preparing myself to touch her for the first time in so long. But when my lips reached her cheek, there was no longing, no physical reaction at being so close to her after so long. "It's been awhile. How are you?"

"Great," she said smiling. "You look good. But then you always did. What are you up to?"

"Here for an event in the ballroom." This stilted small talk was odd, considering this was the woman I'd long considered the love of my life.

"Explains the bowtie," she said. "I'm meeting a girl-friend for drinks downstairs."

"Shall I walk you down?" I offered.

She shrugged. "If you like."

We headed over to the lifts in silence and I glanced over at her, trying to remember what about her had been so special. "Are you still a tennis fan?" I asked.

"More of a spectator these days," she replied. "Although I do play occasionally."

The lift pinged open and I followed her inside.

As the doors closed, she looked up at me. "Dexter, I should have said something years ago when . . . your parents, you know. I'm really sorry I wasn't more supportive to you when they died." Her mouth twitched and she shifted her handbag from one shoulder to the other. "It was just that things had been so casual between us and then this huge thing happened to you and I couldn't handle it."

Had I been so lost during that time that I didn't remember anything about our relationship? David had the impression Bridget was no one special to me and now

Bridget herself was saying the same thing. "It's fine," I said, confused and hoping she'd elaborate. "I can't quite recall the details."

"Well, I'm not proud of myself," she said. "I shouldn't have just finished things with you when you needed someone."

I'd always thought I'd broken up with her, messed it up by being stubborn and stupid. Bridget clearly had a different view of what had happened between us.

"It was a long time ago," I replied.

Part of me wanted to probe, dig deeper, ask more about her memories from that time. They seemed so completely opposite from what I recalled. But here we were—two almost strangers. It didn't seem right to ask someone who didn't know me about the most difficult time in my life.

"It was," she replied. "That doesn't make it right. You had your friends though."

I smiled. "I did. I still do, actually. The six of us are still close."

She turned toward me. "Wow. That's really nice."

More than nice, but if Bridget wasn't lucky enough to have friendships as strong as mine then I wasn't going to make her feel bad about it. I had the most incredible life with the most incredible people in it. I had nothing to regret or feel bad about.

Whatever had happened between us all those years ago just didn't matter.

Whether or not she was important to me at the time or I'd simply mythologized her because she'd come before my parents' death, when life had been good—she was nothing to me now. The woman in front of me wasn't *Bridget*. She wasn't the woman I'd clearly created in my head as proof I'd never be married. Be in love. Have a future with someone.

We stepped out of the lift and stopped at the entrance of the bar where she was meeting her friend.

"It was really good to see you," I said, smiling as if I'd won tonight already.

She half smiled at me, as if she couldn't understand why I might be telling the truth. "You too."

I turned back to the lift. She would never know how good it was to have bumped into her. Only now was I able to say goodbye to a lie I'd been telling myself for so long. Seeing her had cut the last few strands that were tying me to my past.

I'd been set free.

———————

STANDING BESIDE PRIMROSE, I angled myself away from the far end of the room where the entries were displayed. I hadn't even looked at the designs of the other four finalists, and I didn't want to see their finished products. My father always said that comparing yourself to others led to madness, and it was a rule I lived by. Primrose, on the other hand, knew everything about everybody else's designs, which were all showcased on the back wall of the ballroom.

"It's about personal choice at the end of the day," she said to the editor of *The Jeweller* magazine, who had come over to welcome us but had really wanted to know how stressed and competitive we were. "We just focused on designing and making a collection worthy of Her Royal Highness."

"Anything you want to add?" the journalist asked me.

"I'm just looking forward to an enjoyable evening with my team. I hope we raise a lot of money for charity," I said.

To win tonight would be the pinnacle of everything I'd worked for my entire life. But I wasn't about to admit that to a journalist. The winning shouldn't matter. I knew we had produced an incredible collection—it incorporated the heritage of Finland and the royal family as well as raising the profile about global issues. And on top of all that, it was some of the finest jewelry in existence.

But the winning *did* matter. To me at least. My parents would never know—would never get to appreciate it—but I wanted to do something I *knew* they would have been proud of. My fortune wouldn't have impressed them. No doubt it was their lack of interest in money and profit that had left the business on the brink when they died. No, they would be interested in the pieces. In the creativity. In the stones.

And we'd nailed all of it.

I spotted Tristan through the crowd a few meters away, and he headed toward us, glass in hand. "I might not know anything about jewelry," he said. "But if it was up to me, you'd win. Congratulations, mate. By far the best entry in the room."

"I agree," Primrose said as Tristan kissed her on the cheek. "But I'm slightly biased."

Gabriel came up behind him. "Well done," he said. "It all looks spectacular. And no gimmicks. Did you see that first entry as you come in has some kind of graphic scene behind it?"

"It's clever," Tristan said. "But it means you're looking at the film and not the crown thing. Which is probably for the best. Because it was very mediocre." Tristan, like all my friends, was loyal to the core.

"Very mediocre," agreed Beck, as he appeared from nowhere. I hadn't been sure he'd make it. "The Daniels &

Co entry is spectacular, on the other hand." He glanced around. "Where's Hollie?"

Lucky for me, Gabriel distracted him, probably remembering that Hollie didn't want the rest of my business to know we were dating. Not that it mattered. She wasn't here, and I wasn't sure we were dating anymore. After she'd left, I'd checked the flat over and over, but she'd taken every single last thing of hers. And I knew she hadn't left anything at her studio. She had no reason to come back. Was that it? Was I supposed to just say, "Thanks, see you around"?

I'd sent an email to Autumn but I'd heard nothing.

I wanted Hollie here. To see what she'd earned. To see what she was capable of.

We were called to our table and Gabriel, Tristan and Beck headed to the table next to the one where I would sit with the Daniels & Co team. I glanced around to find David before following them.

"Mum and Dad would have loved to have seen you both here," he said as he came up behind Primrose and me.

I pulled him in for a hug. I didn't want to let go. I'd spent so long angry at him I'd forgotten to miss him. But having him back in my life, it all came flooding back. I liked his laugh and the way he was terrible at football. I remembered how he was so grouchy if things weren't fair. I remembered him plastering my knees, giving me Chinese burns and cutting my hair when I was about eight; it had gotten too long and our parents were too busy to notice. He'd been the consummate big brother. When he'd sold the business to Sparkle, all those memories had been locked away. Now I'd allowed them out, it was as if I was more *me*.

I was whole now I had my memories of us back.

"Thanks for coming," I said, trying to keep my voice steady.

"Wild horses couldn't have stopped me," he said as we parted. "This is my wife, Layla."

A small, pretty blond woman stood beside him, beaming. "I'm so happy to meet you," she said and threw her arms around my neck as if she was my long-lost sister. I supposed she was in a way. "I feel like I know you. Primrose always kept us up to date, but it's not the same as being able to see you in the flesh."

I glanced at Primrose. I'd never told her not to talk to David about me. I'd spent years trying to act as if I didn't have a brother, and now I wished I could get those years back.

"Sounds like I have some catching up to do," I said.

She grabbed my hand. "Lots. Come round for supper this week, will you?" I nodded, realizing I didn't even know where they lived. So much wasted time. "And bring someone if you want?" Frustration clutched at my stomach as I imagined Hollie back in Oregon. She was probably home with her sister now. However hard I tried, I couldn't imagine her in America. She belonged in London.

I shook my head. "I'm a party of one," I said.

We made our way to our table, with me fastidiously avoiding looking across the room at the competitors' pieces. I'd look if we lost. But not before the winner was announced.

Our first courses were delivered and as Primrose chatted to David and Layla, I checked my phone, but it was blank. I'd put my phone number in my email to Autumn and was hoping for a message from Hollie. It didn't feel right that she wasn't here. The last-minute changes we'd made to the tiara on her suggestion had elevated the piece to another level. I'd been so fucking proud of her. I knew in that moment she was going to have a fantastic career.

But she needed to learn to put herself and her own needs first.

If she was determined to be drawn back to Oregon at every opportunity, then no doubt, she'd have to make do with an Etsy store. And that would be a waste of talent.

The meal dragged on, intermittently interrupted by short films about the charities that had been supported and speeches on the industry and Finland. The entire room was smiling and feigning interest. I glanced at the next table and saw Beck, Gabriel and Tristan chatting away and then across from me, my brother and his wife. Next to me, Primrose. Not all the guys had managed to come tonight, but other than Andrew and Joshua, everyone important in my life was here. The only person missing was Hollie.

After the plates were cleared and the amounts raised for charity announced, the room began to quieten. Everyone was ready. All heads were turned to the podium and side conversations hushed.

The princess of Finland was welcomed on stage to finally announce the winner. Not just months, but a lifetime of preparation had come down to this moment. Her Royal Highness was going to decide whether or not I'd picked up that baton from my parents and carried it with me.

I was usually quite a patient man—fine jewelry making required it—but right then I wished I could press the skip button on the princess and get to the part where she announced the winner. Instead she talked about the charities being supported. About Finland, her family and her fiancé. With every sentence my insides coiled tighter and tighter, images flashing into my head of me as a boy in my parents' shop, me opening my first business, taking my first commission. I glanced at my brother, whose gaze was glued to the stage.

"And now," she said. "To the winner. As you know, I've been advised by the expert panel who were responsible for selecting the finalists and I've made my choice." I swallowed. I knew we'd done our absolute best. The thought that it might not be good enough gnawed at my throat.

"The winner's design was inspiring in so many ways. I love the way it incorporates the ethereal beauty of the Finnish landscape without compromising on the design."

That sounded promising. She could be talking about Daniels & Co, but because I hadn't seen the other finalists, perhaps it could apply to them as well.

"And the quality of the stones and settings was outstanding."

I imagined she'd say that about whoever won.

"But I also loved how there were small references to my mother's wedding jewelry." She paused and the breath in my chest turned solid, rendering me entirely still. "The winner is Daniels & Co."

The corners of my mouth twitched, the rock beneath my ribcage dissolved and I released the breath I'd been holding. I glanced at my brother, who was on his feet, his arms in the air, cheering. His wife was beaming as if she'd known me for the last fifteen years. Over at the table beside ours, Tristan had two fingers in his mouth and was whistling. Gabriel stepped across and pulled me into a hug.

I was proud and pleased and relieved. But despite being exactly where I wanted to be, with everything I'd been working for . . . it wasn't enough. Because Hollie wasn't by my side to share in it. All I wanted was to turn to her and kiss her.

Instead, I took Primrose's hand and led her to the stage.

THIRTY

Dexter

I lay my hand, palm up, on the shiny mahogany of the bar. "I swear, my skin's about to break I've shaken so many hands tonight," I said, before downing a gulp of whiskey. As soon as we won, I'd wanted to leave, but Primrose made it clear I was to stick around. It wasn't the skin on my hands that truly hurt. It was the stormy darkness swirling in my gut that I couldn't drink away. Hollie should have been here tonight. She should be here now. With me.

"For a guy who just reached the pinnacle of his career, you don't seem very happy," Gabriel said.

My driver had taken Primrose and the trophy home and was going to come back for me. I'd been ready to leave but I didn't want to go home, so Gabriel and Tristan had brought me to a nearby bar. My driver would be outside by now but I wasn't ready to go back to the flat. Maybe I'd grab a room at a hotel. There was no point in going back to empty room after empty room. Not until I'd drunk a lot more. There was no one there to go home for. "I just have a sore hand," I replied.

"Right," he said, and he glanced over his shoulder. "Tristan never misses an opportunity to get a number, does he?"

"He tries too hard," I said. It wasn't true. Tristan didn't need to try—he just liked the challenge—but I was taking my bad mood out on my friends. I needed to go out for a run or take a shower or do something to clear my head.

"I presume the fact that Hollie isn't here has something to do with your demeanor," Gabriel said. "As well as your sore hand." He didn't roll his eyes because that wasn't Gabriel's style, but he might as well have done.

There was no point in talking about Hollie. She was gone.

I finished my drink and ordered another. "You want one?" I asked him.

He shook his head. "Come on, mate. What happened? You should be happier than a pig in shit."

"She had some kind of family crisis at home. Left early."

"Oregon home?" he asked and I nodded. No doubt he had to check because it was so bloody ridiculous that she'd leave London completely. I should have forced the conversation about her staying in London. I'd just been busy with the competition and it didn't occur to me that she'd up and go back to the US with no notice. I didn't know who to be angry with—her for just taking off or myself for not making her stay.

"But she's coming back, right?"

"On the basis I've not had a single message or call since she left for the airport, I'm assuming she's gone for good." As I said the words my stomach churned. Could that be true?

I'd heard nothing. And I didn't believe that bullshit about no news being good news.

"The phone works two ways, you know," Gabriel said.

"I don't have a number for her. She was using a company phone here, and she left it. I've emailed her sister. What more can I do?"

Gabriel beckoned over the barman and ordered another drink. "Do you want her back?"

"I wanted her here tonight." I'd assumed we'd have time to figure things out after we'd won the competition. I'd assumed she wanted to stay. I'd assumed a lot of things. Things had been good between us and she loved London. She wouldn't be going back to Oregon if it had been her choice. She wouldn't have missed tonight.

But it definitely had been her choice not to call me. Or leave me with her US number.

"It's hard not to put family first," Gabriel said. "It's a natural reaction."

Hollie's generosity and thoughtfulness were at the core of who she was, and I didn't want that to change. "I just want her to be happy and stop sacrificing herself for people who should be able to look after themselves. I want her to get what she wants out of the world." She deserved a happy and successful life where she wasn't just looking after other people. But maybe I was being selfish.

"Sounds like you're serious about her."

There was no doubt about that. "Tonight was meant to have been special. I've worked so hard to live up to my parents' reputation, and to have that recognized tonight was all I could have wished for. You're right. I should be fucking ecstatic instead of a miserable bastard, drowning my sorrows at the bar." I took another sip of my drink. "Don't get me wrong, I'd be a hell of a lot more miserable if we hadn't won."

Gabriel chuckled. "Yeah, I probably wouldn't be sitting here if you'd have lost. Or if I was, I'd be wearing body armor."

"I just wanted her here," I said. "I wanted to share it with her." Nothing was right without Hollie. It was slowly sinking in that she was gone. Not just for tonight but forever. Faced with the prospect of Hollie not being around, I was being forced to consider what life felt like without her. It was like a fist to my face.

I didn't want to go home tonight because I didn't want to be anywhere she wasn't. A hotel room wasn't going to be any different. I wanted to wake up next to her every morning and go to sleep, her body tucked into mine, every night. I wanted her in my life every moment of every day.

"Hey," Gabriel said. "Your parents would have been immensely proud. Your brother was there to celebrate with you and so were we. It's a fantastic achievement."

I knew the theory. And of course, it was fantastic my brother had been there tonight. It was fitting. And I was grateful and so happy to have him back in my life. Even though we'd not seen each other for so many years, it was as if he'd never been away. But him being here just made me think of Hollie. If I hadn't seen the way she was completely devoted to her sister, I would never have contemplated that David might have a legitimate side of the story. It was Hollie's example that made me consider getting in contact with him again. If she hadn't come into my life, tonight would have been even more of an empty experience than it was turning out to be. If she was gone for good, did that mean I would spend the rest of my life with something missing?

I shrugged and tipped back my drink. "It will be good publicity with the store opening."

"Do you regret not making things right with David sooner?"

Christ, was Gabriel trying to make me feel worse? "I think we both have regrets." He wished he'd pushed me. I wished I'd not been so pig-headed. "But yes of course I do. We wasted a lot of years."

"Guess you wouldn't want to repeat that mistake," Gabriel said. He thought he was being subtle. Or maybe he didn't—he wasn't a stupid man. But he didn't get it. The situation with my brother was very different. I'd been grieving and desperate to hold on to my parents. We'd both been young and in pain. Time and age had given us perspective. Hollie knew I wanted her to stay in London. She wanted to please her family more than she wanted me. It was as simple as that.

"Hollie and I didn't have an argument. She flew back to Oregon. I can't change that, Gabriel."

"I get the impression that she was important to you. Like more important than anyone for a long time."

"Yes," I said. The days of trying to deny that were long gone. "She was very important. Before Hollie, I was resigned to being on my own."

He chuckled. "Yes, I think we'd all figured that out."

"Hollie was different. She's sweet and caring and funny and talented and fucking gorgeous." There weren't words enough to describe how really wonderful she was. "There's no point dwelling on it. She's gone. There's no bringing her back."

Gabriel put his hand on my shoulder and pushed me to face him. "What are you talking about, Dex? She didn't get married. And . . . she didn't die. You don't have to let her go without a fight."

He made it sound simple. I knew she hadn't died or moved on, but I also knew I had to let go of things in my life that weren't meant to be. "She's a grown woman. I can't make her do anything she doesn't want to do, and she hasn't called."

"So that's it? You walk away?"

"I didn't walk anywhere. I'm right here where she left me." She had my number.

"Dexter, I've never seen you like this. I don't want you to spend your life regretting that you didn't do more."

"What more can I do? If she doesn't feel the same way about me, I can't force her."

Gabriel clapped me on the back. "You won tonight because you were determined and focused. Because you didn't consider that you could ever fail. Am I right?"

"Hollie might be a prize but she's not a competition."

"You owe it to yourself to at least be clear to her about how you feel and what you want."

She knew how I felt about her.

Didn't she?

"We didn't get a chance to talk about next steps. I mentioned her staying in London though. Offered to put her in contact with some industry people."

"How very romantic," Gabriel said, raising his eyebrows.

"But obviously part of the reason I did that was because I didn't want her to leave." She had to know. I'd been the one to suggest she move into my place so we could spend more time together. I'd been the one to broach the topic of her staying in London.

"You have to say the words. Like, make it very clear.

Believe me when I tell you that lots can get lost in translation. You should have learned that from the situation with David."

There was nothing I could do to get back all the years I'd lost with my brother. And I couldn't bear the thought of even one night without Hollie—let alone the rest of my life.

If I'd bumped into Bridget a decade ago, I might be a different man. If I'd picked up the phone to David earlier, perhaps we would have reconciled years before now. I didn't want Hollie to be another "if."

Just as the wounds of David and Bridget that I'd been carrying for years had finally healed, Hollie leaving had ripped my heart apart. And instead of leaving this fresh wound to fester and bleed, I wanted to stop wasting time. I wanted to heal.

I wanted Hollie back in my life.

THIRTY-ONE

Hollie

I abandoned my suitcase, peeled off my coat and collapsed on our second-hand, brown velour couch as if it was good to be home. It wasn't.

"I don't know what you did to Buck Newland, but thank God," Autumn said, handing me a glass of water and coming to sit next to me.

My first stop on the way back from the airport hadn't been our trailer, but Buck Newland's—Greg's dad. I hadn't managed to get him to lower the rent, but I had managed to get us an extra month to find another place to live. Buck had known our family a long time, and he knew the burden of sorting out new places to live was going to fall on me. He'd taken pity on me.

"It's still not long," I said. "Did you find the listings?"

"You think he might still come around?" She handed me a newspaper and flipped to the rentals page.

"I doubt it. We've been here a long time and arguably we should be paying more rent."

"Not triple the amount."

"No. But Buck knows that apartments around here are few and far between. And he's punishing us because . . ." Autumn already felt responsible for what had happened. I didn't need to rub it in. "I need to focus on getting a rent deposit together for an apartment. We'll have to live together and you and I will have to share a room until you leave." The next few weeks I'd have to do a lot of extra shifts at the factory. It still wouldn't be enough. All that extra work to go backward—back to living with my parents. At least Autumn would be able to leave Sunshine. "Mom is going to have to contribute from her work at Trader Bob's and she's going to have to keep working there if we're going to have a hope of making what we need." I was going to have to keep an eye on Mom, make sure she kept her job.

"You think you're going to miss London?" Autumn asked.

That reminded me—I needed to unpack my carry-on and then the last traces of my trip to London would have left me. "It's nice to be back to see you," I said, avoiding the question.

"What about Sexy Dexter? Will you miss him?"

"Oh, I'm sure he's moved on. You saw him." I desperately wanted to know if he'd won the competition. It was late in London. The winner would have been announced by now. There would probably be an article about it online tomorrow. Dexter was sure to win. I'd seen the designs from the other competitors and there was no comparison. Dexter had some kind of instinct or genetic programming that allowed him to see what would work and what would be too much. It was the elegance and simplicity of the Daniels & Co jewelry that I'd take as inspiration from my trip.

I wasn't giving up on jewelry, but I would have to shift

my dreams a little and focus on my Etsy store. We needed the cash, and we needed it fast.

"Did you text him? Call?"

Dexter had emailed Autumn and asked me to call. But what was the point? I needed a clean break. I couldn't look back. The sooner I resigned myself to my life in Sunshine, the better off I'd be.

"No, and you promised you wouldn't respond to his email." If I had something to say to Dexter, I'd say it to him myself. I didn't need Autumn playing go-between.

"I haven't. But you were living with him, Hollie. You two were serious about each other."

"It meant we got more time together, that's all. I'm sure I wasn't the first woman Dexter lived with. And I won't be the last. He's a great guy."

"So, you're not going to do the long-distance thing?"

"You think he's the kind of guy who does FaceTime sex? Long distance is for relationships that are either super casual or super serious. It's either 'I'll see you next time I'm in New York' or 'We'll bear this time apart before our wedding.' Dexter and me? We weren't either. Whatever we had always had an expiration. Long distance would never have worked." I'd thought about it. In fact, I'd thought about nothing else on the flight home. This was easier. No expectations. I'd go back to life as usual. The last thing I needed was to torture myself by pretending things could be different. Because things *weren't* different. As my gramma used to say—deal with what you've got, not what you'd like. It was advice to live by.

My sister was staring at me. "So, what, you shook hands, thanked each other for the orgasms and said 'see you around'?"

"I need to finish unpacking," I said, getting to my feet

and heading to my room. The last thing I wanted to do was pick through the leftovers of my relationship with Dexter. As if leaving him wasn't bad enough, I hadn't even had a chance to say goodbye.

Heat roared in my chest at the thought of not being with him again. I was resigned but that didn't mean I was happy about it. Just because I'd accepted the way things were didn't mean it didn't hurt every time I thought about him. It didn't mean my heart wasn't broken.

"Are you okay?" Autumn said from the doorway.

"I'll be fine," I said, unzipping my backpack. I knew I would recover. Somehow. Someday. I had to. "I just need a good night's sleep."

"Nothing like your own bed, right? Although I imagine Dexter's bed wasn't so bad."

I pulled out a sweater and a pair of sneakers from my bag. "Yeah, I was okay with slumming it for a while." I tried to squeeze out a smile and make a joke of it, but I felt drained—like my battery was running low and my body was fuzzy and my limbs were stuck in mud.

"At least we've got an extra month, right?" she said.

"Exactly." It was the absence of bad news that equaled sunshine in Oregon. Things didn't have to go right—if they just didn't go wrong, that was a good day. I had to push down the memories of my time with Dexter. He'd been from a different time in my life. Now I needed to get back to my reality.

THIRTY-TWO

Hollie

I plastered a grin on my face, trying to stop the hopelessness breaking through, as I ran my finger down the schedule. "And that one there," I said to Pauly.

"Are you sure? It means you'll have four double shifts that week and only one day off."

"I'm sure," I said.

"Babe, it's your first day back and you're one shift in. You've forgotten how you're going to feel after a week back in the saddle."

"Pauly, seriously. Just put me down. I don't want to lose out. And call me before you put the next schedule up, will you?"

"I heard you were thrown out of the trailer park," Pauly said.

Gosh darn it, I was sick of people knowing my business. "So, we're all set?" I didn't want to get into it with him. There was no point. I needed the money and working was the only solution.

He shook his head and typed in my employee ID. "We're all set." Anyone would think I was asking him to do my shifts for me, he seemed so glum about it. I should be the one picking up whiskey on the way home to get me through the next few months.

I squinted as I opened the door into the daylight of the Oregon afternoon to find my sister waiting for me.

"Hey," I said. "You need a hand with that?"

She seemed to be weighed down with a thousand bags. What had she been buying and where did she get the money for any of it?

"You can take the whiskey," she said, pulling out a bottle from her purse. "It was making my shoulder ache."

"What are you buying whiskey for?" I asked as we made our way through the parking lot. Not toward a car, because I walked the ten minutes it took to get to work. Even in the rain, it was fine as long as you didn't try and take the shortcut across the field.

"You got plans tonight?" she asked, setting quite a pace back home.

"You mean apart from that conference call with Paris and pilates at the country club?" I asked.

"Good. You have plans with me then. We're just going to make a start tonight. We won't get it all done, but we can get an idea."

I peered into one of the shopping bags she was carrying. Whatever it was, it wasn't groceries. "Make a start on what?" I said. "I'm happy if whiskey is part of the equation but all I want to do is go home and watch Bravo." Anything to keep me distracted from thinking about London. About Dexter. About the life I'd left behind. At some point I'd maybe start designing again. I had a couple of ideas but no energy to put down on paper something I wasn't going to be able to make.

Buck was at the entrance of the park. "Hey, Buck, can't stop. Gotta get back and pack," Autumn said, pulling me by the sleeve when I slowed to say hi.

What the hell was up with her. "What have you been buying? You better not have thrown away your textbook money on something stupid and whiskey."

"Come on and I'll show you," she said, marching toward our trailer.

It seemed like time slowed with every pace toward home. It was the last place I wanted to be. Being indoors, I was faced with how starkly different my life had been this time last week.

She was first up the steps, through the door and was emptying her bags before I'd even finished taking my hoodie off.

"What are you doing?" I asked as she spread out what she'd brought back on the table. There were about a hundred Sharpies, each a different color, and a ruler and sticky notes. And then a huge roll of paper.

"Is this an elementary school art project?" I asked, pulling out two shot glasses and setting them next to the whiskey.

"Nope. This is planning HQ."

I poured out the whiskey, careful not to spill a drop.

"What are we planning? How to not run out of Sharpies?"

She ignored me, came over, picked up her shot glass and held it up. "Here's to getting out of here," she said and tipped back the shot.

I'd drink to that. And I did.

The warm, sleepy liquid slid down my throat, loosening

my limbs and making the world slightly more bearable. A couple of more shots and I might be able to call Mom and Dad to make sure they were packing.

"So," she said, screwing the lid back on the bottle. "No more until we've done some work. We need to keep a clear head."

I was hoping a lot of whiskey was the plan to get out of here, but apparently Autumn had something else in mind.

"Come on." She shooed me over to the dining table like I was cattle.

Autumn clearly meant business. And I figured it was easier to just play along. I'd sneak a couple more shots and just let her talk. And then I'd go to bed, hopefully before the dark and quiet could leave room for thoughts of Dexter to take over in my mind.

She sat opposite me and rolled open the large sheet of paper. "So, I've been doing some research. We can do flights to London for five hundred dollars as long as you don't mind a bit of a layover."

London? I sat back, the soothing effect of the whiskey lifting like a pigeon when a car backfired. I was totally confused. Autumn removed the lid of the bright pink Sharpie with a pop and wrote "out" at the top left of the page, underlining it twice.

"You want to fill me in on what we're doing here," I asked, a little uncomfortable. I didn't understand what London had to do with a pile of Sharpies, and there was no need to figure out the cost of flights. If I ever went back, inflation would have been around the block a few times and who knew what the price would be. "Because I really want to go and watch some housewives scream at each other."

"Isn't it obvious?" She looked at me as if I was being

deliberately dumb. "We're hatching a plan to get your ass back to London."

I groaned and went to stand.

"Sit down," she snapped. My sister never snapped at me and I could count on the fingers of one hand how often she'd told me what to do.

"I was just going to get the whiskey," I lied.

"I told you. We need clear heads."

"For what? I'm not going back to London." I needed to be here—to earn money, to keep an eye on Mom so she kept bringing in a salary. "I don't have anything to go back for." My internship was over. I'd not made any friends other than Dexter really, and well . . . that was over. And now I couldn't bring myself to find out who'd won the competition. I would be devastated for him if Daniels & Co hadn't, but if they had, I was worried I'd be so bitter about not being there that I'd take that bottle of whiskey and down the entire thing.

"You have the rest of your life to go back for," my sister said. "You have Dexter. And your career."

I watched her, scribbling numbers down on this huge sheet of paper. She wanted to help and my bones ached I was so grateful, but there was nothing she could do. I was stuck.

"I think on this side," she said, indicating the right-hand side of the huge sheet of paper, "we need things that don't cost money but you'll have to do before you go. I'm going to write 'job' up here and then we'll do a bubble where we put all the preparation you need to do to get a job—you know, applications and stuff."

"Honey," I said, placing my hand on her arm. "This is so sweet of you. But I'm not going back to London."

She turned to me, fire in her eyes. "Of course you are.

I've never seen or heard you so happy as when you were over there. And Dexter's there and you've never been into a guy like you're into him. Ever. In. Your. Life."

Into him. It sounded so cute but so completely inappropriate for what I felt for Dexter. I tried to push it down but it kept bobbing to the surface—the realization that I was in love with him. I tried to think back to when I'd transitioned from wanting to rip his clothes off to being in love with him. It was somewhere after I'd started to like him, then really like him, and it had morphed without me realizing into something much deeper—respect and admiration mixed with an understanding that he enjoyed making me happy just as much as I enjoyed doing the same for him.

I loved the bones of the man.

I loved the heart of the man.

I loved the soul of the man.

I glanced at my phone. It would be so easy to call. Too easy.

"I have responsibilities here," I said. "I need to be realistic."

She rolled her eyes at me. "I'm not planning on robbing a bank. This chart is a real plan. We can do this. You saved up the first time. And now I'm about to graduate and get a job, we'll get there a lot quicker. Which reminds me," she said, flipping over the paper. "I need a column because I need to find a job that pays. None of this interning without a salary shit," she said. "I've started applying and I have a couple of interviews lined up. But I'm not going to put all my eggs in one basket. I'm going to keep applying."

It was the first I'd heard about her applying for jobs already. "You're going to apply around here?" There weren't many good jobs in Sunshine.

"No, I thought Portland. And I've even applied for a

couple in New York."

New York? That was more expense. I'd have to pay for her flights and hotels. But good for her that she wanted to spread her wings. There was no point in two of us being stuck here. After all, giving her a future was what the last years of sacrifice had been about.

"And before you start worrying, I got a scholarship to pay for travel and accommodation to and from job interviews. There won't be any additional expense." Autumn was beaming at me.

My heart rose in my chest. "What kind of scholarship?"

"The kind that pays for kids like me to go to job interviews."

"Wow, I had no idea there even was such a thing."

"Well, there was and I got it. And then you're not going to have tuition to pay for anymore."

I nodded. I just had to get past the bottleneck of deposits on our new apartment—first month, last month, security. Once I did that, I could relax a little. Until the next disaster.

"Let's put rent for parents down here," she said, scribbling down a figure in the costs column. It was probably useful to look at my expenses and get a handle on how long it was going to take to get back to something like normalcy, but Autumn's insistence on including a return to London in our grand scheme was wishful thinking.

"That's not the rent," I said, seeing the number she'd put against it. "It's going to be double that just for their apartment. Let alone mine."

"Yeah, but I'm going to be paying half."

God, I loved my sister. And her imagination wasn't even the best part of her. "How do you think you're going to be doing that?"

"I told you," she said. "I'm going to get a job."

"Yeah, and you'll have to pay rent and bills and buy clothes—"

"I know. Which is why I need a *paying* job. I'll have expenses and one of those will be half Mom and Dad's rent."

There was no point arguing with her. She'd find out soon enough that life wasn't that easy.

"What was your rent in that studio in London? We're planning for worst case because you'll probably live with Dexter again, right?"

I wanted to dive into her fantasy and believe what she was planning could be a reality, but I was afraid I'd never be able to pull myself back into real life. And then what would happen? Too many people were depending on me. I couldn't afford to have my head in the clouds. I needed to be real, keep my feet on the ground.

Autumn kept putting down numbers and I sat and watched, occasionally eyeing the whiskey bottle.

"It really hinges on you having a job," she said. "So that should be your first priority. Can you hit up some of the people you met in London and see if anyone's hiring?"

I could call Primrose. And Teresa from Sparkle. They might know where I could start looking. No—what was I thinking? "It's impossible," I said. "Even if we both got jobs and split the rent, I can't just up and move to London."

"Why not?"

"You want a list?" I asked. What about my situation wasn't she getting?

"Sure. Let's hear your excuses."

"I only need two. Mom and Dad."

"They are grown adults. If we're keeping a roof over their heads, they can figure out the rest themselves."

I half laughed, half sighed. "That's not how they work. You know it's just a matter of time before they get into some disaster that I'll need to bail them out of."

"Mom still has her job, which, may I remind you, she got while you were in London. Maybe they got themselves into trouble because they knew you'd be here to save them. Once you left . . ."

I rolled my eyes. That wasn't true. Mom and Dad had been getting themselves into trouble since long before I was capable of cleaning up their messes.

"And even if that's not true, they're not your responsibility."

I pushed out of my chair and headed over to the whiskey bottle. "Now you're being ridiculous. Of course they're my responsibility. Who else is going to look after them?"

"Hollie, they're not children or dogs. They can figure it out. We can come back and visit but you've sacrificed your dreams long enough. Your entire life has been about providing for me or cleaning up after the two of them. I haven't deserved your sacrifices, but I'm forever grateful for them. But you've done what you set out to do. I'm graduating. It's time for you to live your life."

I grabbed the bottle and brought it and the two shot glasses back to the table. Autumn's growing independence had lifted a cloak of responsibility from my shoulders. I'd always be there for her in any way I could be, but the fact I wouldn't be paying tuition would be a game-changer. "I'm so freaking proud you're graduating. You worked hard for this. In and out of class."

"I know," she said. "But it wouldn't have happened if it wasn't for you."

I'd supported Autumn because I loved her, and because it was the right thing to do. It was as simple as that.

"But now it's time for you to focus on you." She turned back to our plan. "You'll be back in London in three months by my calculations. I'll have a job by then. Mom gets healthcare if she stays at Trader Bob's for twelve months."

"Just like that?" I said, pouring out the whiskey.

"No, not just like that. With hard work and double shifts and weekends spent applying for jobs. But you can do it."

I looked at her spreadsheet. It seemed to work on paper. "How can I just abandon Mom and Dad? What if Mom loses her job?"

"You're not abandoning them. You're just making something of your life. You're not letting them dictate your future. They have a place to live and we can both come back and visit."

She made it sound possible, like I could actually have the life I wanted rather than the one that had been assigned to me since birth.

"I suppose I could build up some savings and send them money if things get bad."

"Yes. And you never know—they might actually pull themselves together a little bit if they know they don't have us catching them every time they trip up and knock themselves out."

Maybe Autumn was right. Perhaps I could let my parents figure stuff out themselves. As long as they had a roof over their heads, and I could send money if they got into a scrape, I supposed I didn't need to be in Oregon to make it work.

"Okay, let's go through the plan again," I said.

Maybe I'd even give Dexter a call if I ever made it back.

THIRTY-THREE

Dexter

I thought it rained hard in London, but Oregon made London's precipitation look like amateur hour. I hadn't been able to sleep; the sheeting rain had been so heavy against the hotel windows. Then again, my sleeplessness might have been thanks to my anticipation of seeing Hollie today. I shoved my hands in my pockets, trying to be patient as I waited for the car to be delivered at the hotel entrance.

It had been over two weeks since I'd last seen her, since I'd last slept next to her and felt her warm body next to mine. Each day without her had felt three times as long. In our brief time together, I'd gotten used to rushing out of the office so I could go home and put my arms around her, hear her take on the day and press my body against hers.

Without her, life was laborious and empty. I wanted her and there was no point in pretending otherwise. Gabriel had been right—I needed to tell her how much she meant to me. I had to be completely clear I'd done everything I could to get her back. She was far more important to me than the competition, and if I was prepared to work so hard for that, I was happy to work doubly hard for Hollie.

A black car pulled up in front of the hotel. "Mr. Daniels?" the driver asked me as he got out. He handed me the keys and I got in, putting the trophy Daniels & Co had won the night Hollie had left London on the passenger seat. I'd wanted to share it with her, even if the celebration was delayed.

As I punched the address into the satnav, it came up with a route and an estimate of three hours and twelve minutes to arrival. When I got there, I didn't even know if she'd be in. But I'd wait. For as long as it took.

I pulled out into the traffic and began to rehearse what I wanted to say that I hadn't already perfected in the two weeks since she'd left and on the twelve-hour plane journey over here.

As I got out of town and onto a road that was simply numbered 84, I picked up speed. Driving in America wasn't like driving in Britain. The roads were almost empty, and the monotonous drive gave me time to think. To imagine what it would be like to see her again. I pressed my foot on the accelerator, focusing on my destination.

THE STEPS LEADING up to Hollie's front door were dry because of the yellow awning. After I'd discovered neither Hollie nor her sister were home, I took a seat beneath it. From the top of the fifth step, I could get a better view of the road from the park entrance than I had from the car.

I checked my watch. It was a little after twelve. I could be waiting all day. I had no idea when she'd finish work, but at least I'd found the place. The guy on the gate had been more helpful than I'd been expecting and given me direc-tions right to the door. So, my plan was to sit here until someone came home. It wasn't like I could turn up to her work, even if I did know where it was.

"Hey, there," an older woman wearing a blue housecoat called from the pavement. "You waiting for Hollie or Autumn?"

"Hollie," I replied, grateful for the confirmation I was in the right spot. "My name is Dexter. Do you know when she'll be back?"

Her face broke into a grin and she came closer. "I'm Mrs. Daugherty. You've got an accent on you. Where are you from?"

"England," I replied. "London."

"London? Do you know the queen?"

I stood and stepped down to meet her at the bottom. "I have met her a couple of times, actually, but I wouldn't say I know her."

"You've met her? What does she smell like?"

The first question I might have been prepared for, but being asked about the scent of royalty was a new one for me. "I don't remember a specific perfume but she was very charming."

"Your accent is so pretty," she said. "Can I get you anything? You're welcome to come and wait inside. I could fix you a sandwich? You like bacon?"

"That's terribly kind of you, but I'm going to wait here so I don't miss her coming home."

"They are lovely girls," the lady said. "So polite. And the younger one's at college, you know?" I nodded, glancing up the road to see if anyone with treacle-colored hair was coming toward us. "Did the queen go to college?" she asked.

"I don't believe she did," I said.

"Prince William did," she said. "It's where he met Kate Middleton. Although officially, she likes to be called Catherine, you know. They met at St Andrews University. They were studying the same thing until William changed to . . . geography," she said, poking the air as she remembered. "I like the royals."

"Did you say you knew when Hollie might be back?" I asked.

"Well I didn't see her leave this morning, which must mean she's on an early shift. So . . . she should be back around one unless she's doing a double. But it's a Friday so probably not. One, I'd say."

I checked my phone. If this lady's intel was right, Hollie should be back any minute.

"If you need anything I'm just there." She pointed at a home a few doors up from Hollie's.

"Thank you," I called as she made her way toward a friend calling her over.

The two women chatted while shooting me glances. I kept my eyes fixed on the road into the park. Eventually, Mrs. Daugherty and her friend scurried off, leaving me in the rain and wondering if I was going to be able to convince my love to come back to me.

THIRTY-FOUR

Hollie

The hood of my jacket kept blowing off in the wind. I'd been planning on taking a shower when I got home, but I was getting one for free on my walk back instead. My hair was soaking and my shoulders ached. Pauly was right. Four double shifts in a week was too many. I couldn't wait to collapse into bed.

I pulled up my hood for the nine millionth time, angled my head into the wind to keep it from flying off and turned into the park.

I managed to get to our trailer without it flying off again. I started up the steps, flipping back my hood as I got under the awning and fell back a step when I saw there was someone waiting by our front door.

Not just any person.

Dexter.

"Hi," I said, because what else could you say when the man you were in love with appeared on your doorstep. I was rooted to the spot, unable to process Dexter Daniels against the backdrop of the Sunshine Trailer Park. He looked so out of place. It was as if everything else faded into a blur of gray, but Dexter was every color in the rainbow.

"Hey," he replied, reaching for my hand to pull me up the steps. How did Dexter manage to get sexier, even under the Oregon sky? And here I was soaking wet and aching after too many double shifts.

"You look beautiful."

I gave him one of my best don't-BS-me looks. What was he doing here? "You're a long way from home," I said.

He shrugged. "Maybe not. You're here."

My insides hurt I missed him so much. But he didn't belong here.

I pulled out the keys from my jeans pocket. He'd flown five thousand miles, the least I could do was invite the guy in. The danger was I wouldn't ever want him to leave.

"Thought you might want to know about this." He reached down to the floor beside him and picked up a sleek, glass trophy.

I wanted to throw my arms around him. I was so proud. It was what he wanted most in the world and I'd wanted it so badly for him too. "You deserve it. And the entire team. I'm so happy for you."

"I wish you could have been there."

I sighed. I wished I could have been there too. Although it was wonderful to see Dexter—he was achingly familiar despite having only been in my life a few months—it was almost beyond painful. I'd hated walking out on him and not even getting a chance to say goodbye, but at least I hadn't had to endure this. At least I hadn't had to look in his eyes knowing it would be the last time.

"I had a speech prepared," he said. "I think it got lost in the rain."

"A speech?" I asked.

I didn't need a speech from him. He deserved an apology from me. He'd emailed Autumn over and over and I'd told her not to reply. Although she must have ignored me at some point. How else would he have known where to find me?

"I'd rehearsed it. But now I can't remember how it starts." He stopped abruptly. "I let Autumn have my number and you didn't call."

Shame circled my chest. "I know. I'm sorry. Once I was back here, I couldn't bear to look back. I thought a clean break would be easier."

"Was it?"

I thought I'd go back to Oregon and be able to put London in a drawer. Away from real life. But it didn't fit. I couldn't hide it away, pretend it had never happened. "It was harder than anything I've ever done before."

He sighed, his chest expanding and contracting, his nearness suddenly so much closer. I just had to stretch out my arm and slide my palm up against his cheek.

"Woohoo," Mrs. Daugherty called from across the street.

"Hi, Mrs. Daugherty. I'll catch up with you later," I said, picking up my backpack. "You'd better come in."

I unlocked the door and we went inside.

"What's this?" he said, immediately honing in on the far wall of the trailer where Autumn and I had pinned up my making-it-back-to-London plan.

"My plan to come back to London."

He turned to me, fixing me with a stare. "You were coming back? To me?"

Was I going back to Dexter? Or was it a plan to go after my dreams? Both, I decided. "It's going to take months. Longer maybe. And I didn't expect you to wait, I just—"

He stalked over to me and cupped my face in my hands. "You were coming back? Then why didn't you call?"

I tried to push down the emotion swirling in my belly. I wanted everything but him to melt away, for the world to condense around just the two of us, existing someplace outside of reality. But that's not how life went. I pulled away from him and he looked at me as if I'd lost my mind.

But it wasn't my mind I'd lost.

This man had stolen my heart.

"I had things to figure out, Dexter. I didn't—don't expect you to wait for me. And hoping for you . . . Hope is something in short supply around here. I'd rather deal in facts and certainty."

Dexter pinched the bridge of his nose. "Okay, let's get some facts on the table. If you want to be in London, why are you standing here in Oregon?"

Dexter made it sound so simple.

"I have to find somewhere for my parents to live. For Autumn and I to live. We have to leave the trailer park. It's a long story but I'll figure it out. It's just going to take time."

"That sounds simple enough. If it's just money you need, I can help with that."

I closed my eyes, wishing he wasn't quite so near. Quite so generous. Quite so wonderful. "Dexter, I've got this."

"But, Hollie, why can't you let me help?"

My family wasn't Dexter's responsibility. He wasn't a white knight, riding to my rescue, or even Richard Gere carrying Debra Winger out of a factory. This was real life. "I don't need you to save me, Dexter."

"I'm not trying to *save* you, Hollie. I know you're

perfectly capable of saving yourself. I'm trying to share my life with you."

Warmth gathered in my heart at the thought that he still wanted me. The idea of sharing the rest of my life with Dexter . . . Well, it was more than I could imagine and certainly more than I deserved. "You think you'd want to wait? You know, until I figure out my plan?"

"I don't want to wait a single second. I want to be with you night and day. I'll do whatever it takes, but the plan is bullshit, Hollie."

It looked more complicated than it actually was because of all the different colors. "It's a good plan," I said, defensive and sheepish at the same time.

"I know you don't want to be rescued. I know it's hard to rely on anyone because no one has proved reliable to you. But let me be the first person in your life who you can count on. Yes, you're perfectly capable of saving yourself, Hollie. But you don't have to. I'm here to help."

It was as if I'd been trying to balance a week's worth of groceries in my hands and someone had just fired off a shotgun, made me jump, and everything had come crashing to the ground. I couldn't take anymore. I covered my face with my hands and turned to face the door in a futile attempt to stop him from seeing me cry.

"Hey," he said, smoothing his hand across my back and gathering me in his arms. "I didn't mean to upset you."

He hadn't upset me. I'd just let go of what I'd been holding onto for so long.

"Let me lighten your load," he whispered as he held me. "Now I remember how my speech started out."

I looked up at him, waiting for him to tell me.

"I love you, Hollie Lumen."

I paused, wanting to say the words back. "That's a short speech."

He chuckled. "Yeah, I forgot the next bit. But what I don't have to remember, because it's etched on my soul, is that I've never felt this way about anyone in my life. I miss everything about you. I hate waking up without you. I need to tell you every single thought in my head, and hear about every single thought in yours. I'm head over bloody heels in love with you."

"I just need some time," I said, my head spinning from the idea that Dexter Daniels could love me.

"I want to spend the rest of my life with you," he said. "But that can't start until we've figured out how we get you back to London. What good is any of my money if I can't use it to help the woman I love?"

"I don't want your money, Dexter. It's not why I love you."

He pulled me so close I could feel his heartbeat against mine. "You love me?"

How could he doubt it? "I think I loved you from the moment I first saw you across the ballroom that first night."

He closed his eyes in a long blink like he was drinking down a glass of cool water after being lost in a desert. "We'll figure this out, Hollie. Your parents. Your sister. We'll do whatever it takes. Do you trust me?"

He'd flown halfway around the world to come and find me. And he hadn't slung over his shoulder and demanded I get the first plane back to London. He loved me and I loved him and he wanted to help. How could I say no?

I reached up and clasped his face in my hands. "I love you so much. Will you marry me?"

He grinned. "Every day of the week and twice on Sunday."

I had the feeling it wouldn't be the last time that Dexter Daniels would do anything I asked of him. And that was only one of the reasons I loved him and would do anything he asked of me.

"I just need one more thing from you," I said.

"Name it," he asked.

"Kiss me?"

THIRTY-FIVE

Dexter

Three hours was a long drive when I'd won back the love of my life and all I wanted to do was strip her naked and bury myself in her. But I was a patient man.

"I thought you'd be staying at the Heathman," she said as she took in the hotel room I'd checked into yesterday.

"You want to move?" I thought the place was okay but if Hollie wanted something different, we'd check in somewhere else.

"No, I like this place—it's blingy. And it's big. Like twice as big as our trailer."

"You make it sound like you were living in a caravan." I set down her case and toed off my shoes.

"It has wheels, Dexter."

"Do you think you want to keep living in the flat or shall we move somewhere else? It might be nice to have a place that's been ours from the beginning."

She linked her finger into the waist of my trousers. "You are a sweet and thoughtful man."

"Shhh," I said, putting my finger to my lips. "Don't tell anyone."

"Secret's out. Everyone who knows you, loves you." She pulled out my shirt from my trousers and slid her smooth, warm hands up my torso. Christ, I'd missed her touching me. I'd missed holding her. I'd missed hearing her laugh, listening to her snore, watching her dress and undress.

"Promise me we won't be apart for this long again," I said, pulling at the zip of her jeans.

"I promise. I don't ever want to miss you like I did these last couple weeks." Relief funneled into my chest at the thought that she'd missed me. She'd said she loved me. She'd even proposed, but I wanted more. I wanted her near me all the time. I didn't want to miss out on a second, and I couldn't imagine a time when I'd ever feel differently.

She pulled her hands from my chest and I shuddered at the loss of warmth. She fingered the hem of her top and then pulled it over her head, revealing that silky skin. "You want to eat first?" She blushed. "Not me. I mean like get room service or something?"

I chuckled. She was adorable. "First you. Then room service." I picked her up and she wrapped her legs around my waist.

"When we're back in London, I'm not going to let you leave our bed for a week."

She pulled me closer. "*Our* bed?"

"Yeah. *Our* bed. And no more escaping to the guest room wardrobe if you want to make a call. We can convert a bedroom into an office for you."

"You know how to turn a girl on."

I set her down on the bed and unhooked the bra strap from her shoulder, dropping a kiss in its place.

"Oh baby, if you think that's good, you've not seen

anything yet." I trailed my tongue over the globe of her breast and took her nipple in my mouth, first flicking it with my tongue and then catching it between my teeth and applying increasing pressure until she moaned. God, I'd missed her sounds. Her touch. Her everything. I never wanted to be without this woman.

"I like you like this," I said. "Half-dressed because neither of us can wait." I sank to my knees, opening her thighs and pulling her underwear to the side. I took a deep breath, taking in her perfectly sweet scent, and skimmed my hand up her stomach before I took my first taste.

Making Hollie happy, giving her pleasure, had over-taken everything to become my first priority. I couldn't rest until this woman had everything she wanted, anything that would make her happy. We were going to stay in Oregon until we had her parents and Autumn relocated and then we were going back to London. Together.

Everything was perfect.

She groaned as I pressed my tongue on her clit and then delved into her folds, savoring the velvety warmth, letting her moans move through my body like a roll of thunder. A twist of her hips signaled she was ready for more, but I wasn't sure my fingers were going to be enough. I hooked my thumbs into her underwear and stripped them off in one smooth movement.

"I want you," she whispered. "My entire life I won't want anything more than I want you inside me at this moment."

Blood surged to my cock and I struggled to my feet, my head fuzzy with lust and impatience. I wasn't done tasting her. I'd never be done tasting her. But I wanted to give her whatever she desired. "Flip over," I said, unbuttoning my shirt. If I had to look into her eyes as I pushed into her, I'd lose it. I pulled up her hips, getting her onto all fours. But seeing her like this was a sensory storm and my dick strained against the zip of my jeans. The way her breasts swayed as she shifted—the way her skin glistened like ice and her hair coiled around her body like ivy—was sheer perfection. Watching her was like taking a class-A drug. Too big a dose after enforced abstinence could stop my heart.

I pressed a kiss at the base of her spine, the muscles of her back that created mountains either side of a ravine I wanted to lick dry. Smoothing my hands over her arse, she bucked. "Please," she cried, her fingers greedily grabbing the sheets as she arched her back. "Please Dexter. I can't wait any longer."

Nor could I. I stripped off my trousers and pants and placed a firm hand on her lower back, steadying her. I grasped my cock in the other hand and circled her entrance with the tip—just a hint of what was to come.

"Dexter. For the love of God, will you please fuck me."

"Shit," I said, shifting my hips away from her. "I forgot the condom." The blood pounded in my ears as I glanced around for my wallet.

She turned and sat up on the bed. "Do we need one?"

She was looking at me, her gaze heavy with questions. We were talking about more than condoms.

"I haven't been with anyone but you," she said. "Not since we met. But if you have . . ." Her voice wavered at the end.

"Of course I haven't," I said, crawling over her, onto the bed. "There's been no one since we met." And no one of any importance before her, I understood now. "If you don't want to use condoms, then that's fine."

"You don't want to know if I'm on the pill?"

I shrugged. "What's the worst that could happen?"

She grinned. "Oh, I don't know. You could knock me up."

"Doesn't sound so bad," I said quietly, the confession formulating in my head at the same time as it appeared on my lips. "I'd like to have children with you." I'd never thought of having a family. I'd been so focused on my business, and I'd just assumed that kind of life—a family life—had been out of my reach since Bridget left me. But with Hollie, it was possible again, maybe for the first time. I wanted us to build a life together—to bring new life into the world.

She pushed her fingers into my hair and pressed a kiss to my cheek. "I'd like to have a family with you too. But not yet. I'll stay on the pill for awhile yet. That okay with you?"

Everything was okay as long as I was with Hollie. Storms could rage, frogs could fall from the sky and Daniels & Co could go down—nothing mattered except being with her. Everything else was white noise.

"But we can practice in the meantime?" I asked, tangling my legs with hers and bending to scrape my teeth over her collarbone. I wanted to map out her body with my mouth. I wouldn't rest unless I knew every centimeter in the dark with just a lick of my tongue.

She pulled her legs up, pressing my cock against her clit. "Well you *are* a perfectionist, and practice makes perfect." Her fingertips trailed up my sides and then around to my back, then slid behind and up over my shoulders. I didn't know what it was about that movement that made it feel like such an intimate act of familiarity—as if I was a part of her, and she'd been absentmindedly touching herself. It floored me. It struck me that I wasn't on my own anymore. For the first time ever, I had someone in my life who was part of my soul. Someone who would be with me forever.

"We're going to have the most perfect children because we're going to be doing a lot of practicing." My life was perfect in that second and would be every moment I was with Hollie. I couldn't want anything more.

I pressed up on my hands, driving my cock into her as she whimpered for more. I had to block out everything but the very second I was in. If I thought about how she'd proposed or how she was going to be mine forever, how I'd get to touch her and hold her for the rest of my life—if I thought about anything but that very moment, it would be too much for me to bear. I just needed to focus on the pressure of her heat. On the drag of my dick as it pulled out and then slammed in, deeper this time. I just needed to press my lips to the dip at the base of her neck, eliciting a groan as I licked up to her ear. Then everything in the world was how it should be.

I felt like a clumsy teenager where everything was a new experience and you didn't want to wait, didn't want to hold back. I grabbed her hands and pressed them over her head, and she smiled at me. "I love you," she said.

Would I ever get tired of hearing those words from her? For a split second, I was catapulted into the future, both of us gray and slow, wild horses still galloping across my chest every time I heard those words from her lips.

"I want you every way," she said. "I want you in my mouth and my pussy at the same time. I'm greedy for you."

Lust fizzled up my spine like the fuse on a stick of dynamite. The feeling was entirely mutual. For now, she'd have to wait for my dick in her mouth. My tongue would have to satisfy her. I kept thrusting trying to get closer and closer to her as sweat coated my skin like I was running a marathon.

She twisted her hips, bucking beneath me, and a groan roared up through my chest and echoed through the room. I fucking loved fucking this woman. And I fucking loved her.

"Dexter," she called out, pulling me closer as my head fell to her neck.

"Hollie," I gasped, feeling my climax spiraling and twisting in my body, trying to break free.

She pulsed around me and sucked in a breath, her eyes open and on me as she came. The look of fulfilment in those green-blue eyes was all it took to sever the last delicate strands of my desire, and I pushed in one more time, pouring myself into her and collapsing over her.

"I love you," she said, pulling me closer as I tried to move off her.

"I love you too," I said, moving to the side. "Will you marry me?"

She sat up with a jolt. "I asked you already."

"I know but that can't be *the* proposal. To be fair, the perfect proposal isn't when we've just had sex. Even though it was mind-blowing. We need something we're going to be able to tell our grandchildren about."

"Okay, I'll think of something."

"Hollie," I said, my tone warning. "I love you. And I know you are fiercely independent because you've had to be your entire life, but let me have this, will you? Let me figure out how I'm going to propose, make a ring and surprise you, okay?"

She rolled her lips back. "Relationships are supposed to be two way, Dexter. You should know, because you're the one who taught me."

What Hollie had yet to realize was that just being with me, just choosing to exist in my orbit, was more than I could have ever hoped for. "I want to give you the world, Hollie. But I'll settle for the proposal, for now."

She wasn't just a prize but a jewel, the most precious creation I'd ever held. I'd spend a lifetime protecting her, looking after her and trying to give her half of what she gave me.

EPILOGUE

Six Months Later

Dexter

A year ago, I would have thought the idea of Daniels & Co hosting a party in London, let alone opening a store in Knightsbridge, completely ridiculous. As I glanced up and saw Hollie coming toward me, it was clear to me that this one-woman whirlwind had altered the entire course of my existence. If she'd never been at that launch party and I hadn't noticed her enjoying my parents' jewelry, my life would be very different.

I wouldn't be opening my London showroom.

My brother wouldn't be here to celebrate with me.

And I wouldn't have an engagement ring in my pocket.

But how could I have not noticed her? In a roomful of priceless jewels, she outshone them all.

We had thirty minutes until the start of the party, and

I'd convinced my family to be here early. I was just waiting on the final stragglers.

"Well done, the place looks incredible," my brother said, tipping his head back to take in the glass-domed roof of the triple height ceilings. My mission when it had come to this place was to communicate calm and relaxation. The carpet was a deep, lush cream, the furniture classic and sophisticated, and the jewelry was displayed in the walls, as if it were the art in an expensive drawing room. "Mum and Dad would be so proud of you."

"They certainly would," Primrose said. "They'd be very proud of both of you."

I swallowed down my ever-fresh grief and nodded. "Thanks. I'm just grateful they gave me this passion." The only thing wrong with this evening was their absence.

"But you put in the hard work," David said. "This is all you, Dexter."

The hard work opening the London store hadn't been physical, it had been emotional. Getting to the point where I felt comfortable opening in this city had taken years and longer than it should have done.

"Did you show David the cabinet?" Primrose asked.

I guided my brother over to the middle of the room, where there was a large, waist height, mahogany display cabinet lined in black velvet that was the centerpiece of the store. "Do you remember this?" I asked, pointing at the brass plate screwed into the back of the case. Both the case and the plaque were a replica of the original that had been in our parents' shop.

"Is this from their shop?"

"No, I had it made. But I wanted to honor them, you know?"

Hollie's familiar hands slid around my waist as she

came to stand by my side. "You do that every day by being the man you are," she said.

"You're biased," I replied.

"She's right," my brother said. "But I like this too," he said, brushing his fingers over the brass. "It's a nice touch."

"They're with me in everything I do."

My brother nodded, blinking back the tears. In his eyes, I saw sadness that my parents weren't here, regret that he and I hadn't reconciled sooner, and disbelief at the passing of so much time. It all stuck in my throat too.

"Here's the rest of your crew," Hollie said, glancing over to the door where Joshua, Andrew, Gabriel and Tristan made an entrance. Beck and Stella had already arrived and knowing Beck, by now he'd have convinced Stella she needed another piece of jewelry.

"Thanks for coming," I said as my friends all approached, each of them pulling me into a hug.

"Wouldn't miss it," Tristan said.

"Right," I said. "Now that everyone's here." I slipped my hand into Hollie's and led her to the top of the three stairs that led to the private rooms and overlooked the rest of the shop.

"Are you making a speech?" she asked.

"I think I should, don't you?"

"Absolutely." She twisted her hand out of mine. "But I don't need to come with you. This is your moment."

"Not a chance." I scooped up her arm. "You're the reason I'm standing here with so many people I love. You're staying with me."

"Ladies and gentlemen," I started. Gabriel had asked me if I was nervous and I had to answer no. He'd said when he'd proposed to his wife, he'd shaken like he was jelly. But it wasn't like she was going to say no. She loved me. I loved her. It was that simple.

"You're all here to help me celebrate the opening of the first Daniels & Co London store."

"Finally," someone shouted out. "About time," another person commented.

"I think you'll agree we've found a great space. It doesn't hurt that it's a five-minute commute on foot from where we live. Not that that influenced my decision at all." Hollie and I had found a perfect home on Montpelier Square, which meant I was close to the office and to the new store. I'd insisted that we convert the entire top floor to a studio for Hollie. She'd decided she enjoyed being her own boss and wanted to produce her own line, so she worked on that while I went to the office. I kept trying to invest in her but she insisted on using my contacts but not my wallet. She still didn't get that everything I had was hers.

"But the reason we're here is because of the woman standing next to me," I said.

"Dexter," Hollie whined. She hated to have the spotlight shone on her but she deserved it—tonight and every night.

"Hollie Lumen, you captivated me from the first moment I saw you and you continue to make my world a better place every moment you're in it. You're the most thoughtful, giving, generous, wonderful woman. And I am very grateful that you put up with me.

"The first time we spoke, I interrupted as you were mesmerized by a ring my mother designed and my father made. And I'm pretty sure you were wondering whether it would suit you."

Hollie widened her eyes. "I was not!"

I grinned at her and pulled out the black ring box from my pocket. "I suggest you try it on to be sure."

Hollie's mouth opened like it did when I caught her checking me out coming out of the shower, which I positively encouraged.

"This is for me?"

It turned out the queen of Finland was sentimental. And when I'd met her to present the princess with her wedding jewelry and told them both about my parents, they had offered me the ring. I'd insisted on making a substantial donation to their foundation in return, but whatever I'd paid wasn't enough for the look on Hollie's face now.

I didn't take my eyes off her as I opened the box.

"Will you marry me?" we both said at the same time.

The crowd dissolved into laughter.

"Dexter," she said. "It's so beautiful."

Hollie's eyes and the emerald, princess-cut solitaire were a perfect match as I knew they would be. That ocean-deep green with hints of blue was as ethereal as the northern lights, as unique as Hollie Lumen.

I took the ring from the box and slid it onto her ring finger. A few months ago, she would never have accepted jewelry from me, let alone anything so beautiful. She kept saying that I'd changed her but she'd completely upended who I was.

"All I can do is try to make you happy. And if I succeed, it still won't be enough because you've made me a better man."

"You're perfect to me already," she said. "I love you so much." She looped her arms around my neck and pressed her lips against mine.

"Is that a yes?" I asked.

"That's a yes. In American."

Hollie

I pressed cancel on my phone. "It's impossible. I couldn't have just had that call."

A knock on the door of my office interrupted the conversation I was having with myself.

"You don't have to knock," I called out. Dexter insisted on knocking every time he came up here, even though I'd told him repeatedly he didn't have to. We'd gotten rid of all the walls on the top floor of our four-story house and it was one enormous studio. Dexter had bought me a computer with all the best software for jewelry design, and he'd put me in touch with people who could fabricate my designs so that I could then sell. It took years to perfect the engineering and craftsmanship and that wasn't where my passion lay, so I'd decided to concentrate on designing. If I got a chance to expand, I'd eventually employ someone who could manufacture the designs in-house. Dexter told me I had an eye for what worked, and given I'd never known him to tell a lie, I was prepared to believe him, even if I didn't have the confidence in me that he did.

"Do you know a Clarissa Michaels?" I asked, wondering if Dexter was behind the phone call I'd just received.

"Doesn't ring a bell," he said, stalking toward me, his hair a little ruffled but his starched white collar revealing the most edible neck. "Should I know her?"

"I thought you might. She's the fashion editor of *Vogue* in the UK," I said, trying to sound casual.

"Why would I know—never mind, why are you asking?" he asked, flopping on the small gray couch under the window.

"She just called me." I spun in my chair to face him. "I wondered if you'd mentioned me to her."

"Well I didn't. Did she say I had?"

"No, she said someone had given her one of my bracelets for a birthday present and she loved it. She wanted to talk about me supplying them for a couple of photo shoots."

"In *Vogue*?"

I slid off my seat and went to join him. "Yeah. Is that even possible?"

"Sounds like the kind of advertising money can't buy." He reached out his arms to me.

"Right. And I've only put out those twelve pieces."

"But they're beautiful, Hollie."

I beamed and took a seat next to him, hooking my legs over his while he draped his arm around me.

"You've clearly caught people's attention, which I told you would happen."

London was definitely some magical fairyland where everything that happened was almost unbelievable, it was so amazing. "I can't believe it," I said, giving way to a shy grin.

"Well, I can," Dexter said, shifting to pull me onto his lap just as the doorbell rang.

"That will be Gabriel," I said.

Dexter glanced at his watch. "He's always right on time."

"He's making the most out of the babysitter."

Dexter chuckled. "Speaking of which—"

"I booked in to see the gynecologist a week on Wednesday."

"Who would have thought the word *gynecologist* would make me want to bang my fiancée?"

I sprang to my feet and hauled Dexter up after me. "Come on. It's bad enough we have a chef for nights like these. The least we can do is show up and say hi to our guests."

We rarely took the elevator, although Dexter had insisted on buying a house with one. He said we'd need one when we had kids. But we used it now to go down the four floors to the kitchen.

"Gabriel," I cried, pulling him into a hug. "Thanks for coming." We were having the gang around for a "casual Friday supper" as Dexter referred to it. To me that meant a bowl of Cheerios and a night in front of *America's Got Talent*, rather than a seated dinner for ten with a private chef and a server. I was still getting used to life with Dexter. At least no one was dressing up.

"Did I tell you Autumn is coming over next month?" I said to Gabriel while Dexter answered the door to the next arrivals.

"Really?" he asked. I could have sworn I saw a hint of pink in his cheeks. She'd never mentioned anything but there was definitely something between them when they'd met during her birthday visit.

"She's on a graduate trainee program that has international assignments. She's going to spend six months here."

"That's great," he said, nodding. "She's staying with you guys?"

"I nodded. How sweet is my fiancée to have her here?"

Dexter's arms came from nowhere to circle my waist. "She's family. Of course she should stay with us."

I greeted Beck and Stella and noticed that Stella was wearing the earrings I gave her. They looked beautiful on her. I was still getting used to people actually wearing my jewelry; the thought that *Vogue* might be featuring me was just surreal.

"We should get married while she's here," I said.

"If that's what you want," Dexter said. "But we can get her a plane ticket over anytime. And your parents."

"I just want it low key. Like, you and me and, you know, your gang—"

"That better include me," Stella said.

"You're in the gang," Beck said as he placed a kiss on Stella's head.

"I don't care how we do it as long as I get to marry you," Dexter said.

"Bethany has said she wants to be a bridesmaid," Gabriel said. "I'm warning you because she's probably going to ask you. Don't worry, I'll be the one to shatter my four-year-old's dreams. I seem to do it on a daily basis at the moment, so I'm well practiced."

"Bethany's part of the gang," I said. "We can pick out a pretty dress and a posy," I said. "It will be nice."

I glanced up at Dexter to check he didn't mind but he was just beaming at me.

"So, we'll go to the Knightsbridge courthouse?" I suggested. "We'll pick a Saturday and just have a casual supper back here?"

Dexter grinned at me. "You're wonderful," he said.

"What did I do?" I asked. Dexter seemed to find the wonderful in everything I did, and I was still getting used to being someone's priority. I felt constantly spoiled by him— not just materially, but simply by getting to share my life with a man as special as Dexter. Married or not, it didn't matter. He was the man who saw the light in everything, including me. There was no one else I wanted to spend forever with.

Thank you for reading Mr. KNIGHTSBRIDGE.

Look out for Gabriel's story coming soon!

Have you read Stella and Beck's story in Mr. Mayfair

Loved Dexter Daniels? You'll love Alexander Knightley from **The British Knight**

Sign up to the Louise Bay mailing list at www.louisebay/mailinglist

Read more at www.louisebay.com

BOOKS BY LOUISE BAY

The Mister Series

Mr. Mayfair

Mr. Knightsbridge

Standalones

International Player

Hollywood Scandal

Love Unexpected

Hopeful

The Empire State Series

Gentleman Series

The Wrong Gentleman

The Ruthless Gentleman

The Royals Series

The Earl of London

The British Knight

Duke of Manhattan

Park Avenue Prince

King of Wall Street

The Nights Series

Indigo Nights

Promised Nights

Parisian Nights

Faithful

Sign up to the Louise Bay mailing list at
www.louisebay/mailinglist

Read more at www.louisebay.com